# WALKING

## *the*

# THREADS OF TIME

# GINA MARTIN

WOMANCRAFT PUBLISHING

Published by Womancraft Publishing, 2020
womancraftpublishing.com

ISBN 978-1-910559-59-8

Walking the Threads of Time is also available in
ebook format: ISBN 978-1-910559-58-1

Cover design, diagrams and typesetting by Lucent Word, lucentword.com
Cover art by Iris Sullivan
Author photograph by Lisa Levart, goddessonearth.com

Womancraft Publishing is committed to sharing powerful new women's voices, through a collaborative publishing process. We are proud to midwife this work, however the story, the experiences and the words are the author's alone. A percentage of Womancraft Publishing profits are invested back into the environment reforesting the tropics (via TreeSisters) and forward into the community: providing books for girls in developing countries, and affordable libraries for red tents and women's groups around the world.

# PRAISE FOR GINA MARTIN

*Epic and intimate, mythic and maternal. Reading this book feels like re-membering a legend I've known all my life, buried deep in my bones, but like the thirteen sisters themselves, long ago forgotten. Martin breathes narrative details into the embers of this story that make it crackle to life.*
**Jeanine Cummins, bestselling author of** *American Dirt,* *A Rip in Heaven* **and** *The Outside Boy*

*Author, teacher and priestess Gina Martin has woven together visions of the mysteries of the Sacred Feminine from the past, present and future, with an evocative and sensual urgency... Lush with rich, descriptive lan-guage that carries the reader into the cultures and rituals she dreams into being, one has only to let oneself be carried deeply into the heart of these rites and the important spiritual messages they contain.*
**Sharynne NicMhacha, scholar and author of** *The Divine Feminine in Ancient Europe, Celtic Myth and Religion* **and** *Queen of the Night*

*A generous offering of heart and spirit, expertly crafted as it envelopes the reader in its sweet embrace and has us caring deeply for the women on their journey, with all their qualities – both human and divine. Filled with wisdom and insight, this tale of love, healing and magic is a power-*

*fully moving and transformative story for our time, as we reconnect with our own inner wisdom and knowing.*

*I loved this book.*

Celeste Lovick, author of *Medicine Song*


*Gina Martin weaves a magical tale of possibility. Parting the tides to bring forth a new/old understanding of our shared past; A past in which the goddess – and therefore all life – is held sacred. And that is exactly what we need right now.*

Jessica M. Starr,
author of *Waking Mama Luna* and *Maid, Mother, Crone, Other*

*"We always fulfill our fate; we don't always fulfill our destiny."*


This book is dedicated to Dr. Jeffrey Yuen,
keeper of the wisdoms, 88th generation of his lineage,
he who remembers.


And to my Mamaw, Lena Jones Martin,
who held the witch within.

| | Land of Qin 600 BCE | Alexandria (Egypt) 415 BCE | Comté de Foix, France 1060–1080 CE | Rupertsberg (Germany) 1120 CE |
|---|---|---|---|---|
| Atvasfara | ▲ | ▲ | ▲ | ▲ |
| Parasfahe | ▲ | | | |
| Maia | | | ▲ | |
| Kiyia | ▲ | | ▲ | ▲ |
| Ni Me | | | | ▲ |
| Tiamet | | | | ▲ |
| Awa | ▲ | | | |
| Eiofachta | | | ▲ | |
| Badh | | | ▲ | ▲ |
| Uxua | | ▲ | | ▲ |
| Io | | | | ▲ |
| Autakla | | | ▲ | ▲ |
| Silbara | | | ▲ | ▲ |

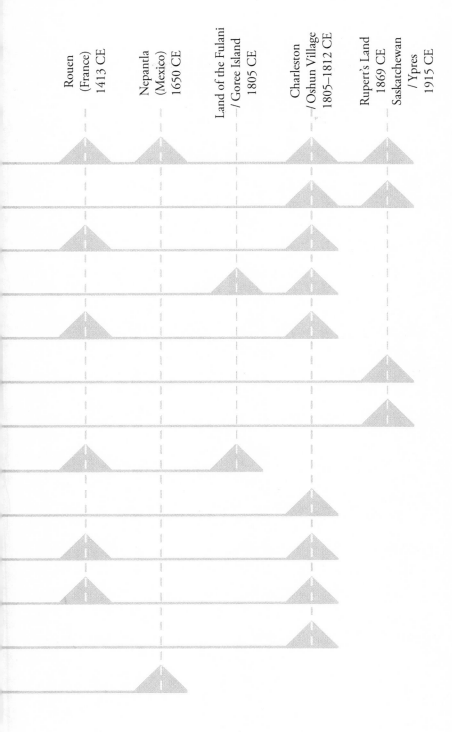

Rouen
(France)
1413 CE

Nepantla
(Mexico)
1650 CE

Land of the Fulani
/ Goree Island
1805 CE

Charleston
/ Oshun Village
1805–1812 CE

Rupert's Land
1869 CE
Saskatchewan
/ Ypres
1915 CE

# CHARACTER GUIDE

Kiyia, *the Guardian of Epona from the Sea of Grasses.*
Uxua, *the Divine Embodiment of Ix Chel from Yucatan.*
Badh *of the Cailleach, the Keeper of Wild Spaces from Eiru.*
Awa *from the Western Shores, devotee of the Goddess Yemaya.*
Parasfahe *of Sumeria, Priestess of the Goddess Inanna.*
Maia, *the living embodiment of Kali Ma from the land of Arya.*
Tiamet *from The Roof of the World, devotee of the Goddess Lhamo.*
Eiofachta *from Great North Woods and the Goddess Nematona.*
Ni Me, *one of the of the Seven Sister from the Pleiades.*
Silbara, *Priestess of the Goddess Brig from The Mystery School at Calanais.*
Autakla, *a selkie from The Sea Without End.*
Io, *maiden of the Wild Hunt from the Temple of Artemis at Ephesus.*
Atvasfara, *High Priestess of Isis from Egypt.*

Li Er — *Atvasfara*
Ra Mien — *Parasfahe*
Lu Ting — *Awa*
Xe Xue — *Kiyia*

## ALEXANDRIA, IMPERIAL PROVINCE OF AEGYPTUS (EGYPT) 415 CE

Merchant — *Atvasfara*

Hypatia — U*xua*

## COMTÉ DE FOIX, FRANCE 1060–1080 CE

Marguerite — E*iofachta*

Mother Monica Maria — *Alama*

Sister Angelica — M*aia*

Sister Dolora — *Atvasfara*

Capitan Juan Miguel de Antonel — K*iyia*

Sister Helena — S*ilbara*

Sister Mary Martha — A*utakla*

Sister Agnes — B*adh*

## RUPERTSBERG, OBER-LOTHRINGEN (GERMANY) 1120 CE

Hildegard von Bingen — *Atvasfara*

Sister Delphinia — *Atvasfara's attendant*

The impudent boy, Petyer Fieldenstarn — I*o*

Griseld — T*iamet*

Sister Maria Stella — A*utakla*

Betterm — S*ilbara*

Alejandro del Marsitel of Sevilla — U*xua*

Sister Catherine of the Wheel — B*adh*

Giuseppe Giardelli de Fuaresca, Cardinal of the Holy See — *Talo*

Theoderic — N*i* M*e*

| ROUEN, NORMANDY (FRANCE) | 1413 CE |
| --- | --- |

Jeanne — M*aia*
John Somerset — E*iofachta*
Friar Isambart de la Pierre — A*tvasfara*
St Michael — N*i* M*e*
St Catherine — I*o*
St Margaret — U*xua*

| SAN MIGUEL NEPANTLA, NEW SPAIN (MEXICO) | 1650 CE |
| --- | --- |

Juana Inés de Ashaje y Ramirez de Santillana (Juana de la Cruz)
 — S*ilbara*
Palle Pelhutezca — A*tvasfara*

| ALONG THE GAMBIA RIVER IN THE LAND OF THE FULANI (GHANA) / GOREE ISLAND (SENEGAL) | 1805 CE |
| --- | --- |

Khadee — K*iyia*
Sailor — E*iofachta*

| CHARLESTON, SOUTH CAROLINA, USA | 1805 CE |
| --- | --- |

Alexander Farley — A*tvasfara*
Martha — A*utakla*
Khadee — K*iyia*
Thomas — I*o*

## OSHUN VILLAGE, UPPER CANADA (CANADA)  1812 CE

Khadee — *Kiyia*
Samuel — *Badb*
Grandmother Prudence — *Maia*
Homer — *Ni Me*
Juba — *Parasfabe*
Bonnie — *Uxua*

## RUPERT'S LAND OF THE HUDSON BAY COMPANY (CANADA)  1869 CE
## AND
## SASKATCHEWAN, CANADA  1915 CE

Kakehtaweyihtam / Sally Standing Bear — *Atvasfara*
Misimohokasiw — *Awa*
Wapiscanis / Walter — *Tiamet*
Tom Fletcher — *Parasfabe*

I had the dream again.

I am entering into the ruins of a building. I can't tell if it was a castle, a temple...? Why can't I remember? I have been here so many times before.

Huge slabs of stone are tipped and fallen, making the floor uneven and the path forward an obstacle course.

The ancient stones are covered in moss. I lay my hands on one and feel the coolness and the texture beneath my fingers. It is the most vivid green, and the pewter rock makes slashes of mineral gray against the living emerald cover. I feel everything. Am I awake?

Cool, cold, soft. I hear running water, and turn a corner in curiosity but only find a small drip down the edge of one cantilevered slab. I pause. Is this safe? I feel danger slither under my skin, but my heart answers, I hear the words, "Go forward."

So I do, sliding down over rough surfaces, down a layer, up another. I am almost able to discern what this place had looked like before, make out what might have been rooms and hallways, crumbling arches...

I almost remember.

I am seeking the water, the triplet music of its coursing, leading me towards voices up ahead: women's voices, girls' voices. I know those voices! I have been with them in the before. I look for them. I ache to find them.

And then I wake up.

# THE TEMPLE OF ISIS 5000 BCE

The Thirteen stood as one in a flight formation like migratory birds.

Kiyia, the Guardian of Epona from the Sea of Grasses.

Uxua, the Divine Embodiment of Ix Chel from Yucatan.

Badh of the Cailleach, the Keeper of Wild Spaces from Eiru.

Awa from the Western Shores, devotee of the Goddess Yemaya.

Parasfahe of Sumeria, Priestess of the Goddess Inanna.

Maia, the living embodiment of Kali Ma from the land of Arya.

Tiamet from The Roof of the World, devotee of the Goddess Lhamo.

Eiofachta from Great North Woods and the Goddess Nematona.

Ni Me, one of the of the Seven Sisters from the Pleiades.

Silbara, Priestess of the Goddess Brig from The Mystery School at Calanais.

Autakla, a selkie from The Sea Without End.

Io, maiden of the Wild Hunt from the Temple of Artemis at Ephesus.

And at their head, Atvasfara, High Priestess of Isis from Egypt.

They were only vaguely aware of the rumbling of the earth beneath their feet, of the shouts of fear and warning coming from outside the high double doors of their sanctuary. They had, bit-by-bit, day-by-day, over these last moons shed their names and titles and let go their connections to others that had made them separate women. Now they stood as a single entity. No longer thirteen women, but the Thirteen. They were focused on one purpose alone – to save what could be saved of Her wisdoms.

They knew what sacrifices had been asked of them.

They had all committed to this path.

And the time was now.

The doors flew open and they moved as a single organism out through the Temple and down the wide stone steps to the river. As one they lifted their eyes, sending love and farewell to the people clustered before them. And as one they turned and boarded the barge that was rocking violently though it was tied to the dock. The rope was released and the barge swirled out into the current of the Naihl.

A sound like the earth giving birth split their ears; a chasm opened in the water. The barge with the Thirteen was sucked down with tremendous force. The water closed over them all. Their spirits lifted, tumbled, were dragged and then flew. The fury of their journey was matched by the ripping pain of loss and the brilliant light pulling them forward, forward. They called to one another.

"Where are we?"

"What is happening?"

"Where do we hide the wisdoms?"

They were without reference, without surety. They reached for one another and felt the others slipping their grasp. Alone! Were they each alone? Where to hide the wisdoms? Where? How? They could see nothing but the light blazing before them. Their panic grew. They had to fulfill their Goddess-given mission!

All was chaos.

And then, in another instant, the tumult ended, and the absolute quiet and tranquility of this new place allowed them to find each other. They found their way on the threads of their love for one another. A moment of stillness. And then.

Into the silence, they asked again.

"Where do we hide the wisdoms?"

And in that fractal of eternity they heard a beloved voice, felt a treasured embrace, knew a divine presence.

"MY DAUGHTERS. BELOVEDS. WELCOME HOME. YOU ARE THE KEEPERS. WITHIN YOUR SOULS OUR WISDOMS WILL BE HIDDEN. AND IN DIVINE TIME, YOU SHALL BRING ALL

And so it was that the ocean of Goddess love, fractured by planetary cataclysm and human weaknesses, branched out into rivers of Her that could flow through the centuries finding eddies of place and time where She could be revered in safety.

As the patriarchy ground down on the power of the Great Mother, the rivers of Her lore became thinner, the safe places fewer and farther between. The wisdom keepers, with Her carried securely in their souls, came into birth and death and rebirth over and over again, seeking each other and sanctuaries for Her. There would emerge those golden miracle places when the Goddess would bubble up, Her voice would be heard, Her memory revered. Those dwindling rivers of Goddess light would bring the Thirteen into contact with each other, like magnets drawn together. And then, the course of human events would splinter them apart once again.

The eternal spiral of existence would be mapped by these Thirteen. All time happening in the same time, all forms of experience illuminating the Source. Each of their souls would seek the fullness of human life, the path to wisdom, and the lessons of pain and love. They would find physical form as female and male and all the exquisite variations of those dualities. They would see life from every angle of status and privilege. They would be alone and be together, always seeking the completion of their mission.

One of them, she who had been Atvasfara, High Priestess of Egypt, she of the golden eyes, had made a soul contract of enormous sacrifice. She would be the memory holder.

It was a great burden. But she had willingly agreed to the task. And so, with her memories also came all the pain of all the loss, over and over again. With each reincarnation she would remember each death and loss and near miss of every lifetime.

Whilst the others had the blessing of forgetting each lifetime, except in fragments of dreams or whispers of synchronicity, Atvasfara would remember. She would seek the others actively and with foreknowledge. She would be the lodestone that their souls would be pulled to.

Hildegard von Bingen — *Atvasfara*

Sister Delphinia — *Atvasfara's attendant*

The impudent boy, Petyer Fieldenstarn — *Io*

Griseld — *Tiamet*

Sister Maria Stella — *Autakla*

Betterm — *Silbara*

Alejandro del Marsitel of Sevilla — *Uxua*

Sister Catherine of the Wheel — *Badh*

Giuseppe Giardelli de Fuaresca,
Cardinal of the Holy See — *Talo*

Theoderic — *Ni Me*

# RUPERTSBERG, OBER-LOTHRINGEN (GERMANY) 1120 CE

Hildegard sat at her desk, golden eyes lifted to the window, but she was only focused on the celestial song that was flowing through her. Her left hand held her quill loosely drooping from her fingers, and a splatter of ink had landed on the paper before her. The music began to swell out of her in her thin true voice and floated on the scent of blown roses and honey-sweet peonies that drifted in from the gardens below. The cup of cider at her elbow was untasted, and the fire was almost burned out in the grate. The moment felt eternal.

"Mother Hildegard? There is a boy here who says he must speak with you."

Hildegard, Abbess of Rupertsberg was deep into the music, so deep into the topography of notes and tones, seeing the landscape made by the music that she barely registered the obviously repeated request for her attention.

With a deep sigh and a remembrance of her most recent vow to herself to act with patience in all things, she lifted her eyes and saw Sister Delphinia looking at her with that particular set to her mouth that indicated frustration.

"I am sorry, but did you say a boy?"

"Yes, Mother." Deep sigh. "A boy! An impudent thing. He demands that he speak with you. Has demanded so for two days. And insists he will not leave until he does. We have tried to keep him at bay, to put him off, but he will not have it. He is underfoot and distracting the Sisters."

"Well, we can't have the Sisters distracted now, can we?" Hildegard replied, laying down her quill with a sigh.

Sister Delphinia looked sideways at the Abbess for a sheer fraction of a moment, suspecting sarcasm in her tone. But Hildegard simply smiled at the red-faced Sister while internally chanting "*Patience. Patience. Patience.*" She glanced out the windows, her pale eyes almost translucent in the late day sunlight.

"Oh, look at how the day is flying! Sister, please send this impudent boy in to me, and have some tea and bread sent along as well. His impudence may be spurred by hunger, eh? Speaking of which, I feel hunger. Have I forgotten to eat again?"

Sister Delphinia's mouth took on its second most common shape when dealing with Mother Hildegard, an ellipse where the down-turned edges warred with the urge to smile.

"Yes, Mother. Again, you have forgotten to eat. How about some cold fowl and cheese with that bread and tea?"

"What an idea of brilliance, Sister! You are too kind to me."

And Hildegard gave Delphinia a smile of surpassing sweetness that caused the nun to swallow and laugh, turn, and exit the airy study that was scattered with parchments and books and an assortment of musical instruments.

Hildegard stretched her arms high overhead and felt the crack in her spine. She had been immersed for hours! She walked to the windows and saw the fields below and the forest edge miles away limned in the last glows of the harvest day. The forest, the forest. It was calling to her. A fragment of a prayer came to her.

*The rich soft body of the Earth.*
*Gives us birth*

*And carries us in death*
*She is divine,*
*the living emerald green*
*Viriditas! Viriditas!*
*The ever living green!*

Hildegard fell into the vision of that green, of that forest, of the freedom of that living green.

# III
# COMTÉ DE FOIX, FRANCE 1060 CE

When she was eleven years old, Marguerite was dragged up the stony hill to the convent of Mater Misericordia and left at the gates by her parents. Her father looked away and her mother wagged a finger imploring her to behave. Then they turned, and without a backward glance trudged down the hill to return to their village. The nun at the gate took the child by the elbow and directed her to wait outside the door to the Mother Superior's rooms.

When Mother Monica Maria opened her door, she took one look at the scruffy, angry, kitten of a girl and burst out laughing. The child was thin, too thin, and dirty with a year's worth of leaves and twigs in her dun-colored hair, a snarl on her lips, and a flash of defiance floating atop fear in her hazel eyes.

"You are Marguerite de'Magdalene, yes?"

The girl only shrugged her bony shoulders.

"Your aunt, Sister Dolora has asked for special dispensation that you might enter this house before the age of consent. She says that you have agreed to this. Is this true?"

The girl again only shrugged, but this time her eyes cut sideways and she bit her bottom lip. Mother Monica Maria bent over to try and catch the girl's gaze.

"Child, look at me. This is not a prison. You do not have to stay here if this is not your wish."

Again, the shrug.

"Come, sit, and tell me why you are here then."

They both settled on the front of the chair and stool the Mother had indicated. A tiny voice composed of equal parts trepidation and steely resolve came through the girl's pursed lips.

"I am unmanageable."

And again, Mother Monica Maria laughed aloud.

"Many of the best are! Is this what your parents say?"

The angry kitten gave a defiant flash of a look up at the Mother Superior.

"I am unbiddable, and untamable also."

"Well, that clears that up. But it beggars the question. Where do you want to be, child?"

"I want to be free!"

Mother Monica Maria straightened and gave the girl a long look of surface placidity while storms of thought and feeling raged behind the nun's dark blue eyes. She could well remember that feeling. She could recall with stark detail the day she had said those very same words. And she remembered, with a pang of love and longing, what the wise woman to whom she had railed had said to her. So, with respect and a certain kind of bitter nostalgia, she repeated what had been said to her over twenty-five years ago.

"The world outside has no place for such as we. For some of us, the world around us makes no sense. It is as if we live in another place, another time. We long for something that evaporates like dew in the harsh sunlight of this world. So for us, the only freedom to be found is within. Within the self. And within these walls. Today this may feel like a cage. But in time, this space will be a sanctuary and a source of liberation for you."

The girl didn't respond, didn't even give indication that she had heard Mother Monica Maria's words. But the two sat in a silence that transformed into a stillness. The sun reached a level where it threw the Mother's face into a clear shaft of pale gold light. The dust motes floated in the air like the celestial bodies floating in the sky. That peculiar quality of peace called grace descended on the two, and time was suspended.

After the light shifted again and stretched shadows across the rushes on the stone floor, the Mother spoke very softly, almost as if to herself.

"What is it you care about, child? What do you love?"

Marguerite responded dreamily.

"I love to run in the woods. I love the bluebells in spring. I ache to hear the plants as they talk amongst themselves. I long to feel the wind tug my hair and the cold bite my ears. I want the touch of moonlight on my skin. I want..."

And she stopped abruptly as if she had revealed too much.

"Ah, yes," Mother Monica Maria replied. "And, so what shall we do with you then?"

"My parents don't want me. They say no man would ever want to let a wild thing such as me into his marriage bed."

"Body of Christ! My dear girl! I should say that is true." But Monica Maria had a smile as she said this. "Now, do you want to learn scripture? Or the arts of calligraphy?"

"Not particularly"

"The distaff arts? Weaving? Embroidery? Spinning of wool?"

"Not likely!" the girl replied with a shudder.

"Singing? Meditation? Devotional practices?"

The girl looked like she would burst into tears, and violently shook her head.

"Then it must be the green arts then. Simples and medicines and such. Sister Angelica is as grumpy as a hungry bear, but at least you can be outside much of the time. Would that suit?"

Marguerite's face lit up at the mention of being outside, and in her head she quickly waved off the notion of 'a hungry bear'. Sunlight, air, the smell of growing things. Maybe this place wouldn't be so horrible after all.

"I guess that would be all right," she said begrudgingly.

Mother Monica Maria sat back in her chair and struggled to keep the wide grin from splitting her face. *This one would be an entertainment to watch. Mayhaps they could keep her spirit whole, not let it be crushed by the world at large.* Monica Maria felt an odd tug, a whisper of a memory, a gossamer wisp of a notion. *This girl is one of mine. There is danger. There will be danger. I must at all costs keep her safe.*

Shaking herself loose from such whimsical notions, Monica Maria stood, and urged the girl up.

"Come my tiny, brave, wild thing, my fierce badger child. Let's go set you with Sister Angelica, and we will see who comes out on top, shall we?"

The Mother Superior led the way along the cool stone corridors, past the open chapel where the intricacies of sacred songs were being practiced, and down a steep flight of stairs to an outside door. She opened the door and the smells of lavender and rosemary and rue flooded them both as they strode across the sheltered herb garden to a stone and thatch hut just inside the high main convent wall. The building had a row of windows facing south, opened to let in the early spring air. Pots and jars of baked clay stood like soldiers, all lined up outside the door waiting to be used. From inside came the sounds of muttering and mortar and pestle.

"'Black pepper poultice', she says. 'I need more black pepper poultice.' Well, who in the name of all the saints is supposed to provide that poultice? 'Me,' I says. As if I haven't sneezed enough for one lifetime. What's a few more hundred sneezes?"

Mother Monica Maria came to a halt outside the hut and waited till that particular diatribe had come to an end. She drew a deep breath, and prayed for diplomacy and equanimity.

"Sister Angelica? I have brought you a young helper, someone to help with all those black pepper poultices for Sister Anna Sophia."

There was silence from within, but the grinding and the grumbling stopped. Small yellow butterflies moved across the newly flowering plants, and the sun felt warm for April inside the protected garden. A very short woman appeared at the door. She was sun-browned and weather wrinkled with deep brown eyes that seemed to flash black as she squinted into the sunlight. There was a moment, a frozen splinter of time when the old nun and the little girl saw each other and remembered the connection between them that had survived thousands of years and a multitude of lifetimes. One saw the scrap of a child as she had been. She had been as scrawny and scrappy then, but with a world of grief behind her eyes. And the scrapper saw the dignity and sovereignty of the old woman – younger in that life and stronger physically, who had commanded a people and embodied a powerful goddess. They nodded their heads in inchoate recognition. And as if it hadn't happened, the moment was freed of the past and burst into the now. Mother Monica Maria saw that moment, knew it had import, and offered it up to heaven.

"This? This is a helper? It looks more like a small woodland creature dragged backwards though a hedge."

Mother Monica Maria felt the girl beside her stiffen and open her mouth to retort so she interjected quickly.

"Ah now, Sister. God assists us in mysterious ways, yes? And this young girl has your love of the outdoors and the living things. You have so much wisdom. Can you find it within you to grant this young charge some of what you know?"

Sister Angelica looked askance at the Mother Superior, perfectly aware that she was being flattered and suspicious of the reasons for that flattery.

"Well, what's wrong with her then?"

Monica Maria grabbed Marguerite's hand to hold her in place and calmly replied.

"Nothing is wrong with her, Sister. She is simply in need of a good teacher."

"Oh, Mother, you and I both know that if there wasn't something off with this child you certainly wouldn't deposit her at my door."

"Sister!" Monica Maria looked at the older nun with humor and compassion and the insight that made her well suited to lead a community of bright and strong-willed women.

Sister Angelica met that look, and acknowledged what all here at Mater Misericordia did, that Monica Maria was the first among equals.

"Mother," she shot her gaze to Marguerite who looked like she was ready to bolt. "All right then, little rabbit. Oh, no. You aren't a rabbit are you? More like a marten or a badger. That's it! A little badger!

More than ready to bite the hand that tries to feed you or capture you, eh?"

Mother Monica Maria laughed a warm generous laugh, and Marguerite almost smiled.

# RUPERTSBERG
# 1120 CE

"Are *you* Mother Hildegard?" The voice was young and male and less than awed.

Hildegard whipped around as if stung. Why did that voice matter? Why did she know it, like she knew the backs of her own hands? She saw a young boy standing just past the doorway, weight on his back foot as if ready to race away at a moment's notice. About fourteen years of age, his clothes were respectable, the child of burghers not farmers, she surmised. His face – that face – she felt that she knew that face – was tinged with suspicion, with brows like wings in flight a black slash above those penetrating wide gray eyes.

"Yes, for my sins, I am Hildegard. What is it you want with me, my child? I hear you were insistent that you must see me."

The boy's chin jutted forward and he flushed a deep scarlet.

"Yes, I… I… Mother…"

"Come now, what is it you want to ask?"

"I… Why do you haunt my dreams?"

Hildegard had the falling sensation that accompanied one of her visions. She saw the boy, but it wasn't the boy. Another face, the face of a tiny girl with wide eyes and wild tawny hair stared through this boy's eyes.

"Io?" the Abbess whispered.

The boy shuddered, as if he clutched a brace of eels.

"That is what you say in my dreams. What is *io*?" The boy's lip

14

trembled for an almost indiscernible moment before he righted himself and demanded again. "What is *io?*"

"Not what, but who," the Abbess said with a small voice. "Not a thing, but rather, a person."

"Who...who is Io?" the boy stuttered.

Hildegard swooped forward and took the boy's hands in hers. His were cold and slightly clammy, hers were warm with callouses from years spent holding quills.

"Sit, my young friend. Sit and have tea, and I shall endeavor to explain the unexplainable."

Sister Delphinia had indeed sent for sustenance, knowing that Mother Hildegard would eat now whilst her attention was diverted, and that after this interlude it might well be hours, if not days, before she arose from her deep prayer and work to take notice of the simple needs of her body. The trays that two young Sisters carried into the Abbess's study were overflowing with cold chicken and partridge, pickles of summer carrots and radishes, several loaves of bread, soft cheeses and fresh butter, and carafes of tea, cider and buttermilk. The young nuns set all the provisions on the low table near the fireplace, and, with sideways looks of curiosity and some disbelief, saw as Mother Hildegard spread butter on bread and poured tea for her guest.

"Thank you, my sweet sisters," Hildegard looked at the young women with a deep gratitude that pierced their hearts with a joyous arrow. The Abbess was not often even aware that others might be in the same room as she, so deep would she fall into her trances. But now, she saw them, golden eyes warm, and smiled that 'you have all of my attention and it is a delight' smile that some of the nuns talked of. What a moment! The sisters stood, transfixed, until Hildegard laughed and gently waved them off.

As the rustle of their skirts left the room, the young boy chewed his bread open-mouthed and slurped his tea with a glare and defiant look under those extraordinary eyebrows as if daring Hildegard to chastise him on his table manners.

*"Oh yes, this one was well brought up,"* she thought. *"He can't even eat without feeling the proprieties constraining him."*

She helped herself to food, discovering that she was well past hungry and far into ravenous. The two, this odd pair, ate and swallowed and ate some more, all the while both were wondering what was to follow. The afternoon shadow that had only touched the edge of the table when they began now covered the entirety of its surface and had spilled onto the slate floor and the carpets strewn across the room. Hildegard took one last bite of pickle, one last gulp of cool tea and placed her palms down on her thighs to begin to say…what?

"Let's start with your name. Sister Delphinia calls you the impudent boy, but I think perhaps that won't serve us well as we proceed together. You know my name. Might I be honored to know yours?"

"Petyer, Petyer Fieldenstarn of Wiesbaden."

"And your age, Master Fieldenstarn?"

"I turned fourteen years at the Feast of St Balthazar."

Hildegard nodded, blinked several times, and then the silence spread. He was clearly waiting for her to answer his – yes, it was a rather impudent question – his query of why she was haunting – had the lad actually claimed she was haunting? – yes, he said *haunting* his dreams.

"Your dreams then, young Petyer."

Again she faltered, and again the boy held his ground. Hildegard found herself amused at his adversarial solidity. She settled herself more thoroughly onto the bench, placed a cushion at her back, and started once more.

"You appear to be a steady sort of young man, not easily swayed or startled. It must be something quite pressing to cause you to travel these seventy or eighty leagues to find me, and for your parents to allow such a journey. Do they know of your purpose? Have you told them of your dreams?"

The boy broke her gaze and looked flushed once more.

"Sweet Jesu, do your parents know you are here?"

When no reply was forthcoming, Hildegard rose abruptly, strode across the room and yanked the cord that was attached to a bell somewhere in the depths of the Abbey that brought her assistance whenever she thought to ask for it. She stood, arms crossed and staring at young Fieldenstarn like an avenging angel. The moments stretched until finally Sister Delphinia came into the room.

"Yes, Mother?"

"Sister, if you would be so good as to send a messenger to the home of the…?"

Petyer replied sheepishly, "Burgomeister."

"The Burgomeister Fieldenstarn in Wiesbaden and inform the family that this young rapscallion, their son Petyer, is here at the Abbey and safe from harm. Let them know that he shall return to them, if, that is, they desire his return after he undoubtedly scared them half to death by disappearing without so much as a by your leave."

Hildegard had run out of steam and the corners of her mouth battled to not turn up into a laugh. She knew she daren't catch Delphinia's eye or that battle would be totally lost. Delphinia harrumphed at the now mortified young man and swept gracefully out of the room. Hildegard took her seat again, fixed Petyer with a gimlet glare, and felt much more confident that she held the high ground.

"So, your dreams propelled you down the byways to me, did they? Why don't you begin by telling me more about these dreams."

"They happen, when I am asleep or no," young Petyer began and Hildegard felt her spine stiffen. "In them sometimes I am running, hunting a stag with a band of warrior girls."

He stopped short. She saw scarlet slashes across his cheeks – stag's blood? – no, the blush of deep embarrassment – and he blazed a look into Hildegard that swept away all her defenses. He was defiant.

"Yes, warrior girls, I know that sounds absurd. But that's what we are. We chase hard, and then we, we do it! We finish the stag! It is glorious. And every time I hear this…" his voice was getting stronger now, as he started to chant:

*"Mighty One. Most Noble of creatures.*
*With gratitude we take your sacrifice.*
*We lift your spirit to return to All That Is.*
*We surrender your flesh to the rich soft body of the earth."*

Hildegard found herself speechless, a wordless state of being very foreign to the woman known as the "Wordsmith of Bingen" as time past collided with time present. She was lost in the sensations of the hunt Petyer had described. She could smell the fear sweat rolling off the stag. She could hear the marked breathing of the warrior girls. She could feel the splatter of blood on her face like drops of hot pewter as the stag was finished. Then the prayer for the stag's spirit – chanted by those young girls, with reverence and jubilation.

The prayer repeated and repeated. Hildegard gradually became cognizant that she was chanting with the boy, Petyer. All felt perfectly right in that moment, complete, and revealed in its fullness.

Their eyes drifted open as the sounds hovered in the still air of the falling light. Young Petyer had tears tracing tracks down his cheeks, and with no sense of embarrassment he wiped a sleeve across his face and stared straight at Hildegard.

"This happens to me all the time! Is this the work of the devil or the Saints? And how do you know those words?"

"My young friend, for my friend you have been and will be again," she stopped short. "My young Petyer, I need to show you something. But it is late, and you must be tired. Tomorrow is another day. For now, you must rest."

Petyer tried to object, but Hildegard had already risen from her chair, gesturing for him to do the same.

"It is enough for tonight, young Petyer. On the morrow, you shall discover what you have come seeking. But for now, rest."

Petyer took a shallow, catching breath, trying to summon the courage to contradict the Abbess. But he could not. Tomorrow would have to suffice.

The Abbey of Rupertsberg ran like a well-oiled machine with many wheels and cogs, all aligned perfectly. A small room, meticulously clean and equipped with warm water and plentiful blankets had been prepared for young Master Fieldenstarn. Hildegard and the boy walked back into the high-ceilinged cloister halls and were met by Sister Delphinia and the two young nuns who had brought dinner hours before. The young women each took one of Petyer's elbows and guided him down the hall, up three flights of stairs and down a long corridor that made a half circle around the outer perimeter of the Abbey's guest quarters. The young boy was wobbly on his feet and tired beyond measure. This day had been an overwhelming mixture of emotions. Nothing was much clearer, but at least he knew he was in the right place. He lay on the bed, eyes open, waiting for the dreams to take him once more.

Delphinia and Hildegard walked side by side back toward the Mother's quarters.

"He is...one of yours, yes?" Delphinia made it a statement, not a question. Delphinia had always taken every odd occurrence and unannounced appearance in her stride. She had never questioned the goings on here at Rupertsberg before. And Hildegard was careful to guard her memories of the past existences, until the time was right.

"Yes, my dear. He is. As are you. You know that we too are joined and destined, yes?"

Delphinia bowed her head. She knew that she felt a special connection to Hildegard, but had always evaded any deeper conversation on the matter. In the Abbey much was left unspoken, idle chatter was not encouraged.

"I know that your soul is precious to me. And I know that all is right with the world when I am able to serve you. For me, that is enough."

But with the arrival of the boy, something had shifted.

"My friend," replied Hildegard. "Do you wish to know all that I know, for I trust no one more than you?"

They walked farther down the corridor, moving from pool of candlelight, to darkness, to pool of light. Delphinia flickered in the wavering light and Hildegard saw her as she had first known her, as a beautiful girl joining the Temple of Isis, becoming a trusted and beloved attendant to the High Priestess Atvasfara. They stopped and Delphinia looked directly at Hildegard.

"I never really wanted to know before. I felt myself skate around the edges of your knowings and felt content in my proximity to you without needing the burden of all you carry. But that boy, that impu-

19

dent boy! It is as if the scales have tipped and some great momentum has accelerated and now, yes, I believe that I do want to know all you remember. I believe that I need to know it all, to serve and guard you best."

And so it was that Hildegard and Delphinia turned, retraced their steps, and went back out into the garden so that the moonlight was the only witness to the tale of their past. The walked high up into the forest and sat at the base of a Grandmother beech tree. They were safe, nestled in the gnarled roots with her strength at their backs.

Ever so softly, Hildegard began to tell the story of the before. It was the story of a land ruled by the rhythms of the mighty River of Life, the Naihl. It was a wondrous story of a beloved Temple, a powerful Goddess of Life Itself, and the women who served Her. It was the memory of a time when women ruled the Temples and the Palaces, and where the Divine Feminine kept balance and justice for all creatures as the prevailing values. It was the dark tale of how an act of greed and violence had tipped the scales and allowed the forces of 'power over' to gain ascendency. It was how thirteen women had answered the summons of their Goddesses and come to that land to preserve what wisdoms could be saved. It was the final note of great magick and sacrifice that had taken the Thirteen, subsumed them into the warp and weft of the tapestry of souls. Hildegard spoke gently of how she had accepted the role, the burden, of The One Who Remembers, and how she walked in each lifetime seeking the others, holding safe the knowledge that they might, once again, serve She of a Thousand Names.

The telling came to an end, with both women and the essence of Grandmother Beech silently watching the peach and raspberry light of dawn peek coyly above the horizon. They could hear the women of the Abbey singing the chants of Lauds that marked a new day.

"And my name was Hatshep?"

"Yes, my dearest. The hatshep is a spring flower, a small blossom the same colors of that sky we see this morning. Once again, you have the name of a beautiful flower."

"When you and the others of the Thirteen perished, did I die as well?"

Hildegard gripped her friend's hand hard and replied, "I don't know! I see and recall everything until that final moment, and then I have no knowledge of what befell you and the others, the companions of the Thirteen. In some lifetimes I find a companion or two, as I have found you in this time and place. But what happened after the ship disappeared, I know not. Do you have any memories, dearest?"

"No, Mother Hildegard. It all sounds like the remnants and tatters of a long-forgotten bedtime story. Familiar, and yet, when I try to grasp it, it all slips away."

With that Delphinia yawned so widely that her jaw cracked and both women giggled.

"Another day begins, Sister Delphinia, and I have kept you from your rest. Why don't you go lie down for an hour or so and let the Abbey spin on without you?"

"And what for you, Mother? Rest?" Delphinia asked teasingly, knowing that Hildegard found sleep a nuisance.

"Ah, no. I believe I have heard a new song this morning. A delight in the small blessings of the new light. And then, I must speak with the boy."

Without any leave-taking, Hildegard wandered out of the forest, through the gardens and down into the Labyrinth, enthralled in the music in her mind that had been seeded by the rising sun. Delphinia gently shook her head and followed, swinging by the kitchens on her way into the Abbey to order tea and fruits to be sent to Mother Hildegard's chambers, and then finding her way to her own chamber, to sleep, and see wide expanses of sand split by a ribbon of dark green, fast-running water in her dreams.

# COMTÉ DE FOIX
# 1064 CE

Days rolled into months. Months blossomed into seasons. Seasons birthed years. Marguerite found a life that afforded her solitude and independence, as long as she paid the toll of regulated prayer times and quiet hours. Quiet hours were no challenge for her, for conversation with other people was always stilted. She didn't build friendships with the other Sisters and her relationship with Sister Angelica was built on grudging mutual respect and the pendulum of moods that afflicted them both. They secretly cherished their time together, but neither was prone to bouts of affectionate display. Sister Angelica indeed had a wealth of knowledge, and how providential that it was the kind of knowledge that Marguerite valued.

"This is the angelica plant. My namesake, you might say. The flowers steeped help bring a new mother's milk. The root, ground and made into tea soothes the womb. One of our Blessed Mother's herbs."

Sister Angelica kept a running commentary while they walked in the medicinal garden. Marguerite interjected. "The priest in my village says women must suffer in childbirth to repent for Eve's sin."

Marguerite posited the statement to see if she could get a rise out of Sister Angelica. And, as predictable as the sunrise. "What utter hog shite! What loving God requires all women to pay for the actions of another?"

On another day near the Feast of the Assumption,

"Charcoal. Add charcoal into the fennel to calm a burning gut."

"Sister, where did you learn all your lore? Was your mother a wise woman?"

"My gran. My mother's mother. So very wise. She taught me all she knew, but I have a knowing that goes beyond that. I have these dreams. I dream of a sundrenched place where it rains and rains as if the land is flowing water upward. I hear music and singing and feel the earth beneath my bare feet. I see a huge creature with a nose like a tree branch and know it to be my friend. It is so deliciously warm there, in my dreams. And when I awake, I remember some bit of herb wisdom, or healing method. It is very strange."

"I wish I could sleep and wake up smarter."

And the two women, one old, one barely formed, chortled.

"Why did you enter the convent, Sister?"

"The world of men was pushing out, pushing at the edges of the old ways held by my gran, and her sisters. They were building towns where once there were fields, and cities where once stood forests. I craved the stillness, the deep night practices of prayer, and the communion with the wild things. I asked for divine intervention, and the Blessed Mother led me here."

"So, She does listen then?" Marguerite said with a tinge of sarcasm. And they both snorted with laughter. And so it was that Marguerite found not only the solace, but the wisdom of green living things, and the lineage of knowledge found a path.

Because she had entered the convent before the age of consent, Marguerite required supervision, a task that Mother Monica Maria eventually took upon herself after the youngster had successfully driven off three competent nuns.

Gradually Mother Monica Maria began to tell the history of their convent, the ways it was organized and the issues found within any community of strong-minded individuals. Mater Misericordia was unique in their region as it held no allegiance to any bishopric and was self-governed, and self-sustaining. There were occasional forays and delegations from the Church hierarchy demanding compliance or obedience, but as the Mother described to Marguerite,

"Each Mother before me has managed to outwit the bishops. I have held firm as well. It makes the bishops extremely uncomfortable that we women are governing ourselves. And still, we stand alone, delightfully unencumbered."

They walked and talked several times a week. Perhaps because Marguerite was standoffish with all the other inhabitants of the convent, or perhaps because the child could hold her own in philosophical and ecclesiastical discussions, Monica Maria found herself using the girl as a sounding board, as a peer, as a friend. She acknowledged to herself that it was the oddest of friendships, but it was a true one and it deepened with each passing year. She watched the fierce little badger child become a wise and educated young woman who had found her niche within the convent and who had been able to adapt remarkably well to the rhythms and strictures of cloistered life. Except for the divine offices, for prayer still seemed a foreign and unnecessary thing to her.

It invariably seemed to Marguerite that just as she was deeply involved in something, anything, the bells rang, and off they must trot to sit in chapel and pray. While the other Sisters seemed to be truly praying, Marguerite usually found her mind to be drifting.

*"The yarrow is in full flower. I must remember to harvest those flowers before the dew dries at the full moon."*

All around her would stand for song, and she stood as well, pulled by the tide of their bodies, yet far, far away in her own world.

As soon as the divine offices were finished she flew from chapel like a quail flushed from the brush, never seeing the exchanged glances from the other nuns or hearing the soft sigh from Mother Monica Maria. She would race to the herb house, or the pasture, or the woods and exalt.

*"I'm free!"*

# RUPERTSBERG
# 1120 CE

"Good morning, young Petyer, how did you sleep? Any dreams?"

Petyr nodded, and brushed away the last fragment of running into the deep woods, strong and free.

Hildegard stood and walked over to her massive desk. It was a deep, rose-gold oak with formidable legs carved at the feet with open-mouthed dragons. There were drawers and shelves, stuffed to the bursting with parchment and old frayed quills. She bent and stretched an arm beneath the surface of the desk, straining to reach a lever. With a sharp click, like a snapping branch, the mechanism shifted and opened a shallow hiding place. With a muted look of trepidation, Hildegard brought out a sheaf of pages, and brought them back to where they had been sitting.

"You read, I imagine," she said.

"Yes," the boy replied with asperity, "I read. Latin and Greek." His face held an air of some pride and a certain churlishness common amongst fellows his age.

"Well done, young Petyer. Or perhaps more true, well done Burgomeister Fieldenstarn, for I surmise he might have played a part in determining your education."

"My father would be content with me knowing simple arithmetic and rudimentary Latin. He believes my quest for knowledge puts me above my station."

Hildegard felt a moment of deep empathy, for she too had struggled against the expectations of family and society that might have limited her access to wisdoms.

"My apologies then, my young man. And I applaud your thirst for more than the simple and the rudimentary. I shall leave you to these pages whilst I take the air in the gardens. When you finish you shall find me among the peonies. Any Sister can help you locate those." She tentatively reached out and placed her fingertips on his cheek. "We shall have much to discuss then."

He looked down at the stack of pages as if it was a nest of snakes. With a slight smile she turned and started to leave him in the study. Suddenly, she halted. "How did you know where to find me in this wide, wide world?"

"I heard your music last Assumption Day at the Cathedral in Mainz. The choir sang your 'In Honor of the Great Queen'. I knew it! I knew it and began to sing along but in a different language until my mother covered my mouth and rushed me out. I asked where that hymn came from, and they all said from the sacred Hildegard of Rupertsberg. After that, every night and day my dreams have you in them. You and many others. How did I know that hymn?"

"Read. Read, and then we will talk."

Hildegard left the room with only a gentle swish of her skirts as the gooseflesh rippled over her skin. Petyer picked up the first page and began to read. He didn't notice when Sister Delphinia came in to stoke the fire. Seeing his rapt attention to the page before him, she only clucked gently and shook her head at his similarity to Mother Hildegard in his ability to be absent from the world.

"Two peas in a pod," she said to herself, "and cut from the same maddening bolt of cloth."

Petyer studied the words written in Hildegard's elegant script.

*The Temple is cool in the middle of the night and the full moon light makes the paintings on the walls come alive. They dance, the Ancient Ones, and speak to me of the women coming to do the great work of magic. They are coming and we will be thirteen.*

On another page was the song that Petyer had heard in the Cathedral.

*"She has come to greet the Dawn.*
*She is splendid in the glory of the Sun.*
*She who holds the key of life,*
*Comes to meet the One."*

And on another page.

*We stand in a Circle and do the work to last thousands of years.*
*Sekhmet and Her lions weave around us and Nut shines Her star-*
*light on us as blessings.*

On another page he read the names, and a tremor began in his
body that could not be contained. Those names, those names!

*In the next world I am committed to remembering the names of the*
*Thirteen. Shall we stand together again? I shall remember. Kiyia,*
*Autakla, Silbara, Badh, Uxua, Awa, Tiamet, Maia, Parasfahe, Ni*
*Me, Eiofachta, and our beloved Io. I, Atvasfara, shall remember.*
*This I pledge.*

*Io...Io...that name...it felt more real than any sound... Io...*
*He was Io!*
Petyr felt that everything he had known and been before dissolved.
He was Io. It was the only truth. And he could see the faces of the
others, the others of the Thirteen. He saw each beloved face.

But if he was Io, then who was Petyer? Petyer Fieldenstarn was only a
suit of clothes that his spirit wore now, just this lifetime's clothing.

Shaken and yet at peace, Petyer looked again at the list of names.
Atvasfara!

It sounded like a bell. Atvasfara. The one who pulled them together again and again. Atvasfara, wearing the clothes of Hildegard,
Abbess of Rupertsberg. He must talk to her!

When he was finished, Petyer was led into the garden by a shy Sister named Maria Stella. He was beyond social pleasantries, but she seemed to understand his distress, taking his hand and showing him the correct path to where Mother Hildegard sat enraptured by the scent of peonies in bloom. As he turned to thank Sister Maria Stella, he looked carefully at her for the first time and felt her face and the world come in and out of focus. She was there freckled and green eyed, then suddenly she had hazel eyes and three blue lines from lip to chin with a head of brown hair that stood up in short spikes from her scalp. Then back again to Sister Maria Stella with compassionate green eyes.

"Wait. Are you...?" he struggled to finish the question.

"Yes," she replied quietly. "Welcome home, Io. There will be time for all to be made clear. It is time to see Mother now."

She who had been Autakla of the Seal Woman People turned to float back to the Abbey, and Petyer took the steps to come next to Mother Hildegard and sink onto the bench at her side. They both sat in poised stillness looking straight ahead.

"We have been together before?"

"Yes."

"Are we all here now?"

"No. Some of us are here now. Some are lost in the threads of time and space."

"Do you remember it all?" he asked in a tight desperate voice.

"Oh yes, I always do."

"What do you mean 'always'?"

Hildegard took in a deep breath and shared the secret of her lifetimes.

"I remember all of you, all of it, every time. It is most lonesome – the knowing and not finding. I search for you all. Always. In this life I have been blessed to find five – now six of you! Io, it is a great joy, finding you.

She reached for his hand and they sat in calm bliss, feeling the contact of souls long separated, feeling the warmth of palms united again at long last.

"It is time to rest, young Petyer. Rest and eat. On the morrow you shall meet some more of us, you have my word."

# COMTÉ DE FOIX
# 1066–71 CE

When Marguerite was sixteen years old she took her Postulant vows that asked her to state her commitment to the path of becoming a nun. Mother Monica Maria had asked her if she truly felt called, but it never occurred to Marguerite to answer truthfully. Was she called to a life of prayer to be a Bride of Christ? Heavens, no. Was she happy enough where she was? Yes. And she was always free to leave any time before her Final vows.

When Marguerite was eighteen years old she took her Novitiate vows, the next step on that path. Again, Mother asked about the veracity of her calling, and again Marguerite didn't see the benefit in blunt honesty. There was always time to leave before the doors closed completely.

When she was twenty years old she took her First vows. It occurred to her then that there was some momentum in her life that she had totally ignored, but her days were filled with herbal preparations and dosing the sick who came to the convent for help. She roamed the fields and forests beyond the convent walls with a gathering basket and a small knife, and luxuriated in the swell of birdsong and the sun on her face. She found fulfillment, and intellectual stimulation, and some degree of independence in her life at Mater Misericordia. In the outside world she would need to marry: all women did. Life outside this place would be filled with childbearing and the constant drudgery of a farmer's wife. No, she convinced herself, better off here.

She could always decide later.

In the month before Marguerite's twenty-first feast day, when she would need to decide if she would take her Final vows and settle in the convent forever, Sister Angelica had an attack of apoplexy that left her right side paralyzed. She had been perfectly fine one moment, grumbling about the need for more beeswax candles, when suddenly she had turned and tipped her head slightly to the left, and dropped like a stone.

Marguerite let go of the mortar and pestle in her hands and only vaguely heard them crack on the floor of the herb house.

"Sister!"

Angelica's face looked like the right side was melted wax and she couldn't close that eye. She made a gurgling sound and clutched Marguerite's hand with her left. They stayed like that while the sun sank lower in the west and the shadows stretched around them. They had both seen this before, and knew that there was no need for urgent attention. Nothing could be done to make anything better. For the first time in her life, Marguerite found herself in what others might label as prayer.

*"Please, may she not suffer! Please, may she not lose her dignity! What do I do? What is to be done?"*

As if in answer a shaft of sunlight slid though the lowest window and rested in a high shelf where the dangerous herbs were kept. Sister Angelica's good eye tracked the sudden illumination, as did Marguerite's. The tincture of poppies lived on the high shelf, carefully marked and sealed in fine cloth and waxed string.

"Is that what you want, Sister?"

Angelica's crabbed left hand tugged on Marguerite's tunic. They both knew full well the power of that tincture. One drop eased pain. Two drops brought sleep. Four drops delivered eternal rest.

"How many drops do you require, Sister?"

Angelica tugged on Marguerite's tunic four times with astonishing strength.

"Oh!" Marguerite exhaled as if in pain. "You would leave me alone then?"

As the young woman looked down on her elder's face, tears flowed easily and dropped onto Angelica's cheeks.

The two women locked their glances, and let the eons of love and memories flow unimpeded between them. They saw the Temple of Isis and the rest of their beloved Thirteen. They saw and felt and heard and breathed in the very aroma of those times. They embraced each other's souls one more time and then let go.

The look that passed between them lasted mere seconds and held the import of their soul missions. Marguerite gently slid Angelica's head from her lap onto the floor, and stood, walking gingerly over to the high shelf as blood flowed back into her legs. She took the step stool, reached up, and clasped the bottle of poppy tincture. As she walked back to where Angelica was lying on the now cold floor, she noticed in an oddly detached way, that her hands were trembling and that they struggled with the string and cloth wrapping.

"Four drops? You are sure? Not one drop for pain?"

Angelica gurgled again, as if begging. Marguerite met her eye, and then closing her own, nodded briefly and with decision.

"Four it is, then."

She took a few moments to straighten Angelica's legs and pull down the skirt of her habit. She gently wiped the drool from the right side of Angelica's face, adjusted her veil and turned her head so that the Sister could be facing the stripes of peach and magenta now filling the sky. She carefully placed the edge of the bottle against Angelica's lower lip and tipped it so that four thick drops fell sluggishly into the waiting mouth. And then she sat beside Angelica and lifted her head once again into her lap. Together they watched the colors of the sky turn to mauve and dove grey. Marguerite counted the seconds between Angelica's breaths, and the pauses lengthened. When at last the last pause became the final pause, she bent and gave the old nun a kiss on the forehead, and night fell.

# RUPERTSBERG
# 1120 CE

Hunger woke young Master Fieldenstarn when the sun was still young in the sky. He followed his nose, and found himself in the vast Abbey kitchens, standing unnoticed as women scurried and carried and stirred and pounded dough. A small girl, perhaps seven or eight years old sat on a low stool close to the wide fireplace, leaning in as if she were trying to soak all the heat from the fire. She looked wan, with pale dun colored hair and sharp features carved by illness or hunger. She spotted Petyer and exclaimed, in a surprisingly robust voice.

"It's a boy!"

Spoons fell with a clatter and heads whipped around and several women swooped down upon him at once, like a flock of roosting hens. They found him a stool, pulled him up to a high, scarred wooden table and placed fresh bread and butter in front of him before he could even ask. The girl, named Griseld, slid off her stool and came to stand across the table from Petyer, staring at him without any circumspection.

"You are the new arrival?"

Petyer, with his mouth jammed full of the most delicious bread he had ever eaten, could only nod in response. Griseld continued to stare as he chewed, and Petyer felt the full heat of the damnable blushes he suffered rise up his face and well into his hairline. The girl watched, rapt, not granting him the courtesy of turning her gaze somewhere else.

"It shall be useful to always know how you are feeling, boy. That blush tells the truth, yes?"

The girl, Griseld, spoke as if she were an adult and he a child. But Petyer, squirming under her scrutiny, knew himself to be her elder. He swallowed sooner than he should have, choked on a wad of bread, and hastily tried to wash it down with the buttermilk that had appeared at his right elbow as if by magic. He choked harder, a hand slammed between his shoulder blades with precision, and the ball of bread flew out of his mouth and landed on the table.

"A waste of perfectly good food," Griseld remarked and turned to walk deeper into the kitchen to disappear between baking ovens and shadows.

The hand that had walloped Petyer in the back was attached to a frighteningly efficient-looking nun of middle years. She reached across him and swooped the bread ball into the cloth in her other hand, pushed a plate of fried eggs in front of him and was gone before his choking spasms had subsided enough for him to thank her. Petyer addressed himself to the food before him, all the while silently muttering about bossy girls and intimidating nuns. When he had eaten as much as he could fit, another Sister appeared at his shoulder, startling him with her demand that he follow her.

They walked out the back door of the kitchens into the walled gardens still ripe with the last bounty of the vegetables and fruits of autumn. The air was thick with bees and the small swallows that burst out from the branches of the espaliered pear trees that lined one of the high brick walls. Petyer thought about asking where they were going, but the nun's wooden heels clicked hard and fast on the stone walkway and Petyer had to speed up to keep apace with her.

The arched gate was dense with clematis blossoms the color of ripe plums, and the bees were extra busy there. Everyone and everything in the Abbey seemed to move expeditiously. She led him into the formal garden, gestured toward a bench and ordered him to sit. With that, she turned and sped away, back the way they had come. Petyer was feeling quite adrift in this sea of rapid and bossy women. He stubbornly chose to not sit down and instead began to wander aimlessly through the gardens until he heard a male voice.

"Aha!" he thought. "A fellow!" and he followed the voice, turning around a hawthorn border and coming across a very old man, dressed as a gardener, kneeling on one knee. The old man was talking to Sister Maria Stella, the nun who had welcomed Petyer home yesterday and called him Io. The man and the nun heard his approach at the same time and turned their heads to greet him with the wide-open smiles one saves for the dearest of friends.

"There you are!" Sister Maria Stella said.

The old man struggled to stand. Sister Maria Stella took his hand and helped him up. She held onto his hand, taking Petyer's with her other. The old man, the gardener, reached for Petyer's free hand, looked deep into his eyes, "Welcome to my heart."

Petyer felt himself tumbling backwards through eons of time with no sense of up or down, held only in place by the hands holding his so firmly. He saw flashes of images. The searing bolt of sunlight on a giant golden statue. The cold dark tunnel of a tin mine. The burn of a lash across his back. The cool star-filled night of the desert, standing in Circle with these two souls, summoning great power. When he came back to himself, he was in the garden holding the hands of an ancient gardener and a kind-faced nun.

"You have met Sister Maria Stella. May I introduce myself? I am Betterm Haus, head gardener here at the Abbey for some fifty years. And you are Master Fieldenstarn, I am told."

The old man had light blue eyes that showed no sign of fading. He held himself erect and his face held a thousand crisscross wrinkles from a life in the out of doors. His gaze was kind, and infinitely patient, and he looked at Petyer as he might have watched a plant, waiting for it to bloom in its own time. Petyer had dropped the hands that had held his, but he noticed that the nun and the gardener had interlaced their fingers and stood connected, watching him and gently smiling as if he were a clever toddler that they loved.

Sister Maria Stella spoke softly, "Betterm has been showing me how to splice the stem from one variety of rose onto another. In this way we can protect and save those varieties that may have been damaged by winter or insects. See young Petyer, different shades of color, all on the same bush."

Petyer felt like her words held some deeper message, but when he looked at her she seemed to be resting in the simplicity of her statement. She continued, "You spoke to Mother Hildegard? You know that we have lived before, yes?"

Petyer nodded vigorously, and blushed yet again when he discovered that he had no words that could meet this situation. The gardener and the nun shared a look and seemed to have an entire conversation between them without speaking. Sister Maria Stella nodded as if in agreement and then spoke aloud to Petyer.

"Let us walk. We have found that walking facilitates the workings of the mind and allows the spirit time to catch up."

The three walked along the garden paths until they reached the edge of the formal plantings. Here the gardens ran to saplings, planted each year by Betterm to create a lush complex forest that held homes for all the wildlife around the Abbey. The trees grew taller as they walked deeper into the woods. Some of the oaks had started to turn a rich gold, and the aspen leaves trembled in the light breeze.

Betterm and Maria Stella still walked hand in hand and had pulled slightly ahead of Petyer in the speckled light. In an explosion of remembrance, as if clouds were blown away from his knowing, he saw who they had been. They held hands! They had always held hands when he had first known them. He remembered them walking alongside a wide green river, two young women whose rhythms matched perfectly. He saw them in his mind's eye as they leaned against one another, sharing plates of lentils and lamb. He knew how they had curled together in sleep and love atop brilliant patterned rugs and cushions, for he had seen that too. They were soul mates, friends of the heart, and had found each other again in very different forms. Autakla, the Shape Shifter from the far northern seas and Silbara, the scholar of Brighid from Calanais, were together again. He saw those two young women moving in the bodies of the nun and gardener, so powerful was their bond that not age nor gender nor social class could keep them apart. Petyer felt himself welling up with sadness and relief and wonder.

Sister Maria Stella and Betterm walked on ahead slowly and gave Petyer the time he needed to catch up. They approached a sturdy wooden bench and Betterm eased himself down onto it, breathing audibly.

"I planted these trees over thirty years ago, before either of you came into this life. They have been my children, my hope for a future, my legacy."

Petyer looked up at the high shade canopy overhead. It was a mixed forest of beech and larch and oak. All the leaves reached for each other in a lacy dance that moved high above, responding to the music of the wind. "This is a peaceful place. You have made a beautiful legacy, sir," Petyer said with a certain degree of shyness.

Betterm nodded in soft agreement.

"It is my belief that the trees of a forest talk to each other, that they share and communicate and know. Oh yes, they know, perhaps more than our minds can know in a single lifetime. But we three, and the others of the Thirteen who are here, we have all the blessings of more than a single lifetime. We possess the knowing of what came before." The old man paused and looked at young Petyer hard. "These blessings must never be squandered, young Master Fieldenstarn. You understand this, yes? You must not share what we know, what we are. There are many, oh so many, who would not understand and would be moved by their fear to do us harm."

Betterm didn't stop his hard stare until Petyer nodded in reply. The old man continued.

"No one. Not your parents or friends or any one whom you may ever love may know these secrets. Mother Hildegard will tell you more, but those of us who have been discovered before in other times have suffered greatly for it. Promise you will hold these secrets!" The gardener gripped Petyer's hand till his knuckles popped. "Promise!"

"I promise! I swear!"

# ALEXANDRIA, IMPERIAL PROVINCE OF AEGYPTUS (EGYPT) 415 CE

The merchant was running and fighting his way through the mob. His lungs were burning and his vision was narrowing but he couldn't let himself slow down. The sound of the mob was like a tidal wave, like the roar of a thousand lions, and he had to get to her before the worst could happen.

He had been traveling to Alexandria for two months now, ever since he heard of the famed Hypatia and her scholarship. He had read her treatise on the movement of the celestial bodies, and he knew with absolute certainty that she was one of the ones that he burned to find. In his dreams he kept company with those he grieved for, the thirteen that he felt compelled to seek out. Only once before in this lifetime had he found one of his beloveds. She had been a house-slave in a fellow merchant's house, and to keep her safe he had made her his second wife. He never flagged in his searching, with no results. And then he had read Hypatia's work.

But nature and mankind had conspired to delay him. Storms along the coast kept him stalled in Tyre. An insurrection in Galilee had forced him to find an alternate route southward. And today when he finally arrived at the Port of Alexandria the rumors spread like wildfire that the Wise One, the Professor, the Witch – all depending on who was speaking – was being charged and tried in the Agora today.

He stumbled and fell to one knee as a throng rushed past him, with an energy as startling as lightening. Struggling to his feet he raced on, and with the crowd he spilled into the large open plaza of the Agora. There she was – standing atop the staircase to the Library, looking out calmly on the mass of people below her as shouts and cries for mercy and screams for her death showered around her. Two men grabbed her arms and trussed her up, like a goat for slaughter.

"No!" the merchant cried, and Hypatia heard his anguish above all the rest. She lifted her eyes and looked right at him with a question, then a light of recognition, then a shimmer of regret. He saw the one-sided smile that he knew of the old days, the imperious humor of Uxua, she who had been the living embodiment of Ix Chel.

For that one moment they are reunited.

Then she was dragged down the steps of her beloved Library, tied to the horse of one of the Christians and pulled through the Agora to the wails and cheers and pulsing sounds of a thousand heartbeats in the merchant's ears.

"I will find you again, I promise."

# RUPERTSBERG 1120 CE

With that vow spoken, the three sat in stillness, such a profound stillness that a fox wandered across the woodland floor not more than fifteen feet away, paused in more curiosity than fear, then continued her walk into the pale shadows of the morning. Finally, young Petyer spoke so softly that his words could be mistaken for the sloughing of leaves in the wind.

"I see flashes of memory. I know who you two are and what you have been to each other. I see places and buildings not like any in this land. I was drawn here, pestered in my dreams by Mother Hildegard, or rather, Mother Hildegard in another form. But when I try to find the surety, it slips away."

Sister Maria Stella nodded and spoke thoughtfully.

"It is thus, for us all. I counsel patience, young Master Fieldenstarn. With patience the mind will relax like a long-held fist that can soften to reveal what treasure rests in the palm. Mother Hildegard will guide you as you regain what is yours to know. The tricky part is to not slip up in front of others. And for that reason, I will call you Io this last time only."

She paused, and began again, speaking past the emotion in her throat.

"Ah, the sweet joy of saying your name. Io. Io."

The gardener wrapped his arm around her, she leaned into his shoulder, and they both looked at Petyer with such joy, the intense joy of long separation and delicious reunion. Betterm the gardener continued when Maria Stella could not.

"Io, you were and will always be in our hearts. But going forward, it is Petyer Fieldenstarn. Or as Sister Delphinia calls you, the Impudent Boy!"

Maria Stella and Betterm laughed, and the chagrined Petyer gradually joined in. With a nod of mutual agreement, they rose and began to walk down the gentle slope back toward the Abbey gardens. Petyer, with the pent-up emotion of his discoveries here and the physical form of an adolescent boy, raced around the trees running forward and back to his companions, like a puppy set free. Betterm stumbled and Maria Stella clasped his elbow to steady him. She looked with worry at his face. He was pale and had a light sheen of sweat across his upper lip. But she was most startled to see the tears that traced down the crevasses of his cheeks.

"Beloved! What is it? Are you not well?"

"I am old Autakla. This body is old. And I wonder if I will live to see any others of us together once more. It will grieve me greatly to have to leave you again."

With that Betterm turned his face down to hers and kissed her on the lips with the tenderness and passion of three thousand years. Petyer saw it out of the corner of his eye, and raced back down the slope. In his mind he saw Silbara and Autakla, one tall and pale with wheaten hair, the other small and compact with a sable corona, leaning into each other and making a bridge with their kisses, a bridge to last all the lifetimes. Petyer Fieldenstarn might have been shocked to see an old man and a nun in an embrace of love, but for Io this was as it should be, now and forever.

When they had returned to the expanse of gardens, they could hear song floating from Mother Hildegard's chambers. There was a lute melody, and then a thin but true voice weaving in and around the notes. The sun was now high in the sky, and Mother Hildegard was still ensorcelled by the song that had graced her much earlier that day. Betterm left to go rest in his cottage at the edge of the gardens.

Sister Maria Stella approached Petyer, "What next for us, young one?"

"Food!" he replied without hesitation, and she laughed and led the way to the kitchens. This was a different path than he had been led along this morning, past rooms filled with books, with another light-filled room with rows of high desks where nuns were bent transcribing something. Then on past a large salon a-jumble with stringed instruments and pipes and flutes of all descriptions.

"We here at the Abbey are encouraged by Mother Hildegard to make music. Truth to tell, most of the women here sought out this place where we may pursue a life of devotion to the Divine through art and intellect. Places like this are very rare, young Petyer. Very rare indeed."

A shadow flitted across her face like a dark cloud pushed across a mountainside by an in incoming storm. Maria Stella gave her head a sharp shake, and gestured for him to proceed with her down the corridor. The hall seemed to run down a slight slope as if burrowing into a hillside. Up ahead the sound of women's voices blended with the thwack of knives hitting wood and iron pans tinging together. It was yet another kind of music here at the Abbey, the sound of the 'busy and bossy' women Petyer had encountered when he broke his fast, but this time he found the clamor reassuring. No matter whatever strange and unsettling information might bubble up to the surface of his consciousness, the kitchens of the Abbey were firmly in the here and now. And he was hungry.

The odd girl he had met this morning was seated at the high wooden table leaning on one elbow and looking askance at the bowl of stew in front of her. She poked without enthusiasm at the food, and, as if under duress, brought a small spoonful to her mouth, then put her utensil down.

"Eat!" came the command shouted across the noisy kitchen, as a general might give the order to 'Charge!' on a battlefield. And the girl, Griseld, gave a surly sideways look, and scooped a spoonful into her mouth. Maria Stella smiled at Petyer and then seemed to evaporate into the mist of busyness. He turned to look at the unhappy girl who had reached a hand to pull up the shawl that had slipped off her left shoulder. In a flash or what he now knew to be true remembrance, Petyer saw her reaching for the edge of a long white cloak of silver wolf. The sliver of vision was gone as she looked up, saw him, and dared him with her eyes to say one single thing. He started to smile, and then thought better of it. Best not to poke that bear, he thought.

As if by practical magic, a generous bowl of stew appeared before him, and in the way of all healthy young mammals, he bent to his work, eating fast and with dedication. When he had finished his bowl, mopping up the last bits with his fourth slice of bread, Petyer stopped and looked under his lashes at the girl across the table. She didn't look well at all. Dark circles lay under her eyes, and her complexion was a translucent grey, the color of river oysters. Feeling fortified by venison and root vegetables, he ventured to introduce himself.

"My name is Petyer Fieldenstarn. I am from..."

"I know," she said abruptly.

Petyer paused, waiting for her to offer her name. The girl looked surreptitiously over her shoulder, saw that her domina of eating was focused elsewhere, and slid off her stool.

"Follow me," she whispered.

They left the kitchens by a back corridor that opened like the maw of a giant fish between two enormous bake ovens. Petyer felt the blast of heat, then the contained warmth as they walked deeper between the brick walls to come to an abrupt ascent up a narrow spiral stone staircase. He touched the walls and they were hot!

"The heat! Where is it coming from?" he asked.

The girl, Griseld, was breathing hard. She stopped climbing and looked over her shoulder and down at him three steps below.

"The clay pipes from the bake ovens run through the walls and up to the infirmary to keep it warm all year round. Mother Hildegard's idea."

"Is there nothing that woman doesn't get into?" he muttered under his breath, still carrying umbrage at Hildegard for pestering his dreams these last months and years.

Griseld's thin voice took on a stern tone and aged decades in an instant. To Petyer it seemed that her tiny form aged too, from young sick girl to wizened crone.

"That woman, as you call her, is a miracle of intellect and wisdom, and if she suffers to let you be here, you are among the blessed on this earth."

Without pausing to see his reaction she turned and began her laborious climb once again. Petyer, well and truly chagrined, followed. They wound around and around, continuing their climb beyond the landing that led to the infirmary. He caught a glimpse of a sunny room with several pallets dressed with stark white sheets. He had a momentary immersion in the smell of vinegar and honey, and the sound of gentle singing in call and response.

In an awkward attempt at reconciliation Petyer asked.

"Is that the infirmary you spoke of?"

The girl only grunted assent.

"Not a bad place to be sick," he ventured.

Griseld said nothing.

"Not that I've ever been sick, mind you. My mother says I am as healthy as a peasant."

The girl stopped suddenly and he almost walked up into her. She slowly turned to look him square in the eye, and her look bore into him. She was not an old woman now, but an astonishingly angry young one. He felt himself flush violently as he belatedly remembered that this girl was patently not well. The thought also occurred to him, too late, too late, that she might also be a peasant.

"Lucky you," she said, her words separate and distinct and burning like acid.

Wishing that the ground would open up beneath him and swallow him whole, Petyer had a moment, an eye blink moment of vertigo, as if the earth suddenly *had* opened and he was dropping hard and fast. Those words that had been his thought, *the ground opened up and swallowed him whole*, had become a real thing, a memory that squeezed the breath from him and blotted out the stars.

It was all sound, clanging, harsh, brutal sound. No notion of being-ness; no sense of self. Just motion faster than light and unimaginable sound breaking the ears. Nothing to hang onto. Nothing to know. Sheer terror.

He came back to himself after a second, an hour, and was awash with sweat. He was clinging to the stones of the wall, leaning on it for his life, whimpering in abject fear. Griseld was watching him with a detached curiosity, like he was an insect in some distress.

"We can only be who we are and who we were, and sometimes those two pieces don't fit together very graceful-like, boy. We can only pray you improve."

She spoke not unkindly but without much warmth. It was as if she paused and took stock, then came to a decision.

"Oh well. You always did have some rough edges, didn't you."

Petyer was clear that she wasn't speaking of Petyer Fieldenstarn, so he could only lift his shoulders in a shrug of begging ignorance. She chortled and turned and climbed. It was clear that she was struggling with the stairs. She had begun to use her hands on the walls to help with each step, and her breathing was starting to catch and rasp, like a saw pulled back and forth across a log.

"May I hel…" he started to ask when she turned back halfway towards him and snarled like a wounded fox. Petyer was stunned into silence. People usually spoke to young Master Fieldenstarn, the Burgomeister's son, with some air of deference, or at the least civility. But this chit of a girl snapped at him like he was a cur.

"All right, then! Sorry I offered!"

She turned and climbed. After what was an eternity of bruised feelings, wounded pride and awkward silence, they arrived at a round room at the very top of the tower. There were windows in each direction that had real glass, a corbeled ceiling, a narrow bed piled high with blankets against the south part of the wall, and a small brazier in the center of the room, lit even in the warmth of the day sending puffs of frankincense out to saturate the air. This was clearly Griseld's room, and she walked into the space with the air of ownership. She took off her shawl and dropped it on the low red wooden chest, carved with what looked like sea monsters or dragons. She sank into a camp chair that she had pulled closer to the brazier and put a pot of water to hang on a tripod over the fire. Petyer stood just inside the room's entrance, unsure of what to do, and afraid to say anything that might encourage another snarl.

He waited while the girl caught her breath, then finally shifted his weight and one shoe scraped against the brick floor. She didn't look up at him, but waved a hand at another camp chair against the wall.

"Sit."

Petyer obliged, dragging the chair to the opposite side of the brazier. He thought about asking if this was her room, the sort of conversational entre that he had been taught so well. But then he remembered that her tolerance for his statements of the obvious was in short supply and just kept his mouth shut, feeling the silence stretch out.

The water came to a boil. Griseld brewed tea that smelled like wet cat, and offered some to him begrudgingly. He declined. She chortled again.

"A wise decision. This tea is another of Mother Hildegard's ideas. For my recovery, she says, even though we both know that to be a polite subterfuge. But I drink it for her sake."

Griseld's humor seemed to improve as she sipped the tea. At length she set down the cup and looked at Petyer, her lips turning up slightly in what, for her, might be construed as a smile.

"So, you are one of the Thirteen, eh?" She spoke the question like a statement.

"It would appear so," Petyer replied.

"Who have you met so far? Mother Hildegard, of course. Anyone else?"

"Is it allowed to speak of these things?" Petyer asked.

"Why else do you think I brought you all the way up here, silly. Of course it is allowed, so long as no one can overhear."

"But, are you one of the Thirteen?" Petyer was oddly reluctant to open up to this strange girl. It was as if she wasn't even a little girl at all, but some creature from a folk tale. She barked a sound that could, for her, be construed as a laugh. But when she spoke, her voice was again as it had been on that staircase, that of someone of great age, not a little girl's at all. Her face became an intricate map of lines and crevasses, and her hazel eyes changed to small black currants sunk deep in her skull. Petyer couldn't help himself. He shivered at the transformation, as if she slipped back and forth between worlds, between forms.

"You know that I am, Io. We lived and died together before, and now it seems we live, and I at least will die when we are together again."

"You are dying?"

45

"I have consumption. And no matter what foul brew Mother Hildegard thinks up, it will, before long, consume me. But we shall have some span of time together, at least. That can be a comfort, yes?"

Again came the barking laugh, but this time the laugh rolled over into a cough that persisted much too long for Petyer's ease. "*There is nothing of a comfort here*," he thought to himself.

But he was wrong. As Griseld's cough subsided and she leaned back into her chair, they both stared into the tiny fire in the brazier. Minutes passed, and an odd kind of comfort happened for Petyer. He was content, not a usual state of being for young Master Fieldenstarn. His body relaxed deeper into his chair, and he didn't twitch and wish to be up and away. His thoughts slowed down. And the silence in the room, only punctuated by the occasional hiss of charcoal and the call of swifts outside the window, became a soothing balm for his soul.

These past months had been a time of continuously escalating confusion and pressure. His dreams had pummeled him at night with increasing frequency until he had felt that his head would split like an over-ripe melon. His decision to make the journey here to Rupertsberg had involved some deception and plotting, unusual behavior from his normal, overly forthright manner. And the week on the road had been quite terrifying, although he would never admit that to anyone. Navigating the world without the automatic deference granted to the Burgomeister's son had been eye-opening. Tough men, uncaring shopkeepers, fleas – all had been assaults to his sense of what the world was. And since his arrival, he had been pulled back and forth through time in a most disconcerting way. So, yes, there was some strange comfort here in the silence of Griseld's eyrie. He looked at the amulet that Griseld wore around her neck. It looked like a wood carving of a feather. He felt his eyes drift shut with the image of the feather imprinted on the back of his eyelids.

Kakehtaweyihtam/Sally Standing Bear — *Atvasfara*
Misimohokasiw — *Awa*
Wapiscanis/Walter — *Tiamet*
Tom Fletcher — *Parasfahe*

# RUPERT'S LAND OF THE HUDSON BAY COMPANY (CANADA) 1869 CE

Kakehtaweyihtam, golden eyes shining, stood before her mother as the final ceremonial ornament, a hawk feather on a leather strap was placed around her neck. It was her wedding day. Well, it was the true ceremony, as far as she was concerned. Tomorrow she would ride into town with the man she had chosen and stand in front of a Christian priest. The folks from the Trading Company said that was a 'real wedding', and she knew that they secretly thought her man was foolish for wanting to 'do it legal' with a Cree woman. But he did, and she wanted to bend enough to give that to him.

Her mother, Misimohokasiw, was the primary medicine dancer for her people, and it was important to her that her daughter was pledged in the Old Way, the true way, to that man, the *moniyaw* that she had set her heart to. This man, this moniyaw, couldn't even say her daughter's name correctly and ended up calling her Sahlee. He looked so strange to Misimohokasiw. He was tall and had hair the color of the sand along the riverbank. His skin seemed always to be pink or red like oak leaves in autumn. And his eyes! They were frightening eyes, pale like the sky with long sandy lashes that lifted too quickly when he directed his gaze right at you. Kakehtaweyihtam had explained that he meant no disrespect. The opposite – he was trying to convince her people of his sincerity and honor. *Moniyaws* were strange like that.

"You make sure he treats you with honor, daughter," Misimohokasiw said softly as she lowered the final necklace into place. "And if he does not, you must return to us at once before the snows set in."

"Mother, I know his heart. And I see my path with him."

"You have always seen so much, my girl," her mother replied. "You are one of the Old Ones. The elders have always known that. And so, I trust your seeing."

Misimohokasiw looked away quickly to hide the brightening in her eyes from the unshed tears. But she felt the need to tell her daughter one more thing.

"Don't let him see you doing ceremony, daughter! Hide your medicine. Don't give him that."

Kakehtaweyihtam, She is Wise, nodded and felt her world shift as she looked at her beloved mother's face and saw the face of a young bird-like girl with ebony skin. She had been so fortunate in this life to be with two of her beloved Thirteen. Her brother, Wapiscanis, now worked as a hunting guide with the *moniyaws* who called him Walter. In this lifetime he enjoyed the freedom of physical strength and the liberty of constant motion, so different than when he had lived for decades in a mountain Temple at the Roof of the World as Tiamet. It had been he who had introduced her to the man who would be her mate, and she knew that he and she could bridge the two worlds of *moniyaw* and Cree. Perhaps there could be some safety for her people. The moniyaws were pushing her people into smaller and smaller areas, limiting their hunting grounds and demanding that they register with the official Indian Agent. Kakehtaweyihtam felt an urgent desire to do whatever she could to protect their ways, their language, their very existence. This marriage might help.

But it would mean leaving her people, her family. She would move away from this sweet good soul, her mother, she who had been Awa of Yemaya. She felt the pierce of loss yet again. How she would miss her mother, her Awa! There was never enough time!

Now the sun was setting and it was the ceremony. They heard the sound of the approaching crowd outside the lodge house. Mother and daughter in the present, friends from ages past, embraced one more time and turned together to move out into late summer evening. The air was rich with the scent of fir and pine and the din of crickets.

There he was, the man that would help her fulfill her destiny, Louis Portreaux, fur trapper, poet, and fiddle player. His face split into a wide smile when he saw her and he couldn't contain his enthusiasm.

"Sally! By god you are beautiful!"

Wapiscanis led Kakehtaweyihtam forward to stand by the fire circle that has been surrounded by rocks. There were two fires lit, one in the north and one in the south. And in the center between the two was a large pile of unlit wood, seven different kinds of wood. Kakehtaweyihtam and Louis stood, each by a fire, and the Medicine Woman came to them both with the sacred pipe. They inhaled the smoke and swept it up over their heads to ask the blessings of Spirit. Then Kakehtaweyihtam and Louis took the hawk feathers that they each wore, and the Medicine Woman bound them together so they could never be separated. Each from their own side, Kakehtaweyihtam and Louis began to push the lit fires into the center until that central fire was burning vigorously. She looked across the fire to watch Louis. He looked so earnest! It was endearing, and childlike.

Their union now made and witnessed, the tribe began to sing and dance, led by Misimohokasiw. The celebration lasted far into the night, and Louis was persuaded to get up and dance as well. Everybody laughed, even Louis, but the people appreciated his sincerity. When the stars were fully out Kakehtaweyihtam and Louis went into the small hut that the tribe had built for them, and found their happiness in love-making deepened. Tomorrow would have to take care of itself.

And so it was that Kakehtaweyihtam, she who had been Atvasfara, entered into her new life as Sally Standing Bear Portreaux.

# RUPERTSBERG
# 1120 CE

When at last he lifted his eyes from the flame he saw that Griseld's little girl face was in place. Her jaw hung slightly open, her eyes were shut and a little snore, like a puppy snuffle, came with each breath. Still he kept quiet, taking the opportunity to study her in repose. Sharp cheekbones, a stubborn pointed chin, and wisps of hair curling in the hot air from the brazier. She was tiny and fierce. Tiny and fierce. Tiny and fierce. Those words kept repeating in his mind until he heard a voice saying them – about him – no, not him – him when he was Io – and had been – tiny and fierce. He woke with a jolt, not having realized that he had been drifting. He looked at Griseld who was now also awake, and torrents of feelings poured back and forth between them like the confluence of two powerful rivers and the swirling currents formed there.

"We were the oldest and the youngest then," Griseld said. "I was older than anyone could remember, and you were but nine sun cycles, so very tiny and so very fierce."

Petyer jolted and then nodded. That all felt truer than true.

"There are moments when your face changes," he said, slightly nervously. "You are you, and then another, an impossibly old other."

Griseld laughed a sound like rocks rumbling, and then a little girl giggle.

"Yes, that is what some called me, the Impossibly Old One. I feel the shifting when it happens, and it happens more and more often these days. When it happens Mother Hildegard looks very sad. So, I am assuming that it isn't a good sign."

Petyer settled into silence again and let the sensation of rightness take possession of his bones. He felt at home with this odd girl and the old gardener and the young nun and the extraordinary Mother Hildegard. He felt more at home with them than with his own parents and sisters back in Wiesbaden.

"What was your name back then?" he asked.

"I was a devotee of Lhamo from the Roof of the World and my name was Tia…"

"…met! Your name was Tiamet!" Petyer exclaimed. "I know that!"

Griseld smiled a small flat smile that narrowed her eyes, and looked at Petyer proudly. He felt proud of himself too, like the day he learned to ice skate and the skills coalesced such that he became fluid on the ice. He now felt he was becoming fluid with the past and moving rapidly and gracefully over the surface of what had been. The sound of the Abbey bells began to ring the Angelus, and Petyer was startled to find that so many hours had gone by since he had followed Griseld out of the kitchens.

"Time is…"

"…a gossamer thing!" she finished his thought and smiled her peculiar smile once again. "It is time now to gather with the others."

She stood with obvious effort, shook off the hand he offered in assistance and led the way out of the room and back down the long flights of stairs. Petyer recalled Mother Hildegard telling him that there were six "of them" here now, so he posited the question to Griseld as they wound downward.

"I met Betterm Haus and Sister Maria Stella, and now you. Who else is here?"

She paused, caught her breath and looked up over her shoulder at him.

"I may not tell you about anyone else. That is always our own singular story to tell. But when we gather you will see what you know, and decide what you will tell."

At the bottom of the stairs they emerged between the big bake ovens into the kitchens that if possible, were even more bustling than they had been earlier in the day. Griseld saw Petyer eyeing a meat pie, and taking a piece of toweling grabbed a hot pie, handing it to him. They exited the kitchens to the sound of that same martial voice from before yelling after Griseld.

"You need to eat as well, you infuriating child!"

Griseld just lifted one shoulder and hurried on, Petyer right on her heels. She took yet another path through the gardens and they came to a small pavilion at the edge of a lake. It had the look of the old Roman ruins in Petyer's home town, but this structure was obviously new and the marble was smooth, shiny, and a pale pink in the late afternoon light. Betterm Haus and Sister Maria Stella were already there, seated on one of the marble benches that circled the raised platform, drinking from a stone water jug. They nodded at the two new arrivals as they sat down on another bench. Sunset was another hour away, but the light struck sparkles on the lake surface and the swallows and swifts were beginning their evening hunt for insects across the top of the water.

Within minutes Mother Hildegard approached, with a bouquet of peonies dangling from her hand, still humming the tune Petyer had heard earlier wafting from her study. She seemed surprised to find them there when she came up the steps of the pavilion and then gave them her smile of unsurpassing sweetness.

"Beloveds! How wonderful to see you here together!" she said as if she hadn't seen them in ages.

"As it is to see you, Mother, each and every day we are granted that gift," Betterm replied.

And Mother Hildegard laughed with joy and with the knowledge that she had been found out in her distractedness and still loved despite, and perhaps because, of it all. She looked closely at Petyer, saw that he was finishing his meat pie and appeared at ease, nodded to herself and took a seat on the bench between Betterm, Griseld and Petyer.

Petyer saw a curious person walking up the path toward them. He assumed it was a man since they wore trousers, but the person walked in a lilting fashion, like a young woman at a mayday dance. He had flowing yellow hair that curled in effortless ringlets and the barest hint of a beard, little wisps of fair hair that speckled his face rather than forming continuous growth. And when he lifted his eyes and directed them at Petyer, the boy was pinned to the spot by the intensity of that emerald stare.

*"Here was power!"* Petyer thought, *"Power wrapped in beauty."*

The man gave Petyer a smile that made him blush hard, a smile that seemed to invite actions that Petyer hadn't even dreamed of in his short life, a smile that incited, demanded response.

"Easy does it, Alejandro. We don't want to scare the young boy off before he even knows you, do we?" Betterm said wryly.

The man, Alejandro, made a quarter turn, executed a magnificent courtly bow to Mother Hildegard, and granted Betterm a half-smile of acknowledgement. He then spun on his right foot and lowered himself onto a bench with the grace of a leaf floating to the ground. Petyer couldn't take his eyes off of this Alejandro fellow with a combination of fascination and terror, as if the man could shapeshift into some giant cat and spring into attack in an eye blink. Griseld patted his hand in comfort.

"Don't mind him. He always makes a dramatic entrance," she said, not minding that Alejandro heard.

Alejandro emitted a low sound like a purr, almost indiscernible, yet it touched Petyer and made the hairs stand up on his arm. *"Power, indeed,"* he thought. Griseld just chuckled that rocks tumbling down a hillside chuckle of hers, and they all settled in to watch the birds skim the water. After some long peaceful minutes, Mother Hildegard seemed to rise up from her reverie and spoke to Petyer.

"We are waiting, young Master Fieldenstarn, for our remaining compatriot. She is…"

"Always late," Alejandro silkily inserted.

"Yes, although she would say, that we are always early," Mother Hildegard calmly replied with a slight smile of bemusement. Betterm exchanged glances with Sister Maria Stella in which an entire conversation took place. Griseld coughed, causing Mother Hildegard to look at her with concern, and Petyer tried not to squirm on the bench.

At length, the sound of shuffling footsteps reached the pavilion and Alejandro stretched his spine and sat up from the lounging position he had acquired. A heavy-set nun of middle years walked up the gravel path accompanied by a small pudgy dog of indeterminate heritage. Both nun and dog were breathing audibly, and both had their faces set in a pattern of grumpiness. No one spoke as the two trundled up the steps of the pavilion and sat with grunts and grumbles. The new arrival looked at those gathered, spotted Petyer among them.

"Who's this then?" she inquired flatly, with no discernable warmth.

The dog eyed Petyer suspiciously, then walked over and sniffed the boy's feet. Suddenly the short stumpy tail began to wag with vigor, and the dog jumped up, putting its paws on Petyer's leg and proceeded to wash his face with enthusiastic licks. Petyer had always liked dogs and returned the welcome with ear-rubbing and soft exclamations.

The dog's companion visibly melted and smiled at Petyer with an awesome display of yellowed teeth. Her name, he would come to know, was Sister Catherine of the Wheel, a name that also conjured up some terrifying imagery. He wondered what, in the name of all that is holy, would direct someone to choose the name of that gruesomely murdered martyr. The flames, the arrows, the spinning wheel, it all gave Petyer the shudders. The dog eventually tired of the attention, or simply tired on his plump legs and went back to rest at his human's feet.

Mother Hildegard smiled at everyone, cleared her throat, and began.

"We are beyond delight at the presence of our new young friend here tonight. Alejandro, Sister Catherine, you have not formally been introduced to Master Petyer Fieldenstarn of Wiesbaden. He found his way to us on the silvery pathway of dreams and memories. He has spent the morning with Betterm and Sister Maria Stella, and the afternoon with Griseld, so I am to assume that he and they shared their stories. Does anyone have anything they would like to add?"

She looked around the circle, connecting with each person there in a time-stopping gaze. Sister Catherine of the Wheel finally spoke.

"Well, Dog likes him, so that's all right by me."

Alejandro simply looked sideways at Petyer and fluttered his eyelashes. Mother Hildegard continued.

"Young Petyer, we six – now seven! – meet here of an evening to be able to openly share what we remember of who we were. For some out in the world, our memories mark us as heretics, so we speak with the understanding that our bond is sacrosanct. Speak at your own discretion, young man. No one here will judge you if you choose not to speak. We begin, if you so choose, by declaring ourselves in present and past."

She looked over her shoulder and surveyed the area nearby. Nodding to herself that they were indeed alone, she continued.

"I am Hildegard, Abbess of Rupertsberg, formerly Atvasfara, High Priestess of Isis."

Griseld stirred from within her shawl and spoke.

"I am Griseld, orphan of the parish of Bingen, formerly Tiamet, devotee of Lhamo."

"I am Betterm Haus, gardener of this Abbey, formerly Silbara, Priestess of Brighid at the Mystery School of Calanais."

"I am Sister Maria Stella of this Abbey, formerly Autakla of the People of Seal Woman."

Alejandro took a long pause and then added.

"I am Alejandro de Marsitel of Sevilla, formerly known as Uxua the Priestess of Ix Chel."

Sister Catherine surreptitiously wiped a tear away from her cheek, and said.

"I am Sister Catherine of the Wheel. I followed Mother Hildegard here to this Abbey from Bingen, and was formerly known as Badh, the Keeper of Wild Spaces and daughter of the Cailleach."

Petyer heard each of their pronouncements as if a loud gong was struck and felt the reverberations of their names push into his bones and beyond. He felt all their eyes on him as he stood, straightened his shoulders, and in his best politician's son voice introduced himself.

"I am Petyer Fieldenstarn of Wiesbaden, formerly known as Io of the Wild Hunt, Dedicant of Artemis."

He surprised himself with those details, but they flowed from his mouth with the surety of the sun rising each day. He stood, stunned for a moment, then sat back down with a scarlet flush spreading up his cheeks.

Mother Hildegard cleared her throat, tightened with emotion, and spoke.

"As you all know, my charge has been to always remember those days from long ago, and to seek out each of us as we revolve around the Wheel of Life. This charge is a privilege that has, at times, accorded me the reunion with some of the Thirteen and those companions from that momentous series of events. In some lifetimes I have met one or two. There was one spectacular life in the land of Qin when there were four of us who gathered and lived and spread our knowledge, and several of us lived together at a convent in Foix. But never before have I been so blessed as to sit with six of you, in some safety and calm, to be able to remember. Why now and for what purpose I cannot say. But I revel in the blessings of your company."

Sister Catherine spoke.

"I am concerned about this boy being here. Doesn't he have family? By his speech and manner of dress, they are family of some standing? What do they say to his being in this place? We need no undue attention given to us here."

Several heads nodded. Mother Hildegard replied.

"It is true that Master Fieldestarn's family is notable. And it is also true, that our young Petyer left his home without notifying his parents."

Exclamations of consternation rumbled around the circle. Petyer felt his face flush vividly again and wished he could sink beneath the bench and disappear.

"Calm yourselves, my beloveds. Calm yourselves. I have sent word to his people of his whereabouts and requested that he be able to continue the studies of Latin and Greek that he so desires here. We will wait and see what response we get. Your concerns are noted, but our Io has found us and we must take the moment to rejoice in that."

Alejandro spoke, his voice deepened by intensity.

"Mother, I appreciate your placidity and trust in the benign nature of the universe. But we all remember the trouble from the Archbishop last year. He has not forgotten, I think we all can be assured of that. He loathes your independence here; he feels it to be anathema. And he is only looking for something to use against you, to drag you and your autonomy before the Pontiff."

Mother Hildegard reached over and clasped Alejandro's hand.

"Yes, my Fierce One. I feel him skulking just outside our sanctuary too. This safety is precious and rare. So we will be smart, and we will be careful, and we will trust that the Goddess has brought us together now for some good and precious reason."

*Goddess.* Mother Hildegard had said it aloud. *Goddess.* The very word was like pearls of sound trembling in the air, dangerous and beautiful pearls. Alejandro's jaw worked hard, but he kept still, leaned over abruptly, and kissed Hildegard's hand. Petyer watched all this and felt guilt, another sensation not familiar to Petyer Fieldenstarn. Had he, without meaning to, brought this group into some danger?

"I am sorry. I didn't mean…"

Griseld patted his hand. Betterm and Sister Maria Stella smiled at him. Sister Catherine made a tut-tutting noise. And Mother Hildegard stopped him by saying.

"We know, Petyer. We know. The voices of the past have made all of us act in rash ways. Haven't they, Alejandro?"

She shot the man a look under her lashes, and he had the grace to look slightly chagrined from this gentle reminder of his own stumbling path to his foreknowledge on his way to find Mother Hildegard. The group seemed to settle, and Mother Hildegard began to sing the song she had been sculpting all day.

*"The Sun, she rises each day anew*
*As Night she folds away*
*We find delights in this new light*
*And grace is sent our way."*

The hymn wound on through eight verses and the chorus. One by one the people sitting around the circle joined in, with Sister Catherine adding a luscious harmony that surprised Petyer. It culminated with them all standing, arms raised above their heads, singing that chorus together with joy and unity. The last line clung to the now twilight air.

*"And grace is sent our way."*

They stood, rooted in the now, with their voices reaching into the past until, with a sigh, Mother Hildegard turned and gently wafted from the pavilion, still trailing her bouquet of peonies snagged on the hem of her habit.

They all felt that grace, and hung suspended in it for infinite crystalline moments. At long last, they lowered their arms and began to amble from the pavilion, back towards the Abbey. Sisters Maria Stella and Catherine of the Wheel were headed to prayers. Betterm took the side turn toward his cottage, knowing that Maria Stella would come to him later with food and some hours of company and comfort. Alejandro swept Griseld up and onto his shoulders to give her a ride back to their evening repast. Some strides along the path he stopped and turned back to Petyer. The man didn't look especially friendly, but he didn't look like he wanted to eat Petyer either.

"Come along then, young fellow. Join us for our meal. You are one of us, there is no denying, and we will face any troubles as they come."

Petyer hesitated. This Alejandro still frightened him a bit, even if he was one of the Thirteen, and therefore supposedly a friend from ages past. But Griseld twisted around, motioned to him to join them, and then turned to face forward again, wrapping her stick thin arms around the fancy fellow's neck with trust and affection. Petyer walked after them, feeling the weight of the day descend on him like a heavy blanket. And despite it all, he was hungry again.

# COMTÉ DE FOIX
# 1071 CE

On the morning of her feast day, Marguerite stood in a simple white shift as the Sisters around her cut her hair. Long hanks of soft brown shot with gold fell to the floor. She was silent and still, and the women around her held their peace as well.

*"What's done is done, and should not be undone,"* she thought.

The day before she had been in Mother Monica Maria's study and said the same words.

"My child, it isn't done yet! If this is not true for you, step back."

"There is no one to take Sister Angelica's place. No one else knows the plants, the herbs, the healing ways. You need me here. You need me."

"In the name of all that is holy! You stubborn girl! I have told you over and over that you may remain nearby and work as a lay sister. You are right that we need your skills in the sick ward, but I can arrange for you to have a separate cottage just outside the walls. You could marry. You can be free from this community, free from the rules of obedience. You don't need to do this!"

Marguerite looked at the Mother strangely. She felt wave after wave of what was almost like memory wash over her. Mother's face and yet another's face. Her voice, yet not her voice. Mother's voice, yet she seemed to speak an unknown though understood language. They stood in Mother's study, yet were standing in a great and ancient forest with the trees around them listening in. This was happening now and had happened in the then. Marguerite spoke quietly.

"There is some thread of time and purpose that is unspooling between you and I. Yes, I need to do this. It has happened before, and needs to happen again. Please, as you love me, let me do this!"

Mother Monica Maria was undone. This fierce little badger of a child had become some force of purpose, some force of nature. And who was she to stand before that force?

"So it is, so it will be," the Mother said. And for a fragment of a moment Monica Maria appeared to be wearing a long deep green cloak. Marguerite had the defiant stare of a fierce young woman with a tattoo of the night sky across her shoulder blade. And it was as it had been, but with the resolve to do it so much better this time.

So, this day, Marguerite walked out into the corridor and down the steps to the chapel. Inside waited all the Sisters of Mater Misericordia, and her family: the mother, father and three brothers who she barely recognized. She knelt, accepted fealty to Christ and took vows of poverty, chastity, and obedience. She lifted her eyes and looked directly at Mother Monica Maria, and without understanding why the words needed to be said, she whispered,

*"It is the very least I can do for you."*

The years rolled on. One became two. Two became four. Four became seven. Marguerite was solely in charge of the green medicines. She supplied the herbs and tonics for the sick ward outside the convent walls, and tended personally to all the nuns inside. She and Monica Maria, both pushed to the limit by the demands of their work, kept up their frequent walks, relying on each other in the listening and refraining from giving advice.

The world outside had become precarious. Conflicts over land and titles had sprung up and the nearby Lords and Dukes had formed mercenary armies to push back and forth, ripping swaths of dark wide ribbons of burnt cottages and trampled fields across the countryside. More and more people showed up outside the convent doors, needing food and sanctuary. Mater Misericordia had always stood independent, holding allegiance to no bishop or secular master. For a while the convent's neutrality was honored. But the day came when the invading army, successful in toppling the local landowner, had demanded that the convent swear fealty to the invader. Mother Monica Maria refused. The army retreated for the winter, and the nuns of Mater Misericordia breathed sighs of relief. Only Marguerite knew that the Mother feared the return and intensified demands of the mercenaries once the spring came.

One night, in mid-winter, deep in the still hours between Compline and Vigil, Marguerite was alone working in the herb hut, straining chamomile tincture into small bottles for use in the sick ward. Sister Agnes, a young nun, newly veiled came and knocked on the door.

"Yes? Who wants what at this hour?"

Sister Agnes had been forewarned that Marguerite was irascible, but nonetheless she was startled into silence by the degree of growl in the voice coming through the closed door.

"Well?!"

"Sister Marguerite! Mother Monica Maria is ill and sends for you."

The door slammed open and Marguerite stood, looking like the avenging angel in the chapel's stained glass window, pale face, scarlet slashes across her cheeks, and a piercing stare.

"What kind of ill? A fever? A gripe? A pox? Well, speak up girl!"

"I don't know, Sister. I heard she fainted, and upon coming to she asked for you."

Marguerite whipped around to grab her medicine basket and flew past the younger woman so quickly that her veil stung the nun's face. She ran full out through the garden, with Sister Agnes right behind, along the corridors and up the stairs to Monica Maria's study and chambers. A small grouping of Sisters stood huddled in the hallway, some looking with relief and some with envy that Marguerite had been summoned and had arrived. She pushed past them and, alone, entered Mother Monica Maria's room. Her eyes took a moment to adjust from the relative bright torchlight in the corridor to the dim circles thrown from a small cluster of beeswax candles on the low chest near the bed.

Marguerite was startled to see another woman, an older nun kneeling next to the bed. It was Sister Dolora, Marguerite's aunt, the very nun who had made it possible for Marguerite to find her sanctuary in Mater Misericordia. She had seen practically nothing of her in her seventeen years in the convent, for Sister Dolora was one of a handful of Sisters who kept complete vows of silence and contemplation, only joining the community at large for special feast days. It demanded a level of devotion and vocation that few aspired to and even fewer could attain. They prayed behind the ornately carved scrim in the chapel, their prayers and hymns floating through the delicate lace-work of wood. They ate behind the screen in the dining hall. They moved along hallways and corridors with eyes cast down and hands folded in prayer. Yet here she was, and she turned her eyes, gold like a hawk's, to Marguerite as she entered the room. And then she spoke.

"She asked for you, niece. But she has little breath for speech. I fear she goes to our Lord soon with the aid of His Blessed Mother."

The older woman's face was awash with tears, crumpled with grief. There was some unknown story here Marguerite thought for a flash of a second, and then she turned her attention to the occupant of the bed. She lifted the brace of candles and brought them closer to the bed. Monica Maria's eyes fluttered and pinched against the light.

"I am here, Mother. What do you require? A tonic?"

"No medicines, child." Monica Maria's voice was soft as fog.

"Mother, let me help you. What is your pain?"

"You need to listen. I have little time left."

"What is wrong?" Marguerite demanded with asperity.

"Hush – it is my heart – it strangles me."

Sister Dolora leaned forward and spoke softly into Marguerite's ear.

"She has had this malady for some time. It increases in severity. And now she has succumbed."

Marguerite flashed fire at the older nun.

"What do you mean 'for some time'?"

She shot her gaze back to Monica Maria. "Why didn't you tell me? I could have helped!"

"I am dying, child. It is not ideal. But it is true. And you must take my place as Mother Superior. Sister Dolora will witness that this is my decision."

For a solid heartbeat Marguerite was stunned silent. Then she exploded.

"Absolutely not! I am totally unsuited for the job. This is a disastrous idea. You must live, instead!"

Mother Monica Maria only smiled a small smile and said,

"It is my command. Remember your vow of obedience."

Marguerite straightened and went colorless. She looked at Monica Maria hard, as if to look through her.

"This is truly a bad idea! Perhaps you have lost your mind!"

Sister Dolora took a sudden intake of breath, but Mother Monica Maria only weakly motioned with her hand for Marguerite to come closer. Reluctantly the young nun inched closer and then closer still until Monica Maria tugged at her hand and pulled her down to sit on the narrow bed.

"Listen! Listen to me!"

Marguerite averted her eyes, then brought her gaze back to Monica Maria's ashen face. The Mother's breathing was rapid and shallow, like the fluttering of a frightened bird in hand.

"There is trouble coming," Monica Maria said very softly. "Trouble when the soldiers return. I need you. It must be you."

"Why?" Marguerite wailed. 'Why me? I have no alliances here."

"Exactly," Mother Monica Maria said. "You stand alone. It is as if you dropped from the sky." She laughed in a squeezed exhale and began to cough. Sister Dolora leaned in to offer water, but Monica Maria shook her head. She had little time and energy left, and this before her must be settled.

"You stand alone, and will take my place with my blessing. They will follow you. Dangerous times are coming, dangerous times."

"I cannot. I have no patience in the way that you do. I have no skill in diplomacy. I am not as capable as you seem to think I am." Marguerite's voice had descended to pleading her case one last time.

"You have the courage of a lion. You will do what needs to be done. Keep them safe! Keep them safe! Promise me! Promise me you will take on this burden!" she clasped Marguerite's hand with ferocity and bore her gaze into the young woman. "Promise!"

# RUPERTSBERG
# 1120 CE

The next five days passed without incident, and Petyer found himself falling into a rhythm that dovetailed with the schedule of prayers and meals within the Abbey proper, and the time spent with his compatriots from the lands that had been. When he arose each morning it was to the sound of singing as the nuns here at Rupertsberg sang all their prayers. They also sang at work, at rest, and at all times in between. Sister Maria Stella had not exaggerated when she said that women found their way here to build lives on devotion that floated on music. There was a constant weaving of voices and instruments that seemed to keep everyone at the Abbey in a pleasant state of being. Smiles were the normal countenance. Kind words the coin of discourse. The only person who struck a discordant note was the sister in charge of the kitchens, and then only when she trumpeted orders to Griseld to eat something. Even Sister Catherine of the Wheel was mostly cheerful except when she had to walk or climb stairs because, as Petyer would soon find out, her knees bothered her "when it was damp...or dry...or cold...or hot."

Petyer ate his meals in the kitchens where there were always ample seconds. He seldom attended the prayers that linked the hours of the day like rosary beads on a strand. Mostly he was in the company of his fellows of the Thirteen. He spent one morning digging daffodil and iris bulbs with Betterm. One afternoon he tagged along with Griseld where she showed him all the fabulous hiding spots and secret staircases that were enclosed in the Abbey.

"Mother Hildegard had these built into the buildings when she founded the Abbey here. She said a person always has need of an escape hatch or two." Griseld smiled at Petyer and he knew then that she was instructing him in some very important knowledge, and he vowed to learn the lessons well.

Alejandro, it turned out, was the scion of a wealthy and minor royal family from Sevilla in Iberia. Although he affected the demeanor of languor, he was, of all things, a sculptor who worked in stone. Petyer watched him work one warm afternoon on a statue of the Three Marys. His lithe, willowy build was belied by strong ropey forearms and Petyer became mesmerized as the huge piece of marble was chipped away to reveal the women who had been, evidently, visible to Alejandro all along, merely hiding inside the stone block. Petyer was too intimidated to ask the questions that he asked of the others of the Thirteen. But as he used the chisel, Alejandro began to speak of his own journey to Rupertsberg and his awakening to his memories.

"Hildegard was correct, young fellow. I too made some graceless moves on my way here. I had insisted that I was a woman, since the time I could speak. My parents and my tutors tried to beat that out of me. At one very low point my confessor insisted that they do an exorcism to rid me of 'my demons'."

Petyer could think of nothing to say in response. Some minutes passed with only the sound of rock being chipped away and the glitter of rainbows made in the air by marble dust.

"Finally, my family settled on me a sum of money, a generous sum mind you, and suggested that I find a nice religious order somewhere far away where I could 'live out my fantasies'. I traveled for many months. I dressed as a man in Iberia, as a woman in Burgundy, and then throwing caution to the winds I came as you see me now to find this miraculous Hildegard of Bingen that people talked of. I knew, I just knew, that with her I would be safe. I came here dragging my own encumbrance of scandal and disgrace, young Petyer. I had no place to point accusations at you. Might you forgive me?"

Alejandro turned toward Petyer and his face dropped all artifice. He took a deep breath and let go of all pretense and dramatic archness. With his miraculous emerald eyes he looked at Petyer, and in all sincerity begged for forgiveness. Petyer took two steps forward and reached out a hand to clasp Alejandro's chisel free hand. The boy looked at the man and saw, for a shimmer, like water rippling over the surface of a lake, the wide cheeks bones and chestnut skin in the strikingly beautiful face of Uxua.

"Of course," was all he said in reply, and it was all that needed saying.

Alejandro's eyes brightened with what in a lesser human might be tears, and returned to his process to reveal the three women standing at the foot of the cross. Petyer sat with him for hours and watched the birthing of the statue – to him a most miraculous birth indeed.

The boy spent several hours each day under the tutelage of two terrifyingly brilliant nuns who spoke fluent Latin and Greek. Mother Hildegard, while she would on occasion skirt the truth, had every intention that Petyer's presence here at Rupertsberg would be thoroughly ensconced in his studies in alignment with the message she had sent to his family. In the event that a parent or their emissary arrived at the Abbey, Hildegard intended for Petyer to be gainfully employed as a student.

So alike that at first Petyer thought they were twins, Sisters Michael the Archangel and Mary of Ephesus drilled him in grammar, ridiculed his pronunciation, and relentlessly drove him to memorize vocabulary. After his first five days with them, he actually began to feel like a scholar. When he voiced this, the two nuns scoffed and then smiled. Petyer was a bright boy; they enjoyed poking at his intellect and making it rise from sluggishness.

On the morning of his sixth day of instruction Sister Maria Stella came to the library and stood with hands folded, waiting for the elder nuns to notice her. She looked pale and worried, and Sister Mary of Ephesus motioned her forward asking if she was in need of something.

"Mother Hildegard has sent for young Master Fieldenstarn, Sister. His uncle and cousin have arrived from Wiesbaden and are awaiting him in Mother's study."

"An uncle and a cousin, eh?" Sister Michael the Archangel queried. "Do they need one for each arm to carry him away?" She spoke jokingly, but Maria Stella only smiled wanly and gestured for Petyer to proceed ahead of her. As he left the room she whispered in reply.

"That is, indeed, what Mother Hildegard fears. Or at least that they will attempt it. They look most formidable."

Sister Mary of Ephesus laughed.

"Then they will have met their match with Mother, eh?"

With a speaking glance between them, Sisters Michael the Archangel and Mary of Ephesus joined Maria Stella as she walked back to Mother Hildegard's study. *"Power in numbers,"* they thought.

At Hildegard's doorway they heard men's voices raised and rolling right over Mother Hildegard's even tones. The sisters walked in at young Petyer's heels, and abruptly broke into the tirade that the men were directing at the Mother.

"What is the meaning of this? I will not allow this student's studies to be interrupted," Sister Michael the Archangel said sternly.

The two men whipped around and reflexively stepped back. Sister Michael the Archangel was looking at this moment like her namesake, ready for battle, and only lacked a flaming sword to be the exact replica of the angel's statue in the chapel.

Mother Hildegard, in a calm sweet voice, made the introductions.

"Sisters, this is Agre and Klaser Fieldenstarn, uncle and cousin respectively of our young Petyer. They have traveled here from their home town to inquire as to his wellbeing."

"His family demands an answer as to what sort of chicanery has transpired to draw him to this place." The uncle, Agre spoke belligerently.

Sister Michael the Archangel drew a deep breath and stood even taller and broader. Ever the defender, she spoke.

"What insolence is this? Rupertsberg is a holy house, a place of prayer, devotion, and scholarship. Perhaps its reputation was sufficient to 'draw' the young fellow here." She laced the word 'draw' with the heaviest of sarcasm.

Mother Hildegard moved between the nun and the angry uncle, gliding on tranquility and otherworldly confidence.

"So, you see, our Petyer is safe and engaged in a rigorous schedule of study. You must be thirsty from your travels. Shall I send for some refreshment?"

The uncle and his son were similar in appearance. Stocky, short, with beaded brows and dark lank hair, they looked nothing like Petyer, whose lean build spoke of the height still to come, and whose soft curls shone chestnut and copper in the light flowing in the tall study windows. All three of the Fieldnstarns were at a loss of how to respond to Mother's query, so Sister Mary of Ephesus rapidly interjected.

"Enough time has been taken from Petyer's studies this morning. We shall return to them now." She turned to direct her comments to Petyer. "Scurry back, young man and work on those conjugations. They are woefully shoddy at present."

Petyer gratefully escaped the room, shooting a quick glance at his cousin who had an odd smile on his face. Petyer had never been able to trust that fellow, and had suffered greatly as a child from his older cousin's teasings and torments. Petyer had a feeling that if his cousin was happy about something at present, it wasn't going to bode well for Petyer. Disquiet flooded him and feeling guided by some inner voice and seeking solace for his qualms, he turned at the doorway and bowed a deep bow to Mother Hildegard. She walked forward and placed her hands on his head in benediction.

"Work hard in your studies for the glory of God, young master Fieldenstarn," she said, her voice almost singing the words. The atmosphere in the room seemed to hold its breath and shimmer with a pearlescent light.

Petyer straightened and his eyes were on a level with hers. He met her gaze and felt peace and grace fill him. Fortified and reassured he left the study and practically galloped back to the schoolroom, followed at a sedate pace by the footsteps of Sisters Michael the Archangel and Mary of Ephesus.

In the study, Mother Hildegard rang for Sister Delphinia. When Delphinia arrived she took in the ever calm and ever elegant Hildegard standing in the center of the room in a beam of sunlight holding the two men present in a trance of equal parts sweetness and steely determination. The two fellows clearly couldn't break from her focus on them and looked dumbstruck.

"May we have a light repast, Sister. Some fruit, perhaps and some watered wine?" Hildegard didn't look at Delphinia when she spoke, but kept her eyes directed at the man and his son. They were mesmerized, and she seemed to be thoroughly enjoying the exercise. It was as if she had caught them on a fishing line and was reeling them in. Delphinia thought that perhaps Hildegard was enjoying this a little too much.

"Of course, Mother. Ah, would your guests like to take a seat?"

The men didn't move. Neither did Hildegard break her gaze. Delphinia spoke again, this time more definitively.

"Mother. Mother! Your guests?"

Like a cat slowly deciding that the mouse before her wasn't worth the trouble, Hildegard shifted her eyes to Delphinia, gave a knowing half smile, and gestured to the elder and younger men toward the low bench across from her desk. She went and sat behind the desk, assuming the position of authority in the room. When it came to maneuvering and playing the game of power, Hildegard had no equal. Delphinia gave a soft chuckle and left the room in a swish of skirt.

Hildegard took several long minutes to simply look at the men before her. They both now had a sheen of perspiration and a slightly stunned demeanor. The silence held until Sister Delphinia returned with two young nuns carrying trays with wine, water, fruit, and pewter goblets. These two men certainly didn't qualify for the glass goblets, but Delphinia had made sure that the wine was decent.

"Gentlemen, help yourselves," Sister Delphinia offered. She raised an eyebrow at Hildegard who shook her head slightly and declined anything from the trays. As the men poured wine and took apple quarters, Hildegard waited until they had their mouths full before she asked, "And how are things in Wiesbaden? A good harvest?"

Petyer's uncle, nodded vigorously and attempted to answer, managing only to garble a reply and spit some apple onto the front of his shirt. Klaser, the cousin, had a flicker of disgust cross his face at his father's display, and flushed hard and deep red.

"Ah," Hildegard thought, "the telltale blush. That is one trait he does share with our Petyer."

"And young Petyer's father, the Burgomeister, your brother I presume? How fares he?"

This time the son, Klaser answered. He stared right into Hildegard's eyes with an air of defiance.

"The Burgomeister is well. But he is concerned for his son, and does not wish to countenance such errant behavior. The boy needs to come home."

Mother Hildegard watched the young man speak, and smiled at him as if he were a clever curiosity, like a dancing pig or a parrot that spoke Latin. When she didn't respond he finally broke the gaze and looked down at his apple quarter, noticing in an almost detached way that his hands were shaking. In her own good time Hildegard replied.

"And of course, God willing and in His good time, young Master Fieldenstarn will return to the bosom of his family. But that will need to wait, of course, until we hear back from the Papal Nuncio. And as you may or may not know, his Eminence is fretfully slow in returning his correspondence."

She shook her head as if to bemoan the frailties of the Pope's emissary in the German states, looking at the two men before her as if they surely joined in her distress.

"The Papal Nuncio?" Petyer's uncle's voice rose and cracked on the final syllable. "What is the involvement of the Papal Nuncio?"

The two men exchanged glances that told volumes of guilt. They hoped that this Mother Hildegard didn't know about their recent troubles with the Archbishop of Mainz and the slight issue of some missing funds that had riled the Church.

"Oh yes. Petyer's abilities and scholarship became immediately evident to the good sisters you met earlier. They insisted that his Eminence be notified of the presence of such a promising mind here at Rupertsberg. The Nuncio has been known to take such potential scholars under his wing. Perhaps there might even be further study possible in Rome for the boy. I know you will understand that I felt compelled, yes, required even, to make such connections that could further young Petyer's fortunes."

She smiled her smile of impenetrable righteousness, and all Agre and Klaser could do was nod and swallow. She had known, of course, through the ecclesiastical grapevine that the 'misplaced funds' were the soft underbelly for these two men. Nobody stole from the Church in the German states and came out unscathed. And these two never needed to know that she had not sent any information about Petyer to the Papal Nuncio, and that she had no intention of letting Petyer into that grubby man's clutches. But she had created a smokescreen through which Petyer's family would hesitate to peer. And it should, Goddess willing, keep him safe here with her.

"I am sure that you must be eager to be returning home, gentlemen, so I will not keep you. I fear the wrath of Sister Michael the Archangel, so I will not summon Petyer to say farewell to you. Please assure his family that he will receive an excellent education and the very best care here at Rupertsberg. And now, I must return to my duties."

She rang the bell that brought Sister Delphinia.

"Sister. If you would be so kind as to see our guests to the Abbey gates. They feel a strong desire to be on their way."

Hildegard pulled a book from her desk drawer and transferred her attention to its pages. The two men stood, looking confused as to whether or not they should bow or say anything to the clearly uninterested Hildegard. Delphinia shepherded them out the door before they could decide either way, and swept them down the corridor and staircase, across the courtyard, and through the gates before they even registered what was happening. They recovered their horses and with a palpable sense of relief, mounted and headed down the road back to Wiesbaden.

Back inside the Abbey, Hildegard spent several serious hours building the magickal wards around this sanctuary, circle after concentric circle of protection and obfuscation that would steer curious eyes and minds away from the Abbey. She worked spells of fog and mist into the minds of Petyer's uncle and cousin so that their memories of Rupertsberg were bland and benign. She drew upon lifetime after lifetime of wisdoms to sculpt a spell of invisibility. And when she had finished, she bent to her work and reinforced it all again and again.

Within this net of safety, as autumn turned to winter, Mother Hildegard dispatched her recently completed treatise on medicinal herbs and cures to the Vatican for approval, as was required, and set to work on her history of women in the Church.

Petyer continued with his studies and excelled, much to the delight of Sisters Michael the Archangel and Mary of Ephesus. Griseld's cough worsened no matter what remedies and prayers were directed her way. Betterm felt the cold in his bones, and Sister Maria Stella watched him with concern, pushing far down an ancient grief. Alejandro finished his sculpture of the Three Marys and began work on a lion lying with a lamb. When Mother Hildegard saw the sketches for the statue she burst out laughing, as the lion's face bore a strong resemblance to the goddess Sekhmet. Sister Catherine of the Wheel with her pudgy dog could be found every morning in the wee hours standing in the gardens and doing an odd sequence of movements she called "the Form" saying that it "chases away my aches and pains." Petyer took to joining her, learning the Form, and finding that his muscles knew what to do before his mind did.

# ALONG THE GAMBIA RIVER IN THE LAND OF THE FULANI (GHANA) / GOREE ISLAND (SENEGAL) 1805 CE

Khadee was being ridden by Spirit. Firelight slipped between the particles of her body. She was a lion; she was a tree lizard. She was part of all that is. She danced and vibrated with the drums, a hundred drums, all the drums in the world, in the culmination of the three-day ritual. The dense foliage whispered its mysteries. Stars wheeled overhead, and the Nsanamfo, the Ancestors, rejoiced. She was the youngest of the priests and priestesses gathered here to honor the Old Ways and to give praise to Anansi Kokuroko, the Sky Father, and to Asase Yaa, the Mother Earth. She and the others gifted with the possession by the abosom, what some called the orishas, danced all night as the drums dissolved the illusion of the separation of things, and allowed Earth and Sky to mate. One by one the spirits drifted away, and the humans gave into sleep, scattered along the jungle floor like fallen petals from a Nandi Flame tree.

This gathering was a very special confluence of peoples and traditions. The wise ones, the elders had agreed that the peoples of the Fulani, the Fante and the Mandinka should come together and share their ceremonies. The Old Ways had come under more and more attack from the followers of Mohammed in the cities, the Portuguese and French Catholics along the coast, and British, the slave buyers. The traditional priestesses and priests were more and more in secret, holding ceremonies and rites of passage at night deep in the jungle.

Khadee, having been initiated as a Priestess just this past year at sixteen years of age, was honored to have been chosen to attend with the Sarrounia, the High Priestess of her village.

When only one lone drummer still kept pace, Khadee danced until light began to seep through the broad deep green. Finally, her abosom lifted, and with a presence like a kiss on her forehead, it floated away. Khadee, returning to herself, shared a silent moment with the drummer. He gave a slow blink, and she delicately bowed her head, and thus they acknowledged a good night's work.

She lay down under the branches of a banana tree and thought about this night. Sleep eluded her, but she let her eyes drift shut while she tried but couldn't recall all of what had transpired. The details were gone, like fog, but the feelings were still pulsing within her. How wondrous! To be so alive and yet so beyond life and death! What a lucky girl she was!

She heard rustling in the nearby undergrowth, and assumed it was someone returning from attending to morning body needs. Without warning, men screamed and raced out of the jungle, catching Khadee and all the others unawares.

Panic. Terror. Confusion. They were all caught and tied, hands behind their backs and forced to sit huddled together in the packed earth circle where celebration had occurred the night before. The slave hunters were armed with pistols and long knives, and set about to rip off jewelry and clothing and adornments, shoving all the stolen goods into big muslin bags.

The oldest among them were left tied to trees, and all the young and hardy roped together like cattle. They were led west, through the jungle, and toward the coast. Khadee looked back over her shoulder, holding the gaze of her Sarrounia, her beloved teacher, as long as she could until a knifepoint in her back forced her forward.

They walked for five days, and the rich loam of the jungle gave way to the sandy soil of the coastal lands. The captives were given minimal food and water, enough to keep them alive, and they were forced to sleep tied to one another in wretched jumbles of arms and legs. On the sixth morning they saw the ocean ahead, and all the captives murmured prayers to Yemaya, the Goddess of Deep Waters. At the shore they were loaded into small rowboats and carried across to an island that reeked of pain and fear.

"What is this place?" they whispered to each other.

An older man, a priest of the Mandinka knew. "It is called Goree." he said. "It is a place of no return."

Khadee saw the light of hope die in the eyes of many of her fellow captives. As they were hurried into the large enclosed keep, the men and women were separated from each other, and several of the prettiest women, Khadee included, were moved aside and forced up the staircase to the rooms above. Khadee didn't know where they were going, or what would happen to them, but her ancestors spoke gently into her ear. "*Survive, daughter! Do what needs must to survive!*"

When she would think back over those next few weeks, Khadee could only remember snippets of action or inaction. Hours, days must have gone by; of those she had no recollection at all. She remembered biting off the ear of the man at Goree who tried to have sex with her. She remembered the exquisite blue of the ocean framed by the Door of No Return as she and the others were loaded onto the big ship. She heard, and couldn't not hear, the clanging of leg irons, Years later that sound would wake her from a deep sleep.

Fever had run through the ship's hold like a bush fire. And of that time, she had only one vivid memory. A sailor, a young boy with a tumble of dried grass colored hair was holding a cup with clean water to her lips.

"Shhh, shush now, drink quick before anybody sees." He spoke in an unintelligible clatter of sounds, but his intent was clear.

Khadee opened her split lips and drank. She broke through her fever haze and looked at the boy again. But now, he was a girl, about her own age in a long green cape, with a mat of brown hair and wide worried eyes. She knew that face, from somewhere, sometime.

"Eiofachta?" Khadee's voice cracked and only a sliver of sound emerged. And then she slipped back into her dreams.

Two other times that boy came to her and brought water and one time, a dried biscuit. It was something. It was enough, and it kept Khadee alive.

By the time the ship docked at Charleston, almost half of those who had been with her at the beginning of the ocean journey had died. And Khadee felt the last bit of her resolve evaporate as they were lined up in the hot sun to be marched into the slave auction. Some essential part of her finally just let go and prepared to float free. At just that moment that boy appeared again. He walked near her as the line of Africans disembarked, and without anyone noticing he slipped a feather into her hand.

"May you fly one day," he said. And again, Khadee understood his meaning but not his words.

# RUPERTSBERG
# 1121 CE

On a foggy day in October, an emissary from the Pontiff arrived with full entourage. Sister Delphinia, working with only a few days' notice, had done miracles, and the Abbey was resplendent with sprays of holly and evergreens bringing the forest freshness inside. Every inch of brass and copper was polished, and dust was banished from every corner. Everyone in the Abbey was on high alert, for papal permission was necessary for Mother Hildegard's medical treatise to be distributed. Papal interference in the life of the Abbey was most scrupulously to be avoided. It was a fine line to walk – for the Abbey and its inhabitants to be above reproach and yet not worthy of excessive notice.

Mother Hildegard met the contingent from Rome in the courtyard of the Abbey on a bitter cold morning. She was draped in a winter cloak with gray rabbit fur lining the hood, her small delicate face peeking through and her golden eyes bright. The papal emissary stepped down from his carriage with surprising grace and no stiffness of limbs, wearing the cardinal's red hat.

*"Ah, not an old man then,"* Hildegard thought. *"Perhaps all the more dangerous for having youthful ambition."*

She glided forward and made a deep curtsy to this delegate from the Pope. Holding the depth of the pose, and diverting her eyes down in assumed modesty, she spoke.

"A profound welcome to Rupertsberg, Your Eminence. We hope

your journey was not too arduous. We are eager to make your stay here comfortable."

"We thank you, Sister. Perhaps you could lead us to Mother Hildegard. Our mission is with her and we have no time to tarry."

His voice was smooth and well educated with thinly veiled condescension. Hildegard rose to standing and lifted her eyes to see him directly. Her eyes, like a hawk's, were direct and piercing. The Cardinal felt himself step back in his own skin, and it was only the training and discipline of a lifetime that kept his feet where they were. The farthest corners of her mouth turned up ever so slightly, and she responded.

"How delightful that we can hasten your mission then, for I am that Mother Hildegard that you seek."

She stepped beside him and gestured with her hand toward the high double wooden doors of the Abbey.

"Shall we?"

The Cardinal was indeed a young man, and indeed had ambition as the cause of his early rise to prominence. He was the second son of the Bishop of Venetia, and his father had spotted his son's intelligence early, sending him to the best tutors. The Bishop was a canny fellow, and soon saw that the boy's beauty was as useful a talent as his mind. When Giuseppe came into adolescence, his father introduced him to men in the highest ranks of the Church and the boy's future was set. Both father and son saw his proximity to the powerful cabals surrounding the Pope as advantageous, and Giuseppe learned quickly when to use which sword – that of his physical beauty or his intellect. In his experience, people in power always responded to one or the other.

But at this moment he was scrambling, trying to organize what he was seeing with what he thought he knew of Hildegard of Bingen. Her scholarly accomplishments had led him to assume she was an aged (and grizzled) woman, but this tiny person striding next to him was anything but old and decidedly not grizzled. She seemed about his own age, perhaps thirty, thirty-two years, and those eyes! He took the span of time that they walked into the Abbey to her study to compose himself and reassess his strategy. He had been sent here to convince Hildegard that her treatise would be best received if it were believed to have been penned by a man. The Holy Father had suggested that he, Giuseppe, could claim authorship. The old and cloistered Mother Hildegard he had envisioned might be easily talked into the need for her to succumb to the 'privilege' of anonymity. At this moment, Giuseppe didn't think that the woman next to him, radiating confidence and power as she did, was going to be easily convinced of anything.

Sister Delphinia had arranged everything perfectly. A fire burned vigorously in the grate, sending any chill to the very corners of the room. A generous spread of food was set out, sliced fowl, sweetbreads in gravy, onions and apples braised with pork. Hildegard noted with an inner chuckle that Delphinia had thought this occasion an appropriate one for the crystal goblets.

"Please, sit and rest, Your Eminence. Your entourage is being shown to your rooms and will be made comfortable and be well fed too. May I serve you something?"

Hildegard had said all of this with her back to the Cardinal. She now turned and handed him a goblet of wine. He noted that she had positioned them so that the sunlight streaming into the room through high lead-paned windows was directly in his eyes, leaving him unable to see her expression. He acknowledged that she was cleverer than he had imagined, and decided that he would be best served if he abandoned guile and went with forthrightness as his strategy.

"You are not what I had thought," he said, sipping what was an excellent wine and lifting an eyebrow in surprise.

Mother Hildegard's face lit up with a smile of genuine amusement. Here was noble adversary then. She moved to a chair and allowed Giuseppe to direct his eyes away from the bright blue white light of winter that flooded the room. With a chuckle that was warm and soft like apple blossoms she asked.

"What was it that you had thought then?"

"From the body of work you have accomplished I thought you to be older. It is the work of many decades, or would be for most."

"Some of us are just early bloomers. Wouldn't you say, Your Eminence?"

She said it softly and with an air of innocence, but Giuseppe knew that she knew. She was making an oblique reference to the fact that his rise within the Church hierarchy was precipitous, perhaps even suspect. *"Well then, thrust and parry,"* he thought.

"The hawthorn blossoms early, yet bears little fruit. You, Reverend Mother, have been most prodigious and fruitful. And this is, indeed, an impressive community you have founded."

Hildegard felt a tiny sliver of alarm. The last thing she wanted was for Rome or anyone with Rome's ear to find her situation enviable. The Holy See floated on avarice. *"Divert and distract,"* she thought. *"Drat the crystal goblets!"*

"Oh, we are but a humble community seeking solace from the perils of the outside world. We have been fortunate that several well-positioned families here in the German States have seen fit to settle their daughters with us. They send gifts, like these very goblets we drink from now, which we hope will honor your esteemed presence."

They both took another sip and the only sound in the room was the crackling of the fire. The Cardinal took these moments to study her face. By God, she was beautiful. And her beauty was dim in comparison to the blinding intelligence that shone from those amber eyes. Hildegard, in her own assessment of Giuseppe, was thinking much the same thing. He displayed extraordinary beauty, thinly containing a sharp and exquisite mind.

*"One wonders,"* she thought.

*"Perhaps,"* he thought.

*"Definitely not worth the risk,"* she thought.

*"Absolutely worth the risk,"* he thought. The clerical life did not often offer up these kinds of possibilities.

More wine was sipped, and Giuseppe tried silence as a strategy. It worked so often, to just sit back and let the silence stretch out until the other person was rattled and spoke or blushed or crumbled. As a means to an end he had found it most efficacious. But he had never tangled with Mother Hildegard before. She seemed to relish the silence, relaxed into it and acquired an aura of deep peace.

*"Drat the woman!"* he thought.

*"This is fun,"* she thought.

He tried another tack. Direct frontal attack.

"The Holy Father feels that it may be an unnecessary disruption for the faithful if your treatise was to be distributed under the authorship of a woman. His Holiness believes that much of the healing wisdom within would be disregarded if seen to be coming from such an unreliable source as a female."

Hildegard felt the spike of anger that he had intended for her to have, and refused to give him the pleasure of seeing it in her eyes. She, who had cut her teeth on political maneuvering with the Pharaoh of Egypt, relaxed even more deeply and smiled that cat-like smile that had confounded many a man before.

"The Holy Father is certainly responsible for such weighty concerns. However, in his latest encyclical he remarked that the faithful should be humble before the Virgin Mother and hold fast to her sanctity, her wisdoms, as the vessel that was worthy of nurturing the body of our Lord and Holy Mother Church. Is that not so, Your Eminence?"

Giuseppe was not sure where she was going with this, and was startled that she had had access to that most recent encyclical here in the wilds of the German States. But he responded cautiously.

"Yes, that was a focus of His Holiness's recent writings, but…"

"And did he not draw connection between the body of the Blessed Mother as the 'House of Bounty' and as a corollary to our earth that feeds us all?"

"Mother Hildegard, you are correct in referencing the Pontiff's exhortation that we submit to the sanctity of our Mother Mary."

"So then, Cardinal, since the herbal treatise only refers to the plants of this earth, and since the earth is seen in the realm of the wisdom of the Sacred Mother, I would hope that the medicinal options held within could be seen to also be under her purview and protection."

Giuseppe was at a loss. This Hildegard had boxed him into a corner with papal logic. She continued, "And as I have the deeply felt honor of being the spiritual head of a community of women dedicated to the Blessed Mother, it is only right and correct that Her wisdoms be seen as coming through her emissary, is it not?"

"Your logic is flawless, Mother Hildegard. And yet I have the unenviable task of conveying His Holiness's discomfort in this matter."

Hildegard rose and walked over to ring the bell. Sister Delphinia arrived, suspiciously quickly.

*"Really!"* Hildegard thought, *"Does she know I will be calling before I do?"*

"Sister, would you summon the Sisters of the Abbey to the Chapel? We are called to pray for our Holy Father."

Hildegard had slightly emphasized the word 'Sisters' to let Delphinia know that the presence of Petyer, Alejandro, Betterm, and Griseld would not be desirous. She wanted to lead the Cardinal away from their eccentricities, not waft them under his nose. It would be best to keep the Abbey and its inhabitants looking as normal as possible for now. She turned to Giuseppe and offered.

"Your Eminence, if you are sufficiently rested and refreshed, would you care to come and join our prayers? We are not a cloistered order and would welcome a presence of such august wisdom as yourself to help guide us in our devotions."

Disconcerted by this sudden change in topic, Giuseppe sounded suspicious.

"Mother Hildegard, why are you praying for the Pope at this juncture?"

"Why, Your Eminence, isn't it obvious? You said that the Pontiff is struggling with discomfort at the earthly manifestations of his own divinely given instructions to his Church. How he must be suffering! We will ask that the Lord Jesus Christ and His Sacred Mother can assist the Pope in his struggles. We will ask that the Pontiff see how to offer up his own human weaknesses and fall into alignment with his own teachings."

Giuseppe stood and looked at Hildegard with no pretense or conceit. His face looked bronze in the light from the fireplace, as if he were some gilded statue. The narrow knife blade nose, the heavy lashed eyes, all combined to a classic beauty that would make Alejandro ache to bring it into form in marble. Hildegard saw the beauty, and knew that if she wanted she could let it move her. She chose to not be moved. He stared at her for several long minutes, and she didn't flinch.

"*Check,*" he thought, and then he blinked.

"*Check and mate!*" she thought.

# COMTÉ DE FOIX
# 1079 CE

Winter clung to the hilltop where Mater Misericordia nestled. The snowdrops didn't bloom till late March, and then the chilly rains fell steadily for weeks. Marguerite was feeling imprisoned by the weather and her new position, but did not want to hasten the warm that would likely bring the return of the mercenary soldiers. The convent had lasted the cold months well, for last year's harvest had been bountiful, and Marguerite had sent word to the country folk to hunt and preserve as much meat as could be found. The Convent's larders swelled with pheasant and duck, with venison and wild boar and rabbit. Bags of foraged mushrooms filled the spaces above the rafters, and the Sisters had been set to filling all available barrels with fresh rainwater and storing it in the cellars. There was talk between the Sisters as to what Mother Marguerite was up to, but she kept her worries to herself, only sharing her fears with Sister Dolora.

"Monica Maria was agitated last summer. She fretted that the soldiers would try to force their way into the convent, that they would lay siege and try to starve us out. They want this high ground, and they want our fealty so as to better control the countryside."

"Yes, she told me of her relief when the early snows sent the soldiers back to Toulouse," Sister Dolora replied.

Marguerite looked sideways at Sister Dolora as they climbed the stone steps after inspecting the cellars.

"For one who lived in the Cloister, you seem to have had a remarkable amount of conversations, Sister."

Sister Dolora's mouth twitched in the ghost of a smile.

"Did you chat with others, or just Monica Maria?"

Sister Dolora only pulled a bit of her bottom lip between her teeth in reply. Her amber eyes grew creases at the corners from her curtailed smile.

"Are you ever going to tell me your history with Monica Maria?"

Without breaking her stride, Sister Dolora simply retorted.

"I doubt it."

It was in the month of the Blessed Virgin that the valley below began to fill with the brown burlap tents of the mercenaries. From the hilltop of Mater Misericordia it looked like an army of ants had swarmed into the fields below.

People from the village came to the Convent and reported that the soldiers had a new commander, a second son of a minor lord of Aragon. He was called Juan Miguel de Antonel, and he had signed up with the Duke of Poitier's army to assist in the Duke's attempts to conquer Gascony. This was a repeating struggle, since the Visigoths had consolidated Aquitaine four hundred years before. The folk of the village found this new officer better mannered than the man he had replaced.

"Mother, he has asked to purchase our eggs and milk! Not just take them! Imagine that!"

"Imagine that, indeed!" Mother Marguerite replied.

"Mother, he has punished one of his soldiers for accosting the young Peltier girl. And declared that our women are to be treated as they would treat their mothers and sisters! Imagine that!"

"Miraculous!" Marguerite replied.

"Mother, he sent soldiers to help repair the mill wheel that had become jammed. Imagine that!"

"Truly unprecedented," Marguerite agreed.

By the third week of the army's encampment, Mother Marguerite was so curious about this officer that when he sent word up to the convent requesting an audience, she agreed to meet with him the following day. He arrived the next midday with a small contingent of unarmed men and a cask of brandy. The Capitan and the brandy were allowed to enter. The soldiers were required to wait outside the gate. Mother Marguerite and Sister Dolora awaited him in the Mother's study.

"Why does this man's decency make me suspicious?" Marguerite asked.

"Because a decent man is as rare as a unicorn!" Sister Dolora retorted and both women were laughing broadly as the door swung open and a postulant announced their visitor.

"Mother? Here is Capitaneus Juan Miguel."

Her face still lit with laughter, Marguerite rose, came around her desk, and stepped forward to meet the captain. He was a man of about thirty years, taller than the average man with dark, sunbaked skin and a surprising head of rich red hair worn long down past his collar and swept back over a high forehead. Marguerite looked up into his eyes and felt a wave of disorientation, a surety of recognition.

"Capitan. Have we met before? I'm sure that I know you."

Juan Miguel bowed from the waist and returned her frank gaze. He gave his head a small shake.

"I have never been in this country before, Mother Marguerite. My people hail from Aragon near a city called Barcelona. Have you been there?"

"No," she said. "I have never been anywhere."

They looked at one another with unabashed curiosity. They looked at one another like friends do, with delight in each other's company. They looked and looked until Sister Dolora cleared her throat, and they fell back to earth. Sister Dolora spoke.

"Capitan, have you come with demands?"

He lifted one eyebrow and looked at her askance, "So much for the social niceties, Sister!"

"Young man, I have spent thirty and more years avoiding those same social niceties and haven't missed them a smidgen. We are busy women, and I assume you also have something vital to attend to, battles to wage, villages to sack. Shall we simply get on with it?"

Marguerite shot a startled glance at Sister Dolora from whom she had never heard a rude comment before. Something had definitely gotten under the Sister's skin. Marguerite had never had an instinct toward peacemaking, so she settled within herself to enjoy the cat and dog skirmish sizing up before her.

"Sister, respectfully, I have finished my quota of village sacking for the month, and so find myself at some leisure. Perhaps we could sit?"

"*Bravo!*" Marguerite thought. "*An interesting and witty counter thrust.*"

Dolora shot right back. "Just like a man! Claiming right to sit in a woman's house before being invited!"

"Forgive me. I simply thought that in deference to your advanced age, we might sit to continue our conversation."

"*Ooooo!*" Marguerite winced internally. "*A step too far, brave Capitan. A step too far.*"

Sister Dolora's honey eyes, the same shade as the sun on the horizon at the gloaming, never faltered as they bore holes into the mercenary captain. Marguerite was startled to see that Sister Dolora appeared to be enjoying this sparring. Marguerite had rapidly shifting thoughts as to what might be near at hand to break up a scrabble, if it came to that. The water in the pitcher? The ashes in the scuttle? The Capitan, for his part, didn't even seem to blink, and returned the stare with determination and a kind of good-humored patience.

"*Intriguing,*" Marguerite thought. "*He is simply going to wait her out. He uses patience as a weapon. I shall pray he doesn't use it against us.*"

After an eternity suspended in the time it takes a swallow to lift from a branch and fly away, Sister Dolora chuckled. She actually chuckled, and the corners of her mouth lifted in a genuine begrudging smile.

"Did you come from a family of women, Capitan?"

"Oh yes, Sister. A grandmother, two maiden aunts, my mother, and," he paused for effect, "seven sisters. My brother and I are conversant in female." He made another gracious bow, less full, but perhaps more heartfelt. When he lifted his face again it was transformed by a sweet smile that brought immediate and unreserved smiles in response to the faces of Sister Dolora and Mother Marguerite.

"Well, then." Marguerite gestured toward the chairs facing her desk. "Shall we hear what a man fluent in female has to say for himself?"

In that first conversation, it became clear that Capitaneus Juan Miguel de Antonel was indeed different than his predecessor. He made no hostile demands. He apologized for the disruption his troops caused in the village below. And he endeavored to impress upon Mother Marguerite that his orders to take charge of the Convent and the lands belonging to it were not the desires of his heart but of his superiors. Since Marguerite had absolutely no intention of granting him control of the Convent, and he was implacable in the imperative that she do exactly that, it could be supposed that they would be in a fractious relationship. But week after week they met, made mutually exclusive statements of what would need to be, and found a rhythm together that was based on respect and an odd sense that they wanted the best for each other.

Three months went by. After the first summer harvest it looked as if the soldier's camp down in the valley was preparing for a winter's stay as they built stone and thatch huts and dug deep trenches for fortifications and latrines. Capitaneus Juan Miguel made visits up the hill to the Convent once or twice a week, and Marguerite and Dolora took to walking in the Convent gardens with him as they talked. Both women came to look forward to his visits, and all parties began to share the small details of their daily lives.

"Am I mad to trust his sincerity?" Marguerite asked Sister Dolora after another of their strange encounters.

"As much as I hate to say it, I do too. I am not exactly sure why, but I fell into trust with him," Dolora admitted.

"Perhaps he is so cunning as to be kind," Marguerite wondered. "Might he think to fool us into acquiescing?"

"I don't believe he think us likely to be fooled. I see a man whose soul is in conflict with his position."

"I can do nothing but say no to him. We shall see how long his amiability lasts then, shall we?"

The two descended to the cellars to check on the food and water stocks. The cool walls held an abundance of cheeses and preserved meats. The beams were laced with ropes of onion and ramps. Marguerite continued to order grain and fruits stored as if for a siege, and the cooper in the village worked late into the night to finish more barrels for storing water and wine.

Three more months went by. After the second harvest the cellars and the larders were so full that the Sisters were storing oat and millet in the choir loft, and the barrels of apples, plums and apricots were on constant conveyance into the kitchens where huge vats produced gallons of jams and preserves. Mother Marguerite had requested that all stray cats in the village be brought up to the convent to battle any vermin who might find the new grain stores worth their interest. The corridors now rang with the off-key songs of cats and the murmurings of the nuns who rubbed the cats' bellies and scratched their ears. The routine in Mater Misericordia was tilted off its axis, but there was laughter and vibrancy and a kind of chaos that most appreciated. Sister Agnes, though young, had proven to be exceptionally competent in finding order in the mayhem, and Marguerite and Dolora found themselves counting on her sense and capability.

Sister Anna Sophia was the only fly in the ointment, and one day Marguerite heard her whisper, not softly at all to one of her young admirers. "I, for one, do not believe that Mother Monica Maria would have liked it one bit."

Marguerite felt the words for the slap they were meant to be.

Marguerite looked coldly at Anna Sophia, while in her own mind hearing those words over and over. *Mother Monica Maria would not like it one bit.*

Three more months brought the final harvest, blessed by good warm weather that lasted till Martinmas. Casks of potatoes and turnips now were stored in the Sisters' sleeping quarters and barrels of cider lined the walls of the chapel. And as if God Himself had presided over the harvest, winter fell hard on the very day after the last sheaf of wheat was brought into the threshing barns.

It was the hardest winter anyone could recall. Juan Miguel's visits continued. As Advent led to Christmas, and Epiphany led to the feast of Saints Perpetua and Felicitas, the Convent prayed and sang and observed the liturgical year as they always had before. The Sisters of Mater Misericordia had food aplenty and fuel for their fires. The people of the village found comfort and hot meals amongst the Sisters as well. The Capitan seemed to want to linger with his visits. He was clearly feeling the cold, and the strain of keeping his company of men in order throughout the idleness of winter.

One day he confided to Marguerite that two young village girls had been "interfered with" by some of his soldiers.

"They both swear that it wasn't rape, that the girls invited them to couple."

"What do you think?" Marguerite sincerely wanted to know.

"One of them is a scoundrel and would steal his own mother's teeth if the opportunity arose. The other, Petrus is his name. Well, I think he has genuine fondness for the girl. And from what I've seen, she for him."

"And what will you do?"

"When we arrived here, I set the punishment for rape at thirty lashes. If the girl will have Petrus, I would rather see them married than see him flogged. As for the other one, if I could, I would see him in perdition. He is a trouble-maker."

"Would you like me to talk to the girl and her family? See if young Petrus is to their liking?"

"Yes!" Juan Miguel's face flushed with gratitude, and before he could help himself, he reached forward and clasped Marguerite's hand. Sister Dolora had been in the hospital ward overseeing an outbreak of croup, and walked into the room just in time to see the clasped hands and the blush rising like newly lit fire up Marguerite's face. Marguerite saw her over Juan Miguel's shoulder and snatched her hand back as if it had been bitten. Seeing her gaze, he turned around quickly, saw Sister Dolora's granite face, and said his farewells with a more elaborate bow than usual. After his footsteps could no longer be heard in the corridor, Sister Dolora came and took the same hand that Juan Miguel had held.

"Caution, child. Caution."

"It's nothing, Sister. He is enthusiastic in his gratitude. I am helping him with a problem in the village."

"Are you now…" Each word from Dolora meant volumes. "Why?"

Marguerite shrugged.

"I don't know. Because I can?"

"And is that motive enough?" Dolora gently patted the hand that she still held. "These are uncharted waters, Niece. Our Lord and his Blessed Mother know your heart. Go. Do some good where you may."

# RUPERTSBERG
# 1121 CE

The Sisters of the Abbey at Rupertsberg gathered in the Chapel, curious about the summons that was extraordinary in their daily schedule. Mother Hildegard led the Cardinal to a seat up near the simple altar and she stood in the center of the dais to address the women who were looking up at her expectantly. Hildegard didn't hold to the notion that suffering accelerated prayer, so she had had braziers installed in all the public and private spaces in the Abbey. The Chapel was warm and well-lit with the thick candles that the sisters made here in the apiary. The smell of beeswax and apple wood filled the chamber, and the rustling of feet came to a stillness when Hildegard began to speak.

"My beloved Sisters, we are honored to have with us today an emissary from the Holy See. He has shared with us that our Holy Father is in the midst of a turmoil between his divine inspirations and the small-minded prejudices of our world. We must join in prayer to assist the Holy Father in this battle, one I know we all have felt, when the life of vocation and prayer pulls us one way, and the foibles of our human selves pull us another. I have asked our guest, his Eminence Giuseppe de Fuaresca, Cardinal of the Holy See, to lead us in our prayers for the Pontiff. Cardinal?"

Hildegard turned to see his face, now a study in rapid decision-making. He could do this – lead these nuns in this prayer and be complicit in Hildegard's plan. Or he could denounce her now and make enemies of all these women who clearly were devoted to her and their potentially wealthy and influential families in these German States who could be a source of support for him in his further ambitions. Biting the inside of his cheek, he chose the former. Better to keep this woman and her supporters happy. And, as he told himself, Rome was very far away.

As he walked toward Hildegard, again he felt that frisson of attraction. She was smiling beatifically at him, but behind her eyes was the question. Which way was he going to jump? He stopped with his shoulder to hers, standing between her and the congregation. He leaned down to speak softly into her ear so that no one but her could hear.

"Well played, Mother Hildegard. Masterfully done. The treatise is yours after all, is it not?"

Hildegard looked upward at him directly with no artifice, no subterfuge.

"But Cardinal, does not all knowledge come from above? I am merely the scribe."

Giuseppe's mouth twitched and he found himself smiling and falling into her gold eyes. He felt – heard – a snap like the crack of thunder. In that instant he knew himself to be now, and forever more, a supporter and protector of this woman. The thought struck him like a sword against his skull. A protector? Where did that come from? His ambition, his personal agenda all fell away, and the need to protect this woman became paramount. It was as if something had broken through the crust of who he was and revealed who he was meant to be.

Hildegard reached out and took his hand, her fingers loosely intertwined with his. His brows drew together, and a look of confusion moved across his face like storm clouds. Their linked fingers, hidden from view, were a lifeline he clung to as the world he knew rumbled and shifted.

"Steady on, friend. All will be well," she said quietly.

Giuseppe turned to face the women waiting patiently for him to speak. He felt Hildegard gently touch his back directly behind his heart, and he opened his mouth to do what, just a few moments before, would have been anathema to him. He looked at the chapel filled with white robed and unveiled women, and paused. These nuns were separate individuals, yet connected in spirit. They looked happy and healthy and with complete identities. Hildegard had not demanded that they hide themselves in a convent and in a habit and veil; rather, she had asked them to fully inhabit themselves. His decision made itself, and he asked the Sisters of the Abbey of Rupertsberg to pray that the Pope would see wisdom as it was relayed by their own Mother Hildegard. And somehow, without knowing how it happened, he knew that he would give his life, if necessary, for her.

The Chapel filled with the voices in prayer and song. Giuseppe was startled and yet not surprised that the music the sisters sang moved him to tears. So this was the music for which Hildegard had become famous. It seemed to him that the ceiling of the Chapel dissolved and the celestial bodies joined the chorus. The sounds made were otherworldly and yet so much of this earth that the particles of soil and the leaf mold on the forest floor joined in descant to the melodies of the stars. Giuseppe had never been a religious man. Rather, he had found the Church a convenient organization in which to climb toward his lofty ambitions. But at this exact moment, with the sacred songs tickling the very marrow of his bones, he thought he saw the Divine, and She had the face of Mother Hildegard.

When the ecstasy of prayer had subsided, all the sisters gently walked from the chapel, leaving Giuseppe and Hildegard alone on the dais. Sunlight shot arrows of saffron through the high windows onto the Chapel floor. The walls still reverberated with echoes of song. Hildegard looked sideways under her lashes to watch as Giuseppe opened his eyes made brilliant by the unshed tears. He felt her gaze, and turned to face her.

"I am undone," he said with a catch in his voice.

"That is a good place to start," she replied with tender humor.

They walked together, footstep paced with footstep, in an unhurried way back to Hildegard's study. Sister Delphinia was there, as was her way, to anticipate Mother Hildegard's needs. She had stoked the fire higher in the grate, and lit several tapers in the corners of the room so that a gentle warmth and light spread like honey. At the sound of their footsteps she asked,

"Shall I send for tea, Mother?"

"Yes. Thank you, Sister, and perhaps something a bit stronger as well. Our friend, the Envoy, is in need of some revitalization."

Giuseppe gave a half smile in acknowledgement of the ribbing, and sank onto the cushioned bench in front of the fire. He stared into the flames, watching intently as if there he would find answers to all the questions swirling around in his head. Hildegard went to her desk and began humming softly under her breath as the flesh began to fall onto the skeleton of a new song. He could hear the snatches of a tune and the sound of her quill scratching across the surface of the parchment, and he felt a peace unlike anything he had ever experienced before flood though his body. Delphinia returned with a tray of tea and brandy, set it down, handed him a glass of the latter, and quietly left the room.

Time seemed irrelevant as an hour or more flowed by. Hildegard poured herself tea, humming all the while and nestled back down at her desk. When she felt she had enough of the song down on paper so that it would not evaporate back into the ether from whence it came, Hildegard came over to join him on the settle, filling up his glass with more brandy and bringing one for herself. She sat down and took moments to smell the wool of his tunic and the chamomile and soapwort with which he had washed his hair. He was breathing in the tang of hawthorn bark and oak gall from the ink on her fingers and the deep green smells of tansy and comfrey that seemed to be imbued in the seams of her habit. They sipped the rather excellent brandy that came from the brother Abbey nearby. Giuseppe could hear laughter float in the window, and had a half thought of how strange it was to hear happiness in a convent.

"Glorious music, laughter and a very fine brandy. This is a good life you have made here, Mother Hildegard."

She only smiled in response, for what was there to say?

"I have absolutely no idea what to do next," he said without looking at her.

"Do you need to do anything?" she asked, genuinely curious.

"It has been my experience that doing *something* usually inspires the confidence of others and assuages my own fears," he said with wry honesty.

"And it has been my experience that when I am unclear of which direction to go, it is better to go nowhere at all," Hildegard replied with a chuckle.

He surprised himself by laughing as well. His was a warm molasses kind of mirth, and Hildegard caught the laugh and added her own. Why it was so funny neither knew, but the joy and release filled the study, perhaps assisted by the brandy. They would wind down and then catch a look at the other's face and fill up with laughter again and again. Finally, wiping her eyes, Hildegard said.

"And so, there you have it."

"What an odd creature you are, Mother Hildegard."

She nodded, and repeated, "There you have it."

Their laughter broke out again, softer and less manic, but full-bellied nonetheless. Giuseppe reached out a hand to her and left it, palm up, resting on the settle between them. Hildegard looked him square in the eye for a long, long minute, found the answer she was looking for, and let her hand drift down onto his. They sat like that till evening shadows stretched into the study and the tapers were burned half down.

"I shall have someone show you to your rooms, Your Eminence. You may have a late supper in your rooms with your traveling companions, or you may all join us in the refectory. It shall be as you wish."

She stood and walked over to the bell pull. Giuseppe looked at her in the fading light and wished the late hour and his entourage of clerks and priests all to perdition. Oh, for more time alone with her!

"It is probably best if my companions and I don't sully the refectory tonight." He smiled and went on, "But perhaps tomorrow I might ask for a tour of your extraordinary establishment?"

Hildegard gave an internal sigh of relief. She might be growing something resembling trust in him, but the rest of his bunch from

Rome was another thing all together. The less they saw the better.

"How long do you plan to grace us with your presence?" she asked.

"I plan to send the entourage on to Cologne tomorrow to attend to some business with the Bishop, but was hoping that I might stay here for a day or two more...to rest."

Hildegard nodded gracefully, lowering her eyes so that he wouldn't see the relief flooding through them at the departure of his entourage...and the joy that his longer stay would bring. Something, a memory, niggled at her and brought that visual blurring that her rememberings often brought. She had a clear-as-day picture in her mind of two stunningly beautiful people, a brother and sister, with elaborate snakes tattooed along their arms and shoulders. They had emerald eyes and tawny skin and looked as alike as any man and woman could. So that was who he had been! And why she wanted to trust him. Here stood the latest incarnation of Talo of the Jaguar People, brother of Uxua, and a warrior who had stood to defend them all. And his Uxua was alive as well! The reincarnation of Uxua was here in the Abbey making beautiful statues come alive from hunks of cold stone.

"Yes. Tomorrow would be delightful. And I have someone I want you to meet. He is sculptor in residence here by the name of Alejandro de Marsitel."

"A resident sculptor? How like you! I will be delighted to meet this artist. And to see more of this world in miniature that you have created."

He sighed now, a deep soulful sound.

"You are most remarkable, Mother Hildegard. And odd!"

They chuckled softly. A young sister came to respond to the summons, and led the Cardinal out the door to show him to his rooms. Mother Hildegard stood in the threshold and called down the corridor after him.

"Do not be alarmed, Your Eminence. To safeguard the safety of all here we lock the gates to the guest quarters at night. You will regain your liberty in the morning."

He turned to look back at her, backlit from the candles and fire in her study. She seemed to be surrounded and infused with golden light, like amber held before a flame. He felt that ringing inside his skull again, and his entire being seemed to vibrate subtly.

"Yes, Mother. Safety is worth safeguarding. And liberty will be that much sweeter come the morning."

She lifted a hand in salute and gently closed the door to her study, throwing the corridor into a darkness only lifted by the single candle that the sister carried. He thought, *She takes the light and the warmth with her.* And he shuddered.

Mother Hildegard stood in the center of her study and looked down at the hand she had lifted toward him in farewell. With a strange sense of dislocation she saw that it was trembling. She took a deep clearing breath and walked quickly out of the study and down to the refectory. She wanted the company of her sisters. She wanted to gauge their reactions to the Cardinal's speech earlier that day. She wanted to feel steady ground beneath her feet.

As she entered the large vaulted chamber, the light and laughter reached out to her like the heat that rolls out as one opens an oven door. Strong and welcomed, heat and joy and the promise of nurturance, she embraced the energy and emotion in the room like a starving woman at a banquet table.

At Rupertsberg the tables were long and communal with no separation between the distinctions of rank or seniority. Mother Hildegard was greeted with smiles, and several sisters shifted over on a bench to make room for her. She helped herself to the root vegetable stew and black bread in the center of the table, and let the conversations swirl around her. It occurred to her that she was really hungry, and she looked up from her plate to see Sister Delphinia at the next table watching her with that knowing look on her face. She smiled back sending the silent message, "Yes, dear one, you are right as usual, I had forgotten to eat today." Delphinia smiled in return, and could relax now that Hildegard's physical needs were being met. She could tell that there were deeper issues roiling under the surface behind Hildegard's eyes. But those needs could wait till hunger was assuaged.

Hildegard began to listen to the sisters near her. They seemed at ease and untroubled. Looking around the refectory she noticed that all of the 'others', Alejandro, young Petyer, tiny Griseld, and their gardener Betterm who usually ate with them of an evening, were not present. So, the message to keep a low profile had been sent, received and understood.

# CHARLESTON, SOUTH CAROLINA, USA 1805 CE

"Martha!" Alexander Farley's voice always harkened back to his Massachusetts's roots when he was in distress. "Maaaaaathaaah!" he bellowed to his housekeeper.

"What is it, Master Farley?" Martha's voice came from just behind his left shoulder and caused Alex to start and turn quickly on his heel.

"Jumpin' Jehosephat, girl! Thee are as quiet as a cat."

"At least one of us is," she said and gave a small giggle that made him smile. He looked at her and the half shadow of the front hallway made patterns of light and dark on her face that were reminiscent of the three lines and patterns of dots that had once, in the way back, adorned her chin. In the today she was copper skinned and deeply pockmarked from smallpox, medium height and solid of build. But on occasion he could see the small lithe creature with the heart-shaped face that had once been at home on land and in the water. He shook himself back to the current urgency.

"Hurry! Blankets and a warming pan! I found another one!" He raced back out the kitchen to the wagon that was waiting in the backyard of his Charleston home. Martha hurried to gather what he had requested and followed him outside. When she saw the pitiable girl huddled in the corner of the wagon-bed she came up short. The girl, for she did look to still be a child, had the shaved head that was the mark of the slave auction. She was so thin that Martha could see her ribs, and was naked except for a string of beads that surrounded her waist. There was a large fist-shaped bruise on her left cheek and, her arms were wrapped tight around her bent knees. She looked at them with eyes devoid of hope.

"Lawsy, Master Farley. She looks half dead!"

"Let us hope that we can tip the scales in the favor of life, then," he replied, although his tone didn't offer much optimism.

"She's one of us? Thee is sure?"

"I saw when the auctioneer lifted one of her breasts. Although shackled she looked as though she would rip his head off. I saw her then, Kiyia, Guardian of Epona."

"This scrawny thing is our Kiyia?" Martha's voice rose an octave and she looked at the scrap of a girl hard. "Kiyia?"

The girl's eyes brightened at the sound of that name, as if she knew it.

"They cut her hair, but did they de-louse her, do you think?" Martha asked.

"I am supposing so. She had been through the house slave auction already, and they always try to clean them up for that."

"She didn't get bought," Martha stated the obvious fact.

"I am assuming it was because she bared her teeth at the bidders like a mountain lion. They all backed off after that," Alex almost chuckled. "Then she went on to the field hand pen. I was able to secure her at that point."

They inched forward towards the terrified girl. Martha was making cooing noises. When almost in reach they dropped the blankets on the bed of the wagon and motioned to the girl to take them for herself. She stared at them for three heartbeats and then snatched the blankets up and wrapped them around her shoulders and legs. Martha lifted her fingers up to her mouth to indicate food and then ran back into the kitchen. Alex stood with the weight on one hip and waited for Martha's return. She came back with a plate of cold meat and cornbread, and slid the plate across the wooden boards toward the girl. She grabbed the plate so fast they might not have seen it, and shoveled the food into her mouth barely taking pause to chew.

"Slow down, girly. Slow down," Martha said kindly. The girl ate like a starving wolf pup, and Alex felt his heart squeeze once again at the horrors that men inflicted.

He and Martha exchanged a look and then walked back to sit on the bench just outside the kitchen door. It was late afternoon and the shade made the bench cooler than the October sun had felt. Birds started to come onto the cobblestones and pick up bits of straw and fluff. The city out front seemed a thousand miles away as Alex and Martha felt the stillness within them grow and spread.

They sat like that for maybe half an hour until they saw the girl poke her head around the back end of the wagon and spot them. She seemed more curious than frightened now, and they sat quietly waiting until she slipped off the wagon holding fast the blanket around her waist and over one shoulder.

Martha pointed at her own chest and said, "Martha. Mar- tha." The she tapped Alexander's chest and said. "Master Farley." The girl looked at them, blinked, and then pointed at her own heart and said in a smoky voice that sounded much older than her years, "Khadee."

Alexander stood very slowly so as to not startle the girl. He placed his right hand over his heart, and bowed low at the waist. "Welcome, Khadee. Welcome to our home."

The girl looked at him with a deep fierce appraisal, as if she was trying to understand his meaning, though she knew not the language. But something in his manner reassured her, and she too placed her hand on her heart and make a much smaller, more subtle bow in response. Martha chuckled and said under her breath. "Oh yes, I see our Kiyia now."

# RUPERTSBERG
# 1121 CE

In the cold months the nightly gatherings of the Thirteen at the gazebo were untenable, and so they met in the greenhouses. Hildegard knew that they would all be present tonight, needing to know exactly what was happening with the Papal envoy.

She felt a momentary disquiet. She trusted her foreknowledge of who the Cardinal had been, and what his connection to the Thirteen was. But in her experience, the memories of that past life were not readily accessible to those who had been Companions of the Thirteen, those beloved companions who had survived the cataclysm. Take Delphinia, for example. She felt a pull, a kinship, a loyalty to Hildegard, but the memories of who they had been before were ephemeral for her, like the wisps of dream. It wasn't possible for her to really remember that time, as if too much knowledge would be difficult or dangerous to her present self. And Delphinia was content with that state of not knowing. But through the centuries Hildegard had met many others of the Companions, and the tug of connection was not always a pleasant experience for them. Some feared it. Some constantly looked with suspicion for ulterior motives and agendas. Some reacted with anger at emotions they couldn't explain. Hildegard wondered how Giuseppe would react when he encountered Uxua/Alejandro. It might go well. Or it might go very badly indeed.

After their meal Hildegard went with the flow of bodies into the Chapel for the Vespers prayers. As was the way at Rupertsberg, prayer was sung, a benediction to the glory of the day. And as usually was, most of the music had been composed by Hildegard. This was one of the more spirited offices of prayers here, a last hurrah of joyous sound that would be followed in some three hours by the more subdued Compline that led the sisters to their sleep. Maybe it was the added agitation from the Papal Envoy's visit. Or maybe it was a mutually understood recognition of how much they had to be grateful for. But whatever the reason, the singing tonight made the rafters of the Chapel tremble, gratitude and bliss amplifying the voices and connecting to the angels above and within. On the far side of the Abbey the Papal Envoy sat near his opened window, pulled into an ecstatic trance by the sounds wafting toward him from the chapel.

Feeling very well nourished, both physically and spiritually, Hildegard felt like she was floating down through the gardens and past the kitchens to the greenhouses. There were three of them built into berms of earth, high on their north side and more open on the south. Two of the structures had woven wicker panels that were arched overhead to make a slightly vaulted roof that kept heat in and rain out. One Sister's very rich and very grateful father had donated actual panes of glass for the last, the third greenhouse, farthest away from the Abbey and hidden from common view by the other two, and it was the regular meeting place for the Thirteen. The day's warmth was held there and gradually released by the packed earth, so that even now in the deepest of winter, the space was warm and smelled of newly tossed soil and green things. There was a small iron wood-burning stove in the center of the space to keep all the plants and people from ever freezing, and it was around this that the six of the Thirteen were positioned waiting for Hildegard's arrival.

They all looked up at Hildegard with varying types of curiosity and inquisitiveness. She thought to herself that the weight of responsibility on her to keep them all safe no matter what happened in the outside world felt very great tonight. But then, even greater was the joy she felt at seeing them assembled here all together. She stopped to simply look at them and said,

"Beloveds."

Sister Maria Stella pulled up another stool for Mother Hildegard who came to sit with them near the stove. Griseld was wrapped in so many shawls and scarves that only her eyes and a tiny bit of her red-tipped nose were visible. Sister Catherine of the Wheel held her dog on her lap. Betterm and Sister Maria Stella were perched close together on a rough bench. Petyer was holding out his hands to the warmth of the stove and munching on a small soft roll he had filched from the kitchen on his way to the greenhouse. Alejandro was sitting next to Hildegard with a studied indolence that barely covered an undercurrent of energy like ground lightening. He spoke first.

"What is it? Something has happened!"

Hildegard felt a quandary for a mere second if she should tell him, tell them all of the incarnational identity of the Papal Envoy. Might it be better if they weren't burdened with that information? But she fell to the side that knowledge was power, and made her decision that they deserved to be forewarned and therefore, forearmed.

"It has been a day, indeed. I assume that you have been informed by Sisters Catherine and Maria Stella that the Cardinal spoke at Chapel today and supported my authorship of the herbal treatise. Evidently, that had not been his initial brief from the Holy Father, so we can be thankful that he is a man with enough of an open mind to hear my thoughts on the matter and make a different decision."

They all nodded, and Betterm snorted.

"I wish I had been a fly on the wall while you let him 'hear your thoughts'!"

"Yes, I was most persuasive," Hildegard replied with the sound of a smile in her voice.

"When are they going then?" Sister Catherine said grumpily. Any variation in her routine elicited grumbles and complaints.

"The entourage departs tomorrow morning, but the Cardinal will be remaining for a few extra days," Hildegard answered.

Alejandro stiffened and sat up straighter on his stool.

"Why? What are you not saying?"

"Prepare yourselves, my beloveds, for he is someone we all knew."

"Is he another of the Thirteen then?" Petyer spoke eagerly.

The possibility of this sent a current of excitement and apprehension through the group. They all remembered enough of what had been before to know that not everyone from that past had wished them well and that some very dark forces had conspired against them. But they all also remembered that they had loved and been lost to some dear souls. Who was it that had found their way here to them now?

# XXI

# SAN MIGUEL NEPANTLA, NEW SPAIN (MEXICO) 1650 CE

Juana Inés de Ashaje y Ramirez de Santillana had a fever. And like any two-year-old, she let the world know her feelings about that state of being.

"Tecitzin! Tecitzin!" she yelled louder than any small body could be thought to be able to do.

Dona Isabella, Juana's mother swept into the room, tall, elegant, distressed.

"Juana, you must quiet down! Your grandfather has guests from the capital here and we can hear you all the way down to the stables." The woman's voice was, like her person, elegant and well disciplined, but completely ineffectual.

"Tecitzin!!! I want Tecitzin!" Juana bellowed, and in desperation her mother gave the command for the Tecitzin to be brought to the child's rooms. A small dark-skinned woman came gliding into the room after an astonishingly short amount of time. It was as if she had been poised just outside, awaiting her summons. She was shoeless, dressed in a simple muslin shift, and brought with her the smell of palo santo and ashes. The very air around her made way for her presence. Dona Isabella gave a half glance toward the old woman, not granting her a full-faced look.

"Tecitzin, she won't have anyone but you. I must get back to father's guests. Please…" and here the younger woman, pale of skin and blue of eye, had the grace to look up sheepishly under her lashes and point her sapphire eyes toward her great-grandmother, "please, keep her quiet! She is enough of an irritant to father. Let us not make it worse." Volumes were spoken in silence. The illegitimacy of this child, the vast fortune that surrounded them all, the need for Dona Isabella to placate the influential men around her to insure the continuation of that fortune.

And the old woman, who was indeed the great-grandmother of Dona Isabella and the great-great-grandmother of little Juana was well used to being a personage that the criollos would like hidden. She nodded her head and moved toward the child's bed. With that, Dona Isabella swept out of the darkened room back out into the blinding sunlight, leaving her daughter behind without a thought.

"Tecitzin is here, little one. All will be well." The old woman, named Palle by her people and known as Maria Luisa by the criollos began to sing in a bare whisper in Nahuatl, the forbidden language. Juana drew one more big draft of breath, as if to bellow one more time, but instead let all the air deflate her little body and lifted her long black lashes to look at her great great-grandmother.

The servants in the room exchanged looks and then quietly left. They knew, better than Dona Isabella, that when Palle was present, all would indeed be well. She sang lullabies in Nahuatl. She sang healing songs in Latin and Middle High German. She sang invocations in ancient Qin and an even more ancient Common Tongue. She filled the room with the presence of the Goddess. She summoned those who she needed, and as always, they answered. The room became filled with those spirits.

Little Juana saw the invisible ones, her friends who stayed by her and protected her. They joined in the singing and began to dance around her, floating above and around her bed, defying the demands of the earth. Her fever began to subside and she drifted off to a peaceful sleep, never relinquishing her fierce grip on her great-great-grandmother's hand.

Palle, she who had been Atvasfara, High Priestess of Isis spoke in that ancient Common Tongue to the assembled spirits.

"The Little One will recover, my beloveds. She has work to do in this lifetime. I will prepare her as best I can with the years this body has left." She tilted her head to listen. The older she got, the easier it was to see and hear them. Her lifetimes were coming one after the other, faster and faster, and she felt the pressure of the needs of the Goddess deep within her soul. She had stood with Jeanne D'Arc, the warrior, she had worshiped Seolmundae in the caves of Jeju, she had been a Taino boy taken as a slave who had fallen to measles. Then in the eyeblink of human understanding she had appeared here as a native of what the arrogant ones called New Spain. So fast, so much suffering. But her companions, her beloveds, her Thirteen, their spirits came more and more easily to her. She answered the question they posed.

"Ah, yes, Juana will be dedicated in her scholarship, as she always is, our Silbara."

She whispered to her beloved spirits long into that evening and night, stroking the hair of her tiny one, her Juana, her Silbara. The gathered spirits laughed and reminisced and prayed over the little one, reveling in being together for this brief time. This life, while it had had its joys, had been hard, so very hard. So now, they could rest, rest in the arms of the Great Mother, rest until...

# RUPERTSBERG
# 1121 CE

Mother Hildegard spoke very softly so that all had to lean in to hear her.

"Uxua of the Jaguar People had a twin brother." She turned to Alejandro and said gently, "Do you recall this brother, my friend?"

Alejandro drew a sharp deep breath and nodded. The ache he felt for that long-lost beloved was balanced with the danger that the loss of that love and twinship might devastate again. He didn't speak; he couldn't.

Sister Catherine, she who had been Badh of the Cailleach and the Keeper of Wild Spaces, voiced what they were all thinking.

"Talo? Is it he?"

"Yes, and he is also the Papal Envoy whose ultimate concerns do not align with ours. Which self will determine his actions we have yet to see."

They all took a collective deep breath. Young Petyer remembered Talo very well. He recalled how Talo had led a group in the warrior dance they called 'the Form', a system of movements distinct from and yet very similar to the 'Dance' that the dedicants to Artemis had practiced in Ephesus of old. He could recall himself as little Io with a young dedicant named Pel traveling together toward Egypt, and how Pel and Talo had fallen in love in the land of the Nile. *"What happened to them after the dreadful day when the Thirteen died?"* Petyer wondered. *"Did they survive and build a life together? Did they each return to their homelands? Were there any homelands left to return to?"*

As they all sat in the warm humid air of the greenhouse, steeped in their recollections of Talo, it was as if his very presence here at Rupertsberg, as if the mere mention of his name flung wide open within them doors to memories and feelings about their own beloved Companions. Sister Catherine felt the arrow sharp, sweet pang of loss over the young man who had been her servant, friend, and lover. Betterm and Sister Maria Stella, Silbara and Autakla that were, held hands and moved deep into their shared grief over their mentors who had come with them from Calanais. Griseld who had been called Tiamet saw the worried faces of the two young women who had been dragged from their mountain Abbey home to serve her on their journey to Egypt. Such love, such loss!

Mother Hildegard never let her gaze wander from Alejandro. When he had lived as Uxua, the living embodiment of the goddess Ix Chel, Talo had been his brother, and even more bonded, his twin. They had never been apart, living every day together till the cataclysm of the planet ripped them asunder. To come together again, for perhaps the first time in three thousand years! What would that be like? Sweet joy? Unexplainable torment? Maybe both. After some time, she spoke softly to him.

"Alejandro? How shall this unfold? It shall be as you wish. Do you want to meet this man who was your Talo? Of course, I have told him nothing of what was before and who we were. He may remember something. He may not. Those who were our Companions in the time that was, well, this can be quite a challenge for them, for they do not have the fullness of memory that we do."

Alejandro lifted his eyes from the floor to her. He took a shuddering breath and made a tiny shrug with his shoulders.

"It seems to be my curse in this life that the body I inhabit is not what I might want. How could he see me, looking like this? How could this..." and he made a flicking motion with his hands down over his torso in disgust, "stir any memories? What would he think of his 'sister' now?"

Those last words came out strangled, wrapped in tears and a life-time's frustration and pain.

Hildegard looked at him with deep empathy.

"Oh beloved!" she replied. "Hard as it may be for you to believe, you are still quite pretty."

Alejandro snorted and Sister Catherine let out a big guffaw, part mirth, part relief. Griseld walked over to Alejandro and crawled into his lap. With her usual pugnacious tone she told him.

"And if he doesn't like the way you look now, I'll just punch him in the nose."

All broke out in laughter and Alejandro wiped his eyes.

"Bring him to the studio tomorrow, Mother. Let us meet there in that clear bright light, where everything is clearly visible. And where I have a ladder for Griseld to climb in case she needs to reach his nose with her fist."

Hildegard smiled as she stood.

"It shall be so, Alejandro. But I will keep Griseld in abeyance, shall I? We can call her in if needed."

"I'll be right outside the studio windows doing some vital pruning, and therefore armed with a good knife," Betterm offered, only half joking. Sister Catherine lifted up Dog and offered him forward as well.

Alejandro rose with Griseld still safely ensconced in his arms.

"My dearest friends. Let's let the man get a good look at me first before we attack him with pruning knives and dog teeth." Griseld rumbled from within her many cloaks. "And little girl fists!"

The group began to leave the greenhouse each softly rubbing Ale-jandro's shoulder or patting him on the back as they left.

"Look for us mid-morning then, right after Terce," Mother Hilde-gard said with a final warm look, and then she turned and seemed to float from the greenhouse.

"How does she do that?" Alejandro asked Griseld. "Her feet never make any sound."

"With all her lofty thought it is a wonder she is anywhere near the ground." Griseld retorted, and the pair made their way back through the garden toward the wing of the Abbey that held their sleeping quarters.

# COMTÉ DE FOIX
# 1079 CE

Mother Marguerite summoned the family and the girl, heard their wishes, and sent a message to the Capitan that the wedding between the village girl and the hapless Petrus could proceed. He sent a cask of brandy in reply. She didn't see Juan Miguel or hear from him for almost a sennight. That was unusual, and she worried that something was wrong in the valley below. One evening, late after Vespers, Marguerite was alone in her study when a postulant on gate duty came with a scribbled note.

*It is urgent. I must speak with you, alone.*
*Back gate after Compline.*
*JM*

Marguerite thanked the young girl and sent a reply.

*Well noted.*
*MM*

With her mind churning she sat through Compline prayers barely noticing that they had ended. Should she alert Sister Dolora? Take her along to meet the Capitan? Why the need for the cryptic note? Her reply had not agreed to meeting him alone or even to a meeting at all. Should she go? Should she be chaperoned? Why the back gate where no one could see him enter or exit? She stayed in the pew as the last of the nuns left the chapel. Her memory flashed to Mother Monica Maria on her deathbed.

*"You have the courage of a lion,"* she had said.

Marguerite felt nothing like a lion at this moment, but just the sheer reminder of the faith that Monica Maria had had in her got her up from her seat, out the chapel door, and though corridors, past the sheep pens and stables to the back gate. She barely registered the soft whinny from the stables, the horses disturbed by the sound of her feet in the stones. She purposely hadn't brought a lantern, but the half moon shone enough light for her to see her way cross the stable yard and unclasp the latch of the gate. He was there, barely visible in the shadows, standing under the stone portico. Marguerite stepped two steps out the convent boundary, to join him in the covered darkness.

"I didn't think you would come," he said, rushed and quiet.

"I didn't either," she replied.

"I come bearing bad news."

"What? What is wrong?"

She heard him curse under his breath. She reached forward in the dark and found his forearm. She followed it down until she wound her fingers in his and held tight.

"Tell me!"

"It is that scoundrel, the rapist. I had him flogged and he sent word to his uncle who has the ear of the Duke of Poitiers. They are sending a massive force here, to relieve me of my command. And to…to take the Convent…by any means necessary. They ordered me not to tell you. They won't stop at driving you out at sword point. They won't stop at murder. I have tried to stop this tide. I have tried…" He broke off and attempted to pull his hand from hers. Marguerite held on.

"What should we do?"

"Leave! Leave tonight! Take the footpath and head down into the woods on the far side of the mountain. The new troops arrive tomorrow, and I can stall them for a day before the new commander will demand an audience with you."

"But I have elder nuns! And sisters in the sick ward!" Marguerite 's head was spinning with the logistics of such an exodus.

"Get everyone out – tonight. It is the only way to keep them safe."

*"Keep them safe!"* Those had been Mother Monica Maria's words, her charge to Marguerite. *"Keep them safe!"*

"What will happen to you? Won't they know, when they march up the mountain and no one is here, that you sounded an alarm?"

"They might suspect, but they won't know. And I too have friends in high places. I will manage. But you must go, now! Don't tarry!"

He lifted his other hand and cupped her face.

"Keep yourself safe as well," he whispered though a tightened throat. He turned her shoulders and pushed her not so gently back toward the convent and the night's work to save them all.

"Go!"

# RUPERTSBERG
# 1121 CE

The next day, after the fast breaking and the morning offices, Mother Hildegard led Giuseppe, the Papal Envoy on a tour of the Abbey. He made dutiful sounds of appreciation at the extensive gardens and apiary, he was truly impressed by the music rooms and the light-filled scriptorium where sisters transcribed Mother Hildegard's works and music. He took careful note of how warm and comfortable all the rooms were. This was not like any other dwelling for religious women that he had ever seen. It did not hold the luxurious appointments that he knew from residences of the high clergy in Rome, but neither was it spartan or bleak. It was lovely and easeful and simple. And even more astonishing, every woman looked happy. Smiles were easy and genuine, song and music filled every corridor, he actually saw three young nuns skipping. Rupertsberg was extraordinary, like its Abbess.

As the sisters filed toward the Chapel for Terce, Hildegard led him in the opposite direction toward the workshops. The sisters of the Abbey made candles in one, jams and preserves and relishes from the bounty of the gardens in another. In one vaulted space a sturdy nun of middle years was crafting stained glass windowpanes depicting the women of the Bible, inspired by and made to accompany the stories Hildegard was writing. At the end of, and perpendicular to, the long building which housed the workshops stood a separate large stone structure. It, like all of Rupertsberg, was made of yellow gold stone that gleamed warm, even in the thin winter sunlight. This building was high with double doors that reached twenty feet, like barn doors, along its south-facing wall and windows that ran along the top of the walls, seemingly hung right below the gutters. Espaliered pear trees lined the sunny side, and an old man in layers of brown and russet stood there, pruning the splayed branches with an odd kind of ferocity. Mother Hildegard bade him good morning as they passed.

"Bright blessings on the day, Betterm."

"Just had to see to these trees today, Mother," he replied.

She nodded and turned slightly to Giuseppe.

"Our gardener rules us all with an iron fist, you see," which he thought was a slightly peculiar statement, but then nothing in Rupertsberg complied with the ordinary.

Giuseppe could hear the sounds of chisel and stone coming from within. Hildegard paused at the doors, like she was poised for some signal, and then knocked three times against the wood. Without waiting for a response, she pulled on the large iron handles and swung the doors toward them. She strode in and Giuseppe followed. He stopped, struck with the sight before him. To his right, bathed in light was a magnificent statue of three women, the three Marys, huddled at the foot of the cross. It was exquisite work. The women's bodies radiated grief and anguish, their faces were a study in love and despair. Giuseppe knew that this statue was the equal, if not superior to any found in Florenzia or Rome. There were other large chunks of marble scattered around the large workspace, and the air was filled with the fine sparkling dust that signaled the creation that happened here. Off to the left the front halves of a lion and a lamb, nestled together in peaceful repose. The lion's face looked motherly and the lamb reminded Giuseppe of the absent-minded Cardinal of Stuttgart. He laughed at the whimsy and humor displayed there. A movement, a shuffle of feet, and the sculptor came around from behind the block of stone that would become the animals' back halves, walking into the bright light that flooded down from the high windows. He stopped and stood as still as his statues, his stunning green eyes locking directly on Giuseppe who felt like he was caught in the stare of a large predator as the hairs stood up on the back of his neck.

Mother Hildegard stood motionless, suspended in the waves of time and love and mystery that roiled back and forth between the two men. Afraid to speak, for fear of interrupting something essential, she asked for divine guidance and felt herself poised on the edge of a fractured beam of light. *"Make me an instrument of peace,"* she prayed.

In this deafening silence, Guiseppe, feeling completely unmoored, reached into his habituated patterns of charm and diplomacy.

"Are you the master of these magnificent creations? I confess, I am stunned at their beauty and power."

He made himself break the gaze with the sculptor and looked aside and down at Hildegard.

"Mother, you have a genius besides yourself here at Rupertsberg."

She saw his valiant attempts to keep the world steady and took pity on him stepping forward to make the proper introductions.

"Your Eminence, may I present to you Alejandro de Marisel of Sevilla. He has found a home here with us these last two years, and his statues adorn our chapel and facilitate our devotions. Alejandro, this is His Excellence, Cardinal Guiseppe Giardelli from the Papal See."

She reached forward and clasped Alejandro's hand. His muscles were rigid and his hand was icy cold. Tugging at him slightly, she gave him direction.

"Alejandro, might you tell His Eminence what your current project is about?" There was an ever-so-slight edge of pleading in her tone, but though it was subtle, it broke through his trance-like state and he gave a small shudder like a fever chill.

"Of course, Mother." He gestured with a wave of his free hand toward the half-finished piece. "As is apparent, this sculpture gives reference to the biblical prospect of the lion lying down with the lamb."

Giuseppe chuckled with his practiced easy grace.

"I don't recognize the lion, but I am teased with the sense of familiarity about that lamb. He bears a striking resemblance to Aldross, the Cardinal of Stuttgart. Or is that perhaps, sheer accident?"

Hildegard laughed lightly and murmured a weak denial. By this point, Alejandro had a sheen of perspiration across his brow from the effort of not throwing his arms around Giuseppe and weeping at the finding of his eons-lost twin. He felt his resolve slipping, but, as he opened his mouth to declare his kinship, Hildegard stepped between them and pointed across the studio to the recently completed statue of the Three Marys.

"Your Eminence, you spoke of Alejandro's sculptures having power. This piece always brings me to tears. It holds such pain and loss. Such loss."

Her eyes filled as she walked him across the studio floor away from Alejandro. As Giuseppe studied the work, she surreptitiously studied him. He showed no indication that something momentous was occurring right now in that space. His face was as placid as still waters, with only a tilt of the head and a tiny narrowing of his eyes to give evidence of how intently he was looking at the sculpture. Like Mother Hildegard, he found this work stunning, and he was amazed to find how moved he really was by the plight of these three women whose devotion to the man on the cross had been matched by their anguish at the loss of him. And he was also exquisitely aware of the heat at the back of his neck, like sunrays focused through a prism, that he knew came from the unwavering stare of the young sculptor. The man was extraordinarily gifted, no doubt, but there was an oddness about him, an intensity that Giuseppe found very disconcerting. In working his way through the labyrinthine channels of ambition and plotting within the Vatican, Giuseppe had become adept at handling uncomfortable characters and situations. Yet here, in this moment, he felt like a fly stuck in a spider's web. Again, as she had done in the Chapel the day before, Hildegard placed her hand on Giuseppe's back at the level of his heart.

"Shall we let Alejandro get back to his chipping?" she said with gentle humor.

Giuseppe looked down into her eyes and saw an ocean of compassion. *"For what reason?"* he wondered, and yet felt inexplicably grateful. They turned back toward the sculptor, and Giuseppe made the necessary compliments whilst the artist said nothing. Hildegard pushed gently on the Papal Envoy's back and they made their way across the studio toward the high double doors. At the last moment, just before they reached the threshold, Giuseppe turned back to see the statues, and the man once more. As if an oil film ran across his eyes, as he looked the man standing there rippled and shifted into the figure of a beautiful woman with a sleeveless tunic of burnished gold and writhing snakes up along her arms and shoulders. He gasped, and felt all the color drop from his face. In a blink, the sculptor reappeared standing frozen with a look of such longing on his face that it sent Giuseppe wheeling around and hurrying out into the cold sharp air.

Neither Hildegard nor Giuseppe said anything as they walked back toward the Abbey proper. He looked disoriented and frantic. Hildegard made silent sigils in the air with her hands to restore balance and comfort. *"Bring him peace,"* she prayed. They passed the old man with his pruning shears again. A tiny girl swaddled in multiple cloaks stood near the entrance to the gardens, with a look of fierce focus on her face. Closer to the back entrance to the Abbey they passed an older stout nun walking a small stout dog. Giuseppe had the peculiar notion that the three humans and the dog all looked upon him with suspicion and an odd familiarity. He nodded and smiled as he passed them all, but their gazes merely followed him as he walked by. Hildegard had murmured greeting to them and implored the little girl to get in out of the cold. The girl had merely shrugged one shoulder but said nothing.

"Some of the inhabitants of Rupertsberg seem to be reticent to converse," Giuseppe offered.

"Perhaps they are deep in prayer," Mother Hildegard answered with a hint of a smile in her voice.

"Well, that would be appropriate, yes?" Giuseppe valiantly replied.

"Oh, my friend, whether appropriate or no, I find prayer to always be a good idea." She looked up at him with a broad smile and Giuseppe felt as if storm clouds had just been swept from the sky and the sun was revealed in all its brilliance. "Come, there is someone else I would like you to meet." She led the way through the door, up the staircase and down a curved corridor toward the room where young Petyer Fieldenstarn studied every morning.

"Perhaps fortune will smile on me and this person will be happier to meet me," he said.

Hildegard laughed and the sound filled the hallway.

"There are many kinds of joy, Your Eminence, and not everyone registers said joys in the same way."

Giuseppe knew that she had layers of meaning in that sentence, but at that moment, with the sound of her laughter still resonating along the stones of the corridor, he found that he simply didn't care to try and figure it out. *"Maybe a simple joy would do for now,"* he thought.

Still feeling light of heart, he followed Hildegard into a room with desks and piles of books everywhere. Two nuns were there, one pacing across the front of the room declaiming in what Giuseppe was startled to realize was ancient Greek. The other Sister sat leaning back in her chair with her arms crossed, her eyes closed and a beatific smile across her face. And in the center of the room, leaning forward with intense concentration was a boy of some fourteen years, brown wavy haired, and lean of build. When they heard the footsteps announcing Hildegard and Giuseppe's arrival, all three occupants of the room turned as one with sharp eyes, smiled at Mother Hildegard and stared at Giuseppe. He in turn stared back at the boy, and had the same sensation of dislocation that he had had at the sculptor's studio. A shimmer, a blur, an impossible shift of form. The boy was now a small sinewy girl of about eight or nine with a riot of russet curls and large eyes the color of a trout stream. And this time, instead of gasping and recoiling, he felt a click of recognition, a knowing. And then it disappeared leaving him feeling like he had washed up on an unknown shore. He rocked a bit on his feet, gathered his composure, and stretched out a hand to the boy who had come back into focus.

"I feel that I know you. Have we met before?"

Hildegard made a small catch of her breath, and young Petyer Fieldenstarn, who had been Io, Dedicant of Artemis, walked forward as if through water and took the hand offered to him. When the two hands joined a current of charge, like lightning hitting the ground, ran through both boy and man. Giuseppe took an involuntary step back, pulled his composure around him like a cloak, and tried very hard not to flick his hand to release the sensation.

Petyer sliced his glance sideways to get some private signal from Mother Hildegard, received it, and replied.

"It is most unlikely that our paths have crossed, Your Eminence. I was born in Wiesbaden and have only known that town and this place all my life. Perhaps I just have a face common to many?"

Giuseppe, whose hand still tingled, made a polite small chuckle and began to enquire about Petyer's studies and what brought him to Rupertsberg from Wiesbaden. Hildegard smoothly swooped in and talked about Petyer's promise as a scholar, and how his family saw and supported his academic talents. Without saying so she implied that Petyer's parents had sent him to Rupertsberg, never letting it be known that Petyer had run away from home without their consent and followed some inexplicable call to find Hildegard.

Giuseppe took note of several sketches that were tacked up on the walls around the room. He walked over to inspect them closely. All the drawings were centered around a figure of a woman of beauty and elegance who was draped in the classical robes of the ancient sculptures of Rome and Greece.

"These are quite striking. Is this your work, Master Fieldenstarn?"

"Yes, the Sisters have been helping me to read the Acts of the Apostles in the Greek. The drawings are inspired by the life of the Blessed Mother, Mary of Ephesus, in her time after the death and resurrection of Our Lord, and of course, to honor my wise tutor here." He gestured to one of the nuns, Sister Mary of Ephesus, who nodded her head and blushed slightly.

"The Acts of the Apostles? In the original ancient Greek? How novel!"

Giuseppe's tone was even but his mind was racing. He knew very few scholars who could tackle such a project, and was also fully aware of how such limited access to that original source material suited the powers-that-be in the Vatican. And here, in the relative backwater of Rupertsberg, stood three bright minds who could not only translate but could clearly understand that information. He took a moment to digest this insight. Was this Abbey a refuge for divine wisdom, safely guarded from the taint of politics and rapacious ambition in Rome? Or was it the first small spark of insurrection against the monolithic power of the Holy See? As he rapidly assessed these thoughts he came to the surprising conclusion that, perhaps, it was both. The next piece of this puzzle to unravel was if this Rupertsberg was his to protect or to exploit. Was it his best course of action to guard this sanctuary or use it to propel his own career? And why was his hand still feeling pins and needles?

Mother Hildegard suggested that Petyer demonstrate his fluency by reading some of this text for the Papal Envoy. Sister Michael the Archangel, proud of her pupil, quickly acquiesced, and the visitors settled down on the wooden bench to listen.

Petyer stood with his back to the windows and the light flooded in, making him an outline of a boy. The melodious sounds of the ancient language seemed to be flowing from the empty space where his face would be, making it feel as if the words were coming from a void of antiquity. For Giuseppe, whose studies of Greek had been visual not auditory, the music of the language struck him like a blow to the heart. As Petyer began his oration, Giuseppe struggled to translate silently.

*"And Mariam of Nazareth went to Ephesus to spread the words of her son, Yeshua. She lived there for forty years in the presence of the sisters of Lazarus, Mariam and Martha. There was born there the settlement of believers who waited for the return of the Messiah. Those followers of her son came often to seek her counsel. She was most beloved…"*

Giuseppe felt his mind slip and he was flooded with images, those same images that the boy had captured in his drawing, of men and women clustered around the central figure of the wise woman of Ephesus. She who spoke the truth, as relayed by her son. She who deserved reverence on her own right. The wisdom holder. He felt the rightness of those thoughts, and then caught himself with a start. That was not the conventional narrative of the Roman Church where Mary's glory was derived only as a reflection of her son, not as a deliverer of wisdom in and of herself. He let his eyes sweep the room. Hildegard was looking at Petyer as if he was an adorable newborn puppy. The two nuns were beaming with the maternal pride not usually accorded to religious women. And while his mind told him that this was divergence from orthodoxy, his heart spoke to him of love and alignment with all good things.

Young Petyer came to an end of his recital. Sister Michael the Archangel corrected his pronunciation of several words, and Hildegard looked on approvingly. Giuseppe approached the boy and asked what his long-term goals were.

"Do you aspire to study in the universities of Cologne or Paris, Rome even? I could make introductions for you."

Petyer looked at Giuseppe with a quiet tenderness that struck the Envoy as adult beyond his years. It was if the boy felt sorry for him!

"Thank you for your offer, Your Eminence, but I have found fulfillment of mind, body and heart here at the Abbey," the boy responded.

Again, Giuseppe had that momentary dislocation, that visual abruption from what was before him. He saw women, and this boy – no, a little girl – standing in a circle with hands clasped as energy and music and power swirled above them like a funnel cloud. And again, he felt allegiance to them and a sense of being in service, with himself standing outside of their deep connection. It was a pang of devotion and loyalty and loneliness that made his knees weak.

For the third time in two days, he felt Mother Hildegard's hand on his back at the level of his heart. And, as before, he felt instantly comforted. When she suggested that they allow young Petyer to return to the rigorous tutelage of Sisters Michael the Archangel and Mary of Ephesus he agreed with alacrity. He and Hildegard returned to her study to find Sister Delphinia waiting with a platter of cold chicken and bread still warm from the Abbey's ovens, dripping with honey and butter. Hildegard gave her a rueful smile and look of gratitude and sat near the fire with a small plate of food and a mug of hot cider.

They ate in silence, and Giuseppe could hear the sounds of nuns walking down the corridors to their midday repast, some in talk and many in song. The fire snapped and spoke of oak and apple wisdoms. At long last he took his final bite, cleared his throat, and decided to speak what was foremost in his mind.

"What is it that you are not telling me, Mother?"

Hildegard lowered her eyes and took another sip of cider.

"I have told you only truth, Your Eminence," she said without lifting her glance.

"I don't dispute that, but I am sensing layers upon layers of truths here at Rupertsberg."

"Is that not the nature of the universe, Cardinal?"

"Drat your politeness, woman. Can you not call me Giuseppe? And I would receive it as the deepest honor if I could address you as Hildegard."

"Well then, I grant you that honor, and the pledge that my words to you will always be truth, to whatever level of those layers that you accept, Giuseppe."

"Whatever layer of truth I accept, or that you deem me worthy of being privy to, Hildegard?"

"Perhaps a little of both," she replied with a small smile that took any sting out of the words.

He sat for a moment to marshal the thoughts swirling in his mind like a murmuration of starlings. Then, surprising himself, he made a confession.

"Hildegard, since arriving at Rupertsberg I have, on several occasions, seen things that are not there. It is unsettling."

His understatement caused Hildegard to laugh aloud. He smiled a crooked smile in return.

"What is it that you desire? My assurances that the visions you are seeing are, indeed, not there? Or my confirmation that they are?" She was genuinely interested to know which he wanted. And this time he laughed.

"Whichever is the deeper layer of truth," he replied.

"It is my understanding that there are many, many worlds present, all around and within us, all at the same time. Is this a perspective that you can hold with some degree of comfort, Giuseppe?"

He knew that this here, this was the crux. From his answer Hildegard would decide to which layer of truth he could be admitted. He had never, in all his years of study and examination, felt the import of finding the right answer so desperately. And so, he took his time formulating his response. He looked at her full on, drinking in the sight of her hawk gold eyes and the brilliance shining out of them. Heretofore unknown desires flooded his heart. It all weighed in the balance here, who he was, who he might become. He reached out and took both her hands in his, vaguely noticing that hers were warm and his were chilled.

"Hildegard, I renounce all constructs of knowledge that I have held before. I loosen my hold on any notions that I understand anything. Take me to see the many worlds that co-exist. I eschew comfort, if by setting myself free of its bonds I can travel through the layers of truth with you."

Hildegard felt the weight of all the lives that she protected here at Rupertsberg. The talented and tormented Alejandro who only knew safety within these walls. The precious love that Betterm and Sister Maria Stella held for one another that could only be expressed here. Petyer and his rapier-sharp mind. Little Griseld whose time upon this earth in this incarnation was to be too brief. Even Sister Catherine of the Wheel, whose conversations with her dog might see her burned at a stake in less safe environs. Could she, should she, risk their sanctuary?

"I believe you that you wish to travel through the layers of truth. I believe you when you abandon comfort and the security that dogma provides. I do believe you, Giuseppe. Believe me when I affirm that."

Hildegard paused, looking into his eyes, and through him, peering to see what was at the core. Giuseppe felt totally exposed and shivered at the sudden chill that that nakedness brought into him. But he did not flinch. It was as if deep within him someone else stepped up to hold him solid in the torrent of her gaze. Buffeted, yet stalwart he met her examination, more open and honest than he had ever been in his life. What she saw gave her some of the answers she needed. She saw his earnest desire to jump into the unknown, and she also perceived the powerful threads of ambition and the need for status and power that ran through his being. He wanted, but he didn't know exactly what it was he wanted. And she didn't trust what he would do with the knowledge once he had it. So, she decided to give some of the truths to him and observe how he fared.

"I see you, Giuseppe," Hildegard said quietly, and somehow he knew he had passed some test. She settled deep into the cushions, rolled her shoulders back and began.

# SASKATCHEWAN 1915 CE

The sweat ran down into Tom's eyes, and blurred the road before him and the tunnel made by corn on either side. He didn't stop running, just lifted the bottom of his shirt and wiped his eyes. His lungs burned and the waves of heat pushing up off the packed earth felt like liquid fire. Another mile to the Palmer place, then three miles back home. He knew he was stalling, putting off the moment when he would have to tell his Ma and Pa what he had done. But he just kept running, urging his legs to pump harder and faster.

This was where he felt like he could be free. The speed, the power in his legs, the absence of voices and people and their demands for him to do this, answer me, don't talk back. With other people, he always felt like he didn't fit. But here, running hard, he could just be.

Just shy of the turn off for the Palmers he made a wide half circle and headed back home. By now the sun was low on the horizon and hitting him in the eyes. Now he felt truly blinded. He stopped to wipe his face more thoroughly, drag some air down into his lungs and rest his hands on his knees. The sound of his heart was so loud in his ears that he didn't hear the horse and wagon till it pulled out of the cornfield on his right and into the road, just a few feet in front of him. The driver of the wagon was as startled as he was.

"Hi there, Tom! Ho boy, you scared me. What ya doing?" Andy Palmer shoved his hat back on his head and grinned that one-sided grin that made him look feeble-minded. His wide face was flushed from a day in the sun, and his blue eyes framed with lashes as pale as his hair. Tom waved a hand in a gesture to 'give him a minute,' and drew some more breaths.

"What's it look like I'm doin'?" He sounded grumpy, even to his own ears, but he just couldn't help it. Andy Palmer got on his nerves.

Andy's grin got bigger and he spoke, again just a little louder than was necessary. "You sure ain't doin' your chores. That's for sure. Why ain't you doin' your chores, Tom?"

A bay horse with rider appeared a bit further down the field edge coming off the small farm track.

"Look, Tom. It's Morris. Hi, Morris!" Andy shouted loud enough to make Tom's skin crawl. The boy and the bay walked toward them on the road, and Tom could see that Morris had ridden that bay hard. Sweat and foam and the smell of a badly used horse wafted toward them.

"Did you tell them yet?" Tom asked Morris.

"Yeah, and it wasn't pretty. You?" Morris replied.

"When I get home." Tom said.

"Tell 'em what?" Andy jumped in. "Morris, tell 'em what?"

"Shut up, Andy, and get on home. Pa wants you." Morris snapped.

Andy's red face flushed an even deeper scarlet, but he didn't answer back. He just swung his head low, slapped the reins and clicked his horse homeward.

"Ah jeez!" Morris mumbled. "I hate it when I'm mean to him. You want a ride back to your place?"

Tom could tell that Morris wanted company, but that was the last thing Tom wanted.

"Nah, going to run. You be at school tomorrow?" he asked.

"Might as well. Ma is just crying and Dad is madder than a wet hen. Home ain't gonna be any place to be, anyways. We'll be leaving soon though." Morris's eyes brightened at the thought.

"That's right. Can't be too soon," Tom replied, and he stroked Morris's bay's neck twice. The mare's sides were still heaving and the steam poured off her. "Easy on this one, eh? No need to take it out on the horse."

Morris looked abashed, and kicked the mare's ribs to start a canter. He shouted back over his shoulder.

"Let's just see how you act after you tell your folks!"

Tom stood in the road for a few minutes. It was September in Saskatchewan, and even late afternoon was like a furnace. He could head back to the farm and the conversation waiting there. Boy, he'd rather break a bone. Without really deciding to, he changed his plan and took off down the farm track that led to the small stand of woods that straddled the river. He was loping, not pushing hard and loving the feeling of his legs, strong and powerful. By God, he loved to run!

He slowed as he approached her cabin. Chickens scattered and her small dog made a single dusty woof. She had the fire going outside under the big cauldron. It looked like she was making soap today. He looked into her garden but she wasn't there. He leaned down to scratch the dog behind the ears and asked him. "Where is she, boy? Down by the water?" The dog didn't answer.

Tom stood in the yard and waited. The door was open to the cabin like always and a quilt was hanging on the line to dry. What little breeze there was didn't even move it. She would only show if she wanted to. He knew that. No matter how much he might want to see her. He smacked a couple of mosquitoes that found his sweaty neck, and went to look in the goat pen. Five knee-high creatures with evil yellow eyes looked back at him. Tom could never figure out why she loved those goats so much. They always made him feel like they could see right into him with those sideways eyes.

One of her many cats wound around his feet and followed him as he wandered among the outbuildings. He'd been waiting about twenty minutes and had almost decided to give up and get on home, when her dry low voice came at him from the shade behind the hen house.

"What have you done, Tom Fletcher?" She was carrying her herb basket full up with cress and coltsfoot. He started to prevaricate, and then stopped. That was no good. She saw everything anyways.

"I signed up," Tom saw her face blanch and she staggered and reached out one hand for the fence. Then she turned on her heel and walked back to her cabin, Tom following slowly behind. She pushed the heavy iron arm that held the big cauldron over the flames, and placed the kettle on the grate that sat lower to the fire.

"You'll have tea," she said and Tom let some sound roll around his mouth like an affirmative. He sat down on the log bench at right angles to her, and looked at her out of the corner of his eye. She was small but sturdy, ageless and ancient. She was wearing the same buckskin trousers she always wore and a flannel shirt that had been Tom's when he was a boy. Her hair, in the long plait as always, was snow white on her head and graduated down to inky black at the bottom of the braid, and age had not dimmed those startlingly golden eyes. She put some leaves in the cups and sat staring at the fire waiting for the water to boil with the patience of rocks. He knew she could wait him out all day and night, so he spoke into the silence.

"Morris Palmer and I signed up together. We leave in a week. They say the war will be over by Christmas, so maybe it will be done before I even get there."

At that she looked up at him with those eyes as warm as whisky. He saw disappointment there, and sadness, and fear.

"What does your Ma have to say about this?" she said slowly.

"I haven't told her yet," he admitted.

She shook her head and gave him a look that could curdle milk. "You should'a told her before you told me. She won't forgive neither one of us."

"She's your daughter! You know what she's like!"

"You are afraid to tell her. That's what you really mean." She took a rag and lifted the kettle to pour the water into the cups. From the trees behind the cabin Tom could hear a woodpecker rat-a-tat-tatting. She handed him the cup – almost too hot to hold and asked. "Why are you doin' this, really?"

"I gotta get out of here!" he exploded. "I gotta go someplace! I gotta be somebody!"

She felt her heart tear, like it had torn so many times before. "You already are somebody, sonny boy, to me."

He put the cup down and slid on his knees to be right in front of her. "Granny Sally, I swear. I'll come back. I swear it!"

She only looked at him with the knowledge of loss and reached to take the strap of leather and her medicine pouch off from around her neck. She handed it to him. "You wear this – all the time. Those army folks, they may say you can't have it, but you hide it. You hear me?" He nodded. "And when the time comes that you need help, you hold it and call for me. I'll hear ya. I promise, I'll hear ya."

"I can't take this, Granny Sally. It's your power, ya always said."

"My power best go with you, Tom." She stood abruptly and he struggled to get to his feet. She grabbed him around the waist and hugged with her wiry arms so hard he wondered if he could breath. "Now you head home and tell your Ma. And tell your Pa to send for me when he needs."

"You think she's gonna blame you, Granny?"

"Oh, don't you worry, boy, I know she will."

The next morning at first light Sally Standing Bear, known as Kake-htaweyihtam to her people, woke to the sound of screaming.

"You did this! You stole my son! You took him from me with your ways!"

Tom's mother, Hannah Fletcher, was still in her nightdress, barefoot and wild-haired. Sally opened the door of her cabin and stood at the threshold looking at her daughter.

"He has always had his own mind, Hannah. You know that. Come inside and let me make us some coffee."

"I know he turned from me. I know he wanted to be out here in this shack with you! This is your fault!" Hannah screeched.

Sally looked at the woman she had given birth to and never really understood. When Louis Portreaux had died in the blizzard of '78, Sally had found life among the moyiwans a bigger burden. She had her Hannah, only two years old, but she longed to be among her own people again. The Cree had been pushed into reservations, but Sally had ownership of Louis's land grant out by the river. She had moved there in the summer of '79 and found a kind of peace. Hannah had wanted the white people's life, and she looked like her daddy with blue eyes and sandy hair so she could pass. For the child's safety, and to avoid the possibility of her being sent off to a residential school, Sally had left her in the care of Louis's sister Meredith. Hannah never told the town children where her mother lived; she had hidden her mother and her native family from view. She had thrived living with her Aunt Meredith, and though Sally had longed for a connection, this woman child had always been a stranger. But when Tom had been born, Sally had known from the minute she first held him that he was 'one of hers'. One of the ones she always looked for. One of the Thirteen.

"I don't want him to go any more than you do, daughter," Sally said.

"You stole my son!' Hannah flung at her and then raced back along the track, nightdress flowing behind her like clouds.

# RUPERTSBERG 1121 CE

"What exactly do you understand about the transmutation of souls?"

Giuseppe felt his brain scrambling at the abrupt turn in direction, and by the obscure topic Hildegard was mentioning. Not trusting himself not to babble, he simply pressed his lips together, grinned, and shrugged apologetically. One side of Hildegard's mouth lifted in an almost smile, and she took a deep breath.

What followed was a primer of metaphysical and alchemical knowledge that pushed at the edges of Giuseppe's grasp on reality. Hildegard led him through a discussion of Aristotle's treatises to the young Alexander of Macedonia, the fellow who would later conquer the known world. Giuseppe seemed to follow, nodding his head with enthusiasm. She stood, reached her laced fingers above her head, and he heard the small crackings as her spine stretched. Pacing back and forth before the fire, she wove in the teachings of the messianic cults of ancient Judea and Rabbi Akiva, as well as the foundational underpinnings of dichotomous good and evil as laid out by the Zoroastrians. Hours passed and Hildegard was gesticulating broadly, tracing connections between dynasties and belief systems as if painting them in the air. By the time she had reached back so far into human history as to approach the First Kingdom of Egypt, Giuseppe looked wan and somewhat desperate.

"Shall we pause for today, Giuseppe? I fear that my enthusiasm for these topics can be overwhelming."

Hildegard poured him a tankard of watered wine and looked closely to see if he revived a bit. The light of the afternoon was waning and the candles threw long shadows against the tapestried walls. They had been deep in study for several hours and while Hildegard looked fresh and bright, revitalized by their discourse, Giuseppe had just had his entire worldview diced and shredded, and seemed the worse for wear. He ran his hands through his hair, blinked hard several times, and began, looking like a man preparing to run a gauntlet.

"If I am correct in my understanding, Hildegard, you are saying that the wisdoms of the Holy Mother Church stand on the strong shoulders of the ancients, and these precepts have been carved and manipulated to uphold the world of men, not of the God of Heaven." He yanked on his hair. "And that the Council of Nicea expunged all mention of copious other transcripts of the life of Jesus of Nazareth, as well as the position of women as disciples and clergy," he took a long draft of breath, "as well as the very notion of the reincarnation of souls," and tugged his hair again, "in addition to the purposeful destruction of libraries filled with tomes of philosophy, mathematics, science and legal constructs." He looked at her with eyes filled with despair and hope. "Am I correct? This is what you are saying?"

"Yes."

"I see." Giuseppe found that words were now failing him.

"Let's take a walk," Hildegard stood abruptly, grabbed a cloak and strode off, out the door, and down the corridor. Giuseppe hurried after her, cloakless, with his hair askew from him having tormented it over the last few hours. He looked uncharacteristically disheveled.

Hildegard led him out into the walled gardens. It must have drizzled at some point in the afternoon, for all the twigs and branches looked newly washed, leafless and silver rimmed. She turned her face to the lines of salmon and coral that made horizontal stripes on the horizon. Giuseppe watched her as she prayed, silent but with her lips moving. A smile of great peace and completeness swept across her face.

"The Church offers us the structure of the holy offices, by which we can measure and honor the passage of time. I find that a comfort. Do you not also, Giuseppe?"

"Hildegard, I find that you hop and skip through the definitions of the word 'time' with an alarming dexterity."

She threw back her head and laughed till her eyes were wet with tears.

"Alarming. Yes, that is often a word people use in connection with me."

But the truth of that didn't seem to trouble her. Rather, it seemed a point of pride. Giuseppe started to speak again, but she gently shushed him.

"Enough of the notions of people for today, my friend. Let the setting sun and the soft damp earth be your teachers now."

She set a vigorous pace and they traversed the gardens and set off across the orchards. The ground slowly sloped up, and with the recent rain the ground beneath their feet was slippery. It took all of Giuseppe's focus to keep up with Hildegard and stay upright. The orchards ended at an open meadow, winter flat and brown. Hildegard pressed on until they walked into a sparsely spaced woodland on an even steeper incline. She told him how the Abbey's gardener, Betterm, the man he had seen earlier in the day vociferously pruning the espaliered pear trees, had planted this woods over many decades to replenish the native forests that had been harvested by the Romans hundreds of years before for their ships and fortresses. It had been Betterm's life's mission to restore and repair these woods.

"A peculiar and yet noble enterprise," Giuseppe said, noticeably short of breath.

This caught Hildegard's attention and she slowed her pace. They climbed onward. The woods thickened. By now the light was almost gone and the woods seemed animated. Giuseppe felt the presence of some things, some ones, as if the trees had spirits that had come out to join them. He noticed that Hildegard made nods of her head and slight waves of her hands, as if in greeting. And still they climbed until they reached a giant tree with a massive trunk and a high arched canopy of limbs. Hildegard walked up to the trunk and placed the palms of her hands and her forehead and chest right against the bark. Giuseppe stood a few feet back, instinctively not wanting to intrude on what was clearly a private moment. The branches overhead creaked and groaned in the wind, and small woodland creatures scurried in the leaf loam. Time seemed suspended. And in the fullness of all things, Hildegard turned to Giuseppe and said.

"Grandmother Beech, may I present Cardinal Giuseppe Giardelli, son of Matrisia Giardelli, grandson of Beatrice Buonoto Giardelli, great-grandson of Romola Fuerza Buanoto…"

And she proceeded to list his maternal lineage back seven generations. Giuseppe's jaw actually dropped open. Even he didn't know the progression of women she was listing. How did she?

"Giuseppe, I introduce you to Grandmother Beech, the Anima Mundi of this land."

She took his hand and drew him toward the tree trunk. As she pulled him forward and placed his palm against the trunk she whispered.

"Say hello."

Well-schooled since infancy in the social graces, he responded with aplomb.

"How lovely to meet you, Grandmother Beech!" he said, and was astonished to feel a chuckle emanating from the tree into the palm of his hand. He pulled his hand away quickly, but was only momentarily disconcerted, and replaced his hand to continue their dialogue.

Hildegard was leaning sideways against the trunk with her right shoulder and side of her head tipped to meet the bark. She watched with amusement and tenderness as the beech, the Anima Mundi, held his attention. She watched as his face was transformed into that of a child filled with wonder.

*"Oh Giuseppe,"* she thought. *"You are dangerously likeable."*

She pondered. So far, in all fairness, the Cardinal had passed all the tests she had placed before him. He had listened with scrutiny but no abject denial, to her descriptions of the theories and philosophies of the ancients. He had allowed himself to experience dislocation in time and space without calling her or himself mad. And now, he was absorbed in conversation with a tree, much to his obvious delight. She liked him. She wanted to trust him, as she had trusted Talo, the man he had been before. But she couldn't let herself forget the scorpion's nest that was his home turf: Vatican City. He had thrived there, as was demonstrated by his rapid rise to high status at such an early age. The skills he honed there could override any temptation to enter her world. Which persona would rise triumphant – the voice of Talo, the twin of Uxua raised in the temple of Ix Chel to honor and protect the Goddess – or Cardinal Giuseppe Giardelli, the beautiful and brilliant bastard son of the Bishop of Venice, masterful manipulator of Vatican politics?

# CHU JEN, KINGDOM OF QIN (CHINA) 600 BCE

The dam burst and a wall of water roared through the village. Little Li Er was swept out of his mother's arms and pulled into the torrent. A child of the fisherfolk, he had known how to swim before he had learned how to walk, but even with that he was having great difficulty keeping his head free of the brown choppy waves. He kept flailing, trying to find something to hold on to. His arm encircled something – a bucket – not good enough. Then he saw the old tailor being swept by him, face down in the water. Li Er was tossed and bounced and flipped over and over until he bumped into something warm and loud. The bleating was like a miracle in his ears, and he flung his arms around the scratchy neck of a goat. The animal seemed to find comfort in the boy's connection and he didn't struggle to get free. The two were hurled down what had been the lane, past the mill and fields, and along the path that lead to the Wise Women's sanctuary. They bounced off rocks, felt the slap of branches in their faces, and clung together for dear life.

Three women stood on the wide steps that led up to the Sanctuary watching the stampede of debris and corpses and silty water. They were looking for something specific, and then the youngest of them spotted it.

"There! There! It has two heads?"

The tallest of them reached out with a rake and caught the back of

139

Li Er's jacket, dragging him and the goat over toward the steps. The eldest of them ran down several steps and grabbed hold of the goat's hooves, and the youngest stepped in and pulled on Li Er's shoulders. They dragged the sodden pair up onto the staircase and pried the boy's hands loose from the goat's neck. Recognizing salvation for what it was, the goat sprang to his feet and clambered up the steps and away onto even higher ground. The three women picked the boy up, one at his feet, and the other two each with an arm and struggled up to the higher pavilion.

"Lay him here!" the eldest, Ra Mien, said and they gently lowered him onto the reed mats.

The youngest, a tenderhearted woman of only eighteen years known as Lu Ting, was softly patting the boy's cheeks. When he showed signs of awakening she turned him onto his side, he coughed out a substantial volume of water, and then opened his eyes. They were golden, like citrine, and oddly, considering the circumstances, showed no fear. A very old soul looked out of those eyes.

"Am I alive?" the boy asked in a thin voice.

"You are, by the grace of the Goddess," replied Ra Mien. "And whom might we have the honor of having rescued?"

"I am Li Er, son of Li Su. Are you the Wise Women?"

"We are called so, little one," the very tall Xe Xue answered with a touch of laughter in her voice. "For one so recently snatched from death, you ask a lot of questions!"

"I have always wanted to be here with you. I have run from my home three times, but my mother always caught me before I got here." He closed those hawk eyes hard, then opened them again. "Do you think I made the flood happen by wanting to be here so? Is my mother gone?" His lip quivered and in an eye blink he was a very tired, and very alone six-year-old boy.

Ra Mien summoned assistance and they carried the boy up into the sanctuary. They stripped off his wet clothes, rubbed him dry, and tucked a soft blanket around him snugly as they positioned him by the small charcoal grate. A tiny trickle of tears made ghost marks on his face and he never took his eyes off the Wise Women. At last, warm, safe, exhausted, he fell into the deep sleep of a bear cub.

Outside, the storm raged and sheets of water fell through the rest of that day and night. The bear cub boy slept through it all. The three Wise Women took turns sitting by him. Dawn was a mere hint of rose in the east as Lu Ting saw the boy's eyelashes flutter against his cheeks. She held her breath as he struggled to lift the heavy lids. And then he opened those old-soul eyes and looked directly at her.

"Good Morning, little one. You are safe and here at the Sanctuary," she said softly, as if afraid to startle a wild creature.

"Where's my mother?" Li Er asked with a quaver.

"Ah, little one, the rain still falls and we cannot tell for sure. It is likely that your village is gone. But it is possible that your mother survived," she replied, infusing her statement with more hope than she felt.

Li Er shook his head twice. "No, I can feel it. She is no longer on this plane of being." And he closed his remarkable eyes and fell into another deep sleep.

Several hours later the three women stood at some distance from him and whispered to each other.

"He spoke with such conviction!" Lu Ting said.

"And he spoke about 'planes of being'? You are sure?" Xe Xue asked for the third time.

"We were told in our dreams that one was coming to us. Why should that one not also be aware of the other worlds as we are." Ra Mien spoke calmly as was her way, but she looked worried.

"We didn't think that the one would be such a little child. And he's a boy!" Xe Xue retorted. "What are we to do with a man child? This is a women's house!"

*Everything is perfectly revealed, exactly as it is,*" Ra Mien quoted from their wisdom tradition, reciting the words that had been passed down to them by a long line of Wise Women. That truth set them free from their fears and they moved toward the boy as he stirred in his blanket. He sat up and squirmed.

"I need to make a pee," he said as he looked around for a doorway to the outside.

"And then that is what you must do," Xe Xue said as she led him by the hand to the privy.

When the two returned from the garden, Lu Ting and Ra Mien had a small kettle hung over the charcoal brazier to make tea. They were sitting on cushions and gestured for him to join them.

"Young Li Er, we have some sad news for you. Our servants have heard from the folk downhill that nothing and no one remains from your village. It is a miracle that you survived and were delivered here to us. We are terribly aggrieved for you. Do you have other family that we might notify of your situation?" Ra Mien spoke gently, but with a matter-of-fact tone. The boy pressed his lips together as if to hold back sound and simply shook his head.

Lu Ting reached forward and clasped his hands.

"We would like to offer you a place here in the Sanctuary. The waters brought you to us; we have asked the wind to not blow you away."

*New beginnings are often disguised as painful endings,"* the boy replied, reciting words from their wisdom tradition as if he had always known them.

"Who are you?" Xe Xue exclaimed.

"In the now or in the then?" Li Er replied.

# RUPERTSBERG
# 1121 CE

Giuseppe was so engrossed in his dialogue with Grandmother Beech that he didn't notice the footsteps coming up the hillside though the woods. But Hildegard did.

"Well, we are in it now," she thought.

She must have communicated something to Giuseppe, something to alert him to what was about to unfold. He stood up, brushed off his knees, and turned his head toward Hildegard. He spoke sotto voce, "Grandmother Beech says we are not alone. Are we in danger?"

"That depends," she said, unhelpfully.

"Depends on what?" he asked with some asperity.

"You," she replied.

The suggestion of a man floated through the dimness.

Giuseppe had his back against the tree trunk, leaning on her for support.

"Hildegard, what danger is possible that I may be the source of here?" His voice had gone flat and tight. He coiled his muscles, ready to pounce if necessary.

"I wish I could say," she replied, almost to herself. She closed her eyes for a sliver of a moment, to pull energy from the roots beneath her feet. Then she reached out, took Alejandro's right hand, and drew him toward Giuseppe. She placed Alejandro's hand in Giuseppe's, squeezed hard and then slipped around to the back side of the vast trunk to await whatever was to happen next.

The two men stood in frozen silence. Something was alive at the juncture of their hands, a trembling, pulsating, sentient thing.

Alejandro, who had been drawn up the hill as if he were sleepwalking was shivering from the cold. Giuseppe too now felt the winter slip into his bones. Both wanted to let go of the other's hand with a kind of desperation to shake off the oncoming future. And yet, neither would relinquish the connection.

Slowly, slowly, their breathing became deeper and more measured. They stood in the dark, linked through their palms and their memories. Two unformed souls swimming in the same internal sea, hands linked. A blazing hot sun and two children, a girl and a boy, racing each other through a sea of green leaves and palm fronds. Two young people connected through pain as one retched violently and the other held her hair back. A wrenching dislocation, eyes locked, as one fell into an abyss and the other screamed.

"You?" Giuseppe spoke through a vise-gripped throat.

"You!" Alejandro replied.

They both fell to their knees and wrapped their arms around each other. Alejandro began to cry softly. As his sobs stilled they started whispering to each other in a language long forgotten, not the once widespread common tongue that Hildegard remembered, but a language of their people, that spoke of jungles and hot rains, vivid scarlet parrots and parents barely known. Hildegard listened and thanked all the powers of light that they could be together again, for now, for however long this reunion could last.

She left them there, leaning against each other, remembering, and she walked down through the woods, the night illuminated by starlight and the fingernail moon. She headed toward the greenhouse, and, as she knew she would, found the others of the Thirteen waiting there for her. They had all heard the peeling bell of recollection. It had pierced their hearts and they needed each other tonight, for comfort and to hold for as long as possible the tremulous joy that was rolling down the hillside. Uxua and Talo. Together. At last. Reunion as a sacrament in this sacred space.

# CHARLESTON
# 1805 CE

Alexander waited in the shade of the courtyard until the women were inside the house, then walked quickly to the stables that took up the back wall of the courtyard. His boots made a hard clip clop on the cobblestones, but even that didn't awaken the old man sleeping inside on the straw bales.

Alexander approached him and tapped the old man gently on the shoulder. "Thomas! Thomas! Wake up, man. Thee is sleeping through all the excitement."

Thomas slowly opened rheumy eyes that now had a milky film, reached up to scratch the cloud of white crowning his head, and cleared his throat with a rolling rumble of phlegm and pipe tobacco. "Master Farley, life with thee is wearing me out. What new 'excitement' has thee found for us now?"

Alexander sat down next to Thomas on the straw bale and took his hand, linking their fingers with an affection born of years and lifetimes of trust. Their hands were a study in contrasts. Thomas's a hand of deep bark brown with knobby knuckles from arthritis and hard labor, and ribbed yellowed nails; Alexander's with pale fingers, well-polished nails and callouses only born from riding. Their connection in this lifetime went back to Alexander's first trip to the southern state of South Carolina with his father when he was fourteen years old. Farley senior was a devout Quaker who strove to rid the world of the evils of slavery one human at a time. He wanted his son and heir to witness this "scourge upon the earth" firsthand, so the two went to the slave auction together. It had been a furnace hot day and both Farleys pulled at their collars to get more air.

It was then that the swirling started, and Alexander had a sensation of being in many places at the same time. This wasn't new to him. He often felt like he saw and heard things others didn't. Since he was a boy he had conversed with his unseen friends and 'known' things he shouldn't have been able to know. But today it was terrifying. He saw the men and women of today standing on auction blocks and roped together in pens. But he also saw and heard and smelt the same inhumanity in a Roman amphitheater, and a Burgundian prison cell, and an Alexandrian agora. He stumbled and ran to the alley to vomit and felt the screams of the ages flooding through his brain. He felt his father's hand on his back, gently waiting. With shaking hands he wiped his mouth with the perfectly laundered handkerchief his mother always insisted he carry, before straightening up to walk back into the maelstrom.

"Son, today we can save one poor wretched creature out of all this misery. Only one, but one is better than none. So, I am asking for thy assistance to make this terrible decision. Let the Light inform thee, Alexander. What does God want from thee today?"

Alexander looked up at his father and their eyes met, golden locking with hazel and identical in the recognition of the horror they were seeing. They walked through the market and were shoved and buffeted as the men around them shouted and cursed and raised fists gripping money to secure the purchase of another human. Suddenly Alexander came up short. He saw a man of middle years with thick ropey arms and downcast eyes. The auctioneer was claiming him to be a "first rate field hand", but a man in the crowd demanded to see the slave's back.

The auctioneer poked the slave with the handle of his whip to make him turn around and Alexander saw the flash of hate in the slave's eyes as he jerked and then turned. There were gasps and articulations of "there you go!" "I knew it, not 'first rate' at all!" The man's back was a crisscross of scars, layers upon layers of scars from whipping. All interest in the slave evaporated when he could be seen as clearly

146

a trouble to own. Alexander stepped up quickly and spoke loudly, "I have interest in this slave!" His father came to his side and motioned to the auctioneer that sale could be quickly made. Documents were signed and the Farleys, father and son, were now the owners of a male, aged approximately fifty years, named Thomas.

Twenty years later and manumission papers long signed and certified, Alexander and Thomas sat together with linked hands as the younger told the elder about their newest 'family member'.

"She is very young, Thomas. Perhaps fifteen or sixteen at most. Fresh off the slave ship and starved close to death. But that spark is there. She is our Kiyia; there is no doubt of that."

"Has she any English, young master?" Thomas asked in a low rumble.

"I doubt that. I don't think she even knows where she is. We shall let her settle, and then we will see how to proceed."

"Thee cannot free her until she can understand all of this. She needs language and skills, a trade perhaps. Then thy father can help her make passage to join the others."

The 'others' Thomas referred to were living in a small community just across the border into the British territory of Upper Canada. Farley Senior, when he saw the depth of commitment to the cause that his son held, had helped to raise money to purchase land and settle the newly freed into a little town the former slaves had named Oshun. Alexander had been able to find seven of "his thirteen" as he called them, souls born onto African soil and caught up in the inhuman slave trade. Martha and Thomas had insisted on staying with Alex, but the other five now comprised the core of a growing community of folks from that African diaspora.

Alexander sighed and leaned his head on the old man's shoulder. "Oh, Io. Where is the Goddess in all this pain? Where is Her Temple where all might be free?"

"In our hearts, Atvasfara. In our hearts." Thomas replied.

"And when can She return? When will it be Her time?" Alexander sent his plea out to the universe, and was met with silence.

# RUPERTSBERG 1121 CE

Worried that the reunion could spark a dangerous backlash reaction from Giuseppe, Hildegard found no rest that night. She frequently would, when in the thrall of one of her visions, stay awake for days at a time. She had, when having her 'spells', been without food and water, totally motionless for weeks. Time meant nothing to her then. But this night, each minute felt like a century. She made her way to the Chapel, sang each of the Holy Offices of Lauds and Prime, and remained there when the other sisters had gone to their breakfast. She was still kneeling, deep in prayer when Sister Delphinia came to find her well after dawn.

"Mother! There you are! A storm is blowing in. Freakish for this early in the autumn. The cold is rolling in and it feels like snow! Had the Cardinal hoped to depart today? If so, I am afraid his wishes are for naught. No one is going anywhere today."

Hildegard rose to her feet wearily.

"I don't know what the Cardinal had planned. Send someone to his quarters and tell him I will be available in my study…if he wishes to talk." For the first time in the years that Delphinia had lived by and served Mother Hildegard she saw a flicker of something in the Mother's eyes that she had never seen before. In a lesser human that might have been called fear, not a quality one associated with Hildegard. But it was enough to disconcert Delphinia.

"Mother, has something happened? Is the Cardinal…a concern?"

"Not yet, my friend, and perhaps, not ever."

With that cryptic reply Delphinia was only slightly relieved, and the two walked back toward Hildegard's study, to await the Cardinal's response. Coal black clouds in the sky outside prevented any light from illuminating the hallways, and all the torches were lit. They stopped outside Hildegard's sleeping chamber, and Delphina saw clearly now the dark half moons under the Mother's eyes. Something was not as it should be.

"Hot water for bathing, Mother?"

Hildegard softly exhaled a "Yes!" and looked at Delphinia with extreme gratitude. Within the next hour, Hildegard, washed and with fresh underclothes, a full belly and a very large fire burning behind her, was fortified and standing at the windows of her study watching the winter-like fury outside. Sleet stung the glass and winds high, then low, rattled the panes in the window frames.

A knock came at her door, and not knowing if she wanted or feared it to be Giuseppe, Hildegard gave the command to "Enter".

Footsteps came into the room and then stopped halfway. Taking a bracing breath, Hildegard turned to face her visitor, and was stopped short to discover that it was not Giuseppe, but rather young Petyer Fieldenstarn.

"Petyer, how fare you?"

"Mother, that Cardinal, the one who was Talo. You said he remembers. I was wondering, I mean, how much? He knows that Alejandro was his sister Uxua. Does he remember the end, our end?" he faltered, before continuing in a more hesitant voice. "Does he recall, can he know, what might have happened to Pel?"

Hildegard and Petyer, he who had been Io, shared a long look as recollections of the young woman named Pel flooded back to them. When they had known her as a young woman of eighteen years she had been a dedicant to Artemis and had traveled from Ephesus and the Temple there with the girl Io. Io, headstrong and driven by her vision didn't want a guardian or companion, an opinion she shared frequently. She was rude and obstreperous to Pel at every chance. But Pel had protected and guided Io, even when Io had made it very difficult to do so.

Strong, sun-kissed and golden haired, Pel had caught the eye of Talo, and they had found in each other a safe harbor in the tempest that had swept them all up in Egypt back then, back when.

"Since I have been here with you and the others, since I have begun to remember, I think about Pel often. What happened to her, to them all on that awful day? She wouldn't have been there, so far from home, if not to guard me in my journey. She was patient with me, and kind. Did I...did I... bring about her demise?" his voice was tremulous with lifetimes of emotion.

"Come sit with me, young Peyter and I will share with you what I have been able to discover over all this time."

As the wind slammed against the windows and the ice froze them shut, Hildegard and Petyer, wrapped in thick wool blankets, sat by the fire. She told him what, over the course of many lifetimes she had heard from others of the Companions that she had found. She told him of a life in the kingdom of Qin when she had met two, reincarnated then as a pair of sisters. They had once been the father and son Smiths who had been kidnapped by the fierce Kiyia of the grassy steppes, and brought to Egypt. Those two could recall the years of famine and warfare that followed the cataclysm. They had survived together then, as they were surviving together when Hildegard knew them as servants in the household of the one who would become known as Lao Tse.

She knew from a brief interaction in the library in Alexandria with the one who had been Ndeup, mother of the deaf girl Awa, that all the Companions had survived the earthquakes and floods, and had remained in Egypt for the rest of their lifetimes. It had been tumultuous there, but the outside world had been nightmare and chaos with hunger and disease run rampant, so the Companions had clung together and helped rebuild the court of the Pharaoh.

But of Pel and Talo, she had heard nothing specific, in all these thousands of years. And in today's life she was also short on information. Until now.

"No one has seen the Cardinal or Alejandro since I left them last night. I have sent word for one or both of them to come see me. I can't tell you, Petyer, what state either of them may be in today."

# KINGDOM OF QIN
## 600 BCE

In the weeks and months that followed, the three Wise Women felt as though their world kept slipping sideways without warning. They had begun to call Li Er "Bear Cub" as his cheeks filled out from the good food of the Sanctuary and his hair always stood out in all directions like fur. He continued to sleep profoundly deeply all curled up in a ball on his stomach with his knees pulled up under him. He was a patient student, but would confound them by quoting the wisdoms that had taken them years of study to memorize. Sitting in the orchard he would stroke Lu Ting's pale skin on her arm and marvel at how she had "been as dark as mahogany." He called Xe Xue "Firetop", even though her hair was like black silk. And he repeatedly rushed to help Ra Mien stand and walk as if she needed help, even though she strode quite competently.

When he had been with them for six cycles of the moon the year had flowed through summer and into autumn. They were all sitting around the brazier one evening, pulled close to keep the night's chill at bay.

"Who *are* you, Bear Cub, really?" Xe Xue asked in the dim light thrown by the coals.

"Don't you remember?" came his little voice from the half dark.

"Sadly, we do not," Lu Ting replied, "but we are thinking that you do."

A long silence followed, so long that the women sighed, thinking that he wouldn't answer them. But finally, he began to tell them a story in a voice that was his and not his.

"We live now in the age of men," he said, and he cleared his throat and took a swallow of tea. "But the world was not always so. There was a time when the wisdoms you cherish were known by everyone, and all peoples strove to live in balance as the Way tells us to. We knew each other then."

"What happened?" Lu Ting asked quietly.

"The epoch ended, the pendulum swung, the earth roared. The age of the Great Mother was erased with only small strongholds such as this Sanctuary to keep the wisdoms."

"Why do we not remember this?" Xe Xue asked in anguish.

He didn't directly answer them but instead asked. "Why did each of you come to the Sanctuary?"

"I met a Wise Woman in the market one day and followed her back here. I was eight years old," Ra Mien said with a hint of a laugh. "My parents wanted me to return to the farm. They said they needed my work, but the Wise Woman paid them a sum for me so I could stay. She said she had 'seen me' in her dreams and knew me."

"My father arranged a marriage for me with a man in the next village. After he beat me the first time, I hit him on the head with an iron pot and he returned me to my family. I was in disgrace, but a Wise Woman heard about me and convinced my father that he could be well rid of me if he let me come to the Sanctuary," Xe Xue barked a laugh. "I think he was relieved, for he feared I would hit him on the head with a pot next!" The women chuckled, and Xe Xue tossed more charcoal onto the fire. For a while the only sounds were the dripping of the rain off the gutters, the ping of droplets hitting copper bells.

In the silence Lu Ting spoke so softly that they all needed to lean in to hear her.

"My father died of bloody flux when I was nine, and my mother married another man but two months later. He was a dark brooding man with a temper like a snake. We lived never knowing when he would strike. One day when Mother was in the fields, he took me into the forest and forced himself on me. I came home bloody and torn, but my Mother made no sound. She simply took me by the hand and walked me here and left me at the front gate. She turned and walked away without ever saying a word. The Wise Woman who opened the gate simply said, 'Finally.' And I was home here."

Ra Mien rose and went to kneel behind Lu Ting, wrapping arms around her, and remembering the day the girl had been discovered shaking and weeping at their door.

"And do you feel as if you are in your right place, as if this is your spot in the world?" Bear Cub asked them.

*"At the center of your being you have the answer; you know who you are and you know what you want,"* Lu Ting recited. An owl hooted in a tree nearby and they could hear the distant response from farther up the hillside.

Xe Xue poured more tea for them all as they listened to the owls' conversation. A gentle peace descended on them, and it was from that place of peace that she spoke at last. "Bear Cub, our memories are tattered, without substance. But yours, yours are complete?"

"Yes, they are complete," he answered.

"Why?" Xe Xue continued to press.

"Because they always are. It is my blessing and my curse." And the six, almost seven year old boy, looked at each of them with eyes of ancient origin, with his yellow sapphire eyes that had known the splendor of a forgotten world, with the weary eyes of Atvasfara, she who had been the High Priestess of Isis.

# RUPERTSBERG
# 1121 CE

As she opened the door to go to Terce, she was startled to find Giuseppe standing there, hand raised, ready to knock. He was pale, almost translucent from fatigue, but had regained his usual well-groomed appearance. His hair was tidy and his clothes were impeccable. His eyes were haunted. "Ah! You gave me a fright. Would you like to come in?"

"That was my intention." Giuseppe said wryly.

She gestured him into the room, and both felt an awkwardness that had not existed between them before. It fell to Giuseppe to break the weighted silence.

"It looks as if you were leaving, Hildegard, but might I have a few moments of your time?"

"As much as you need, my friend." she replied, sitting gracefully on the bench before the fire and patting it to draw him down beside her.

He sat and the silence stretched. They both stared at the flames as if answers could be found there. What to say? What to ask? What to acknowledge or deny?

"You..."

"I..."

They both began at the same time.

"Please."

"No, You first."

Hildegard's lips struggled to contain the smile that threatened to erupt. Giuseppe saw it and grinned in reply.

154

"Well, this is a vat of pickle and brine," she said, and he laughed.

Giuseppe reached a finger under her chin and turned her to face him.

"Hildegard, you ascertain that I absolutely cannot believe what I now know to be true."

"Yes, you are in a pickle, alright!" she replied and then chortled. "Pickle!" She let the word roll around in her mouth.

"And if we follow your metaphor that would make you the brine, I suppose?"

"I have been called worse things," Hildegard said.

"I had thought I might slip away this morning without bothering with unscripted farewells," he confessed.

"Fate is capricious. You might say fickle,… Pickle." And with that, Hildegard lost control and began to laugh with gusto.

Delphinia, walking along the corridor outside the study, heard the laughter and felt the worry of the morning slide away. Giuseppe reached out and wiped the happy tears from Hildegard's face. He looked at a teardrop clinging to the tip of his finger and started to slowly recount what he had remembered last night, he and Alejandro/Uxua. As he spoke he began to pick up speed until the words were falling from his lips, tumbling like boulders in an avalanche. The memories had inundated him, all the details of a life in the jungle, at the Temple, dedicated to protecting his sister and serving his Goddess. The trip over oceans to Egypt. The sense of impending doom building for months, and then, almost a relief and yet an exquisite anguish, the breaking apart of the world and the loss of his twin whose every breath he had always shared.

"What do I do now?" he asked.

"What do you want to do?"

"Hildegard, you are a most exasperating woman! You answer almost every question with a question," he responded with a note of asperity.

"Why would I do that?" she retorted.

And they laughed.

"But seriously, Giuseppe. What is it you want? You cannot, a man of your intelligence, unsee what you have seen. I doubt you can ever forget what you have remembered. I am not dodging your question.

155

I sincerely want to know what you want to do. Will you return to Rome as soon as the weather clears? Race to Cologne and denounce this Abbey as a house of heretics? Build a cottage on the grounds and move in? What do you foresee? What do you want?"

He paused, and then looked at her directly.

"What I really want is to take your hand and run out of here. We could renounce our vows and live as humble beekeepers in Hibernia. Or follow the trade routes to Turkmenistan and sell cinnamon and saffron in the marketplace. Or run far north and herd reindeer with the Lapps."

She knew he was being truthful, so she kept her gaze steady, and said quietly.

"And what do you foresee?"

"That for today, and perhaps the next and the one after, the snow will have constructed a fortress, and I do not need to decide."

She stood up, offering him her hand.

"In that case, shall we go find Alejandro and see what happens next?"

He took the hand, and felt the thrill of her warm palm, keeping him tethered in the now.

"Wherever you lead, I shall follow."

The weather continued to bluster, and for the next three days the Abbey was in a cocoon of snow. No pilgrims or tradespeople arrived; no goods crafted by the sisters of the Abbey made their way to the local markets. That first morning of the storm Hildegard and Giuseppe had found Alejandro feverishly at work in his studio. When they had left Hildegard's study they had bundled up and walked through snow, already eight inches deep, to the cluster of workshops. All were dark except Alejandro's. He had braces of candles lit, many dozens of tapers throwing wildly moving shadows to offset the sunless day. He had been at his art ever since he and Giuseppe had parted ways in the wee hours of the morning. When Hildegard and Giuseppe arrived they struggled to open the high doors, pushing back mounds of snow to make their entry. What they saw inside the studio struck them speechless.

Five new sculptures were scattered around the vast space, in varying states of completion. Two were of structures. The one both Hildegard and Giuseppe recognized was a five-foot-high replica of the Temple of Isis, the temple that had been standing before the cataclysm in their ancient world. The pillars were roughly worked, but the design of sequential spaces leading from public to most private and sacred was clearly visible. Hildegard gasped when she saw the detail on the door to the inner most chamber. The Wings of Isis were as beautiful as she remembered, and her eyes clouded with tears.

There was another piece, taller and wider, that was resting on a wooden platform. Similar to the pyramids that Hildegard knew from Egypt, and yet different. She felt Giuseppe start, freeze, then rush to it, gently brushing his fingers over all the levels, remembering and whispering the names of the deities carved on its surface. Alejandro had faithfully recreated the Temple of their youth, the Pyramid of Ix Chel.

"You're here. Good. I need you both. Look at those carefully and tell me what I'm missing."

He turned back to his work and left them to study and remember and weep and rejoice. Wiping her eyes, Hildegard roamed the studio and looked at the other sculptures that Alejandro had birthed in just these few hours. One was a statue of a woman. Hildegard was startled to see herself as she had been, Atvasfara, High Priestess of Isis. She remembered ruing that sharp chin and that high forehead. Alejandro had begun the details of the elaborate hair and headdress that she had worn to signify her position. She saw the hint of the diadem and the merest suggestion of what he would, no doubt, finesse into the marble version of peacock feathers. Had she really looked that haughty? She chuckled to feel the rankle of vanity, and moved to the next piece.

The statue was a cat, a very large cat, the height of a pony with small rounded ears and a long tail. Alejandro had used a marble with thick black veins, and the big cat's muscles seemed to ripple in the candlelight. Its head was turned slightly, as if it had just heard a sound and the tilt seemed to suggest that it was judging the danger in that sound. It looked alive and Hildegard felt the hairs stand up on the back of her neck.

She came to join Giuseppe who was standing in front of the last statue. This was more stylized than the images of Atvasfara and the giant cat. This work seemed ancient, formal and formidable, made to exact awe and instill respect. Two figures were discernable, standing back to back. A man and a woman, about seven feet tall, they wore tunics that came to the middle of their strong thighs and ropes of necklaces and armbands. Hildegard could make out the designs of snakes that swirled up their arms and onto their chests. They were so alike, the representation of the female and the male principles, more like divine beings than people. And yet, Hildegard knew them, had known them, as the living and breathing twins, Uxua and Talo.

To see them like this fanned her memories. She remembered how their mouths had moved and the hard consonants of their accent when they spoke the common tongue. She saw them again in her mind's eye, arm in arm, bronze and beautiful, walking along the banks of the Mother River Naihl. She could smell their skin, moist with the butter from a tree they had called cacao.

She looked to Giuseppe, and saw the tracks of tears streaming down his face.

"Do we hide these or celebrate them?" Hildegard asked softly, as if speaking to herself.

"First the latter, then the former," Giuseppe replied, equally quietly.

They walked over to Alejandro, now chiseling at the pillars of the Isis Temple. The three spent an hour recalling that edifice.

"The statue of Isis was taller than the roof of the surrounding portico," Hildegard pointed out.

"Ah, yes, I recall sunlight striking the head and radiating the gold there," Alejandro muttered.

"I remember the lions," Giuseppe said suddenly, as if the memory was shot into his head. "Sekhmet's lions."

Hildegard smiled wistfully. "And your Jaguar. I don't remember. Did they ever get along?"

"Better than they ever did with that giant Hound of Badh's. Or Maia's elephant." Alejandro and Giuseppe caught each other's eye and smiled broadly.

Then the three fell into silence again, thinking of all that had been lost.

# COMTÉ DE FOIX
## 1079 CE

"Sister Dolora! Wake up!"

Marguerite held the shielded candle in one hand and reached down with the other to shake Sister Dolora's shoulder. The older woman, after a lifetime of rhythms with the daily prayer cycle, knew in her deep sleep that it wasn't time yet for Vigils, and rolled away from the insistent fingers.

"Auntie! Wake up!"

Something in Marguerite's whispered panic sliced through the fog of dreams and reached Dolora, dragging her up to the surface.

"I need you to wake and help me!"

Dolora struggled against her blanket to sit up. "What is amiss?" she asked, adopting the lowered whisper that Marguerite was using.

"We must abandon the convent, and I need your help to rouse everyone and keep the calm."

"Abandon? What? Niece, is this a nightmare? What dream of terror leads you here?"

"I wish it were a dream," Marguerite cried. "The Capitan sent word that we are in grave danger. We must all leave under cover of darkness. Now!"

"What do you mean, he sent word? This sounds like nonsense designed by our enemies. Calm yourself, Niece."

"We don't have time. You need to trust me. As I trust him."

And a lifetime of obedience pushed all resistance out of Dolora's mind. She swung her legs out of bed and stood, bare feet feeling the chill of stone floor.

Sister Dolora and Mother Marguerite divided the tasks and raced in different directions to wake the other sisters, novitiates and postulants. Each woman was awoken with a hand placed over her mouth and frantic instructions to dress warmly, gather what foodstuffs they could carry, and gather in the hall in front of the chapel. No candles or torches were to be lit, and each woman was exhorted to be silent. Marguerite took the job of raising the nuns in the infirmary, helping them to wrap themselves in warm cloaks and boots, encouraging those who could walk to begin the journey to the hall, and arranging for a stretcher for Sister Perpetua, the convent's oldest nun, whose mind wandered in the fields of her youth.

When all one hundred twenty souls were gathered in the hall, Mother Marguerite stood part way up the staircase and told them of the dire threat approaching their door.

"We must leave, and leave tonight, to let the darkness cover our escape. We must help each other over the pass and down into the woodland there. I believe…I know…that we can make this perilous journey if we assist each other and keep our constant faith in the Blessed Mother to guard our steps."

This extraordinary news was met with sobs and gasps. There was no surprise that Sister Anna Sophia had an opinion.

"This seems madness! Where did this intelligence come from in the middle of the night?"

Several nuns began to nod their heads.

"Capitan Juan Miguel gave us this warning, for he fears that the new officers will take the convent by force. Our lives are in danger! We must go!"

"Because the handsome Capitan says so, in the night? How did you receive this message?"

Mother Marguerite felt an iron rod shoot up her spine. She must not waver, if she were to lead all these women to safety. Speed and blind obedience were needed now. In her most imperious tone she directed her words over Sister Anna Sophia's head and addressed them all.

"This is the moment that Mother Monica Maria foresaw. She entrusted you all to my care. And in my judgment, we must leave our home, and not look back."

Sisters Helena and Martha Mary, the very same sisters that had stepped forward in support of her when Marguerite had been announced as the new Mother, stepped to the front of the group and Sister Helena spoke for them both as she always did.

"Mother, all must look as if our usual routine is ongoing. If we leave and the torches aren't lit, and the bells aren't rung, the men down below will know something is awry. Sister Martha Mary and I will stay behind and attend to the observable details."

"Sisters!" Marguerite cried.

"It would be best, Mother," Sister Martha Mary spoke. All were surprised at the steadiness and surety in the voice of this woman who always had deferred to others. She continued, "Sister Helena and I are aged. We would only slow you down, and our efforts here may buy you time."

"Sister, the Capitan will not be in command. He will not be able to ensure your safety," Marguerite implored.

Sister Helena now spoke again, quiet and firm.

"We entered this convent at the same time as green girls of fourteen. We have been here almost sixty years. We have served and prayed and known this place, these stones, to be our only home. Grant us the honor of serving Mater Misericordia one last time."

Marguerite swallowed tears. When she could trust her voice she simply responded.

"Your request is granted."

Sister Dolora had appointed Sister Agnes and five young nuns to be in charge of smaller groups of twenty. Sister Helena and Sister Martha Mary stood still, like rocks in the center of a swift stream, as each woman whispered goodbye or clasped a hand when words wouldn't come. The one hundred and now eighteen souls all began to move out of the hall, back along the corridors toward the kitchens, and out the door to the stable yard and the back gate, the only sounds were muffled sobs and shuffled feet.

Mother Marguerite stayed till the last, taking the hands of Sisters Helena and Martha Mary. In the flickering half light thrown by the lit rushes their shapes wavered. She thought she saw two young women in their place. One was tall and reed thin with pale eyes, cornsilk hair and a sickle moon on her forehead. The other was small and tan with blue lines between chin and lip, and slanted eyes of the warmest hazel. They held hands like the dearest of friends, and the shorter one rested her head on the other's shoulder. Marguerite felt the click of recognition in her heart, and then in the rush of emotions and the demands of the moment she pushed it aside.

"I hope that we see one another again in this life, for I treasure your friendship and example of piety. But in the event that we do not, know that you have my deepest regard and respect. May the love of our Lord and his Blessed Mother fill your hearts till your very last breath."

She leaned forward and gently kissed the two old women on the cheek, then turned with such determination that her habit swirled like a falling leaf, as she tore down the corridor, hearing their prayers following her as she ran.

The line of women snaked up the mountain trail in deepening darkness as the half moon set in the western sky. Only the most discerning eye in the valley could have made out the black dots, like a line of ants, moving up and across the limestone cliff faces. The young nuns coaxed, urged, and tugged each of their charges over rocky outcroppings and stretches of path that seemed to fall away down the slope.

They were not long from the convent when the bells rang for Vigils. Mother Marguerite stopped and looked back at Mater Misericordia and saw the light burnishing the waxed paper windows of the chapel. Sisters Helena and Martha Mary were there, constant as the Northern Star, keeping up the appearance of normalcy. One of the sisters on the trail had very softly begun the decades of the rosary, and Marguerite took a moment to add her whispered voice, "*Save us sinners now and at the hour of our death*".

At one point, about two hours into their exodus, Sister Anna Sophia stumbled and Marguerite, walking nearby, reached out to take her arm and help her up. Anna Sophia wrenched her arm away and snapped.

"May you be right! For if you are not, and you ask this outrageous thing of us, I will see you stripped of your office."

"If I am not right, then I will willingly abjure," Marguerite quietly replied. "You cannot think I do this carelessly!"

"I think your head has been turned by a tall man with a too easy smile, and our welfare is a secondary concern."

Without thought, without pause, Marguerite swung her hand and slapped Anna Sophia across the cheek. The smack was as sharp as a breaking branch, and all the women nearby froze at the sound. Marguerite gripped her stinging palm. She could barely make out Anna Sophia's face in the dimming light.

"Your words are poison! You are poison!" Marguerite spat out. "I command you to silence!"

Sister Anna Sophia almost smiled, a strange smile of victory, and turned to continue walking on, limping dramatically. Moments later Sister Dolora came up, helping the women with the stretcher that precariously held old Sister Perpetua. They ran in danger of falling behind the rest of the caravan, since they needed to stop and rest frequently.

"What was that?" Sister Dolora was breathing hard.

"Sister Anna Sophia," was all Marguerite needed to say.

"Our Lord had his crown of thorns, and we have her," Dolora said.

A snort, and strangled giggle, and both women covered their mouths to smother the sound of the nervous release.

"I only pray that we have a less disastrous end," Marguerite said when she could speak without laughing. At that moment they could hear the distant bells of Mater Misericordia ringing for Matins. Night was disappearing. They must hurry!

Mother Marguerite raced back and forth along the line of walking women, urging desperate speed. They were traveling north and east over the small mountain and the last three nuns crested the top of the peak as the dawn light rose to the rocky top. Their outlines were limned in a raspberry hue as they took the last steps up and over, and Marguerite's heart clenched at the thought that they might be seen from the valley behind. Her thoughts flew back to those last moments, standing in the shadows under the back gate portico with Juan Miguel. He had told her to run, to gather all the sisters and to run. His words came back and flooded her again with the panic she had felt only but a few hours ago.

"Run, and keep on running. I know the kind of men they are sending to replace me. They cannot bear to be thwarted." Juan Miguel had looked as if his next words were composed of ground glass and exquisitely painful to bring forth. "Marguerite, these men, they *like* killing. Do you understand? God forgive them, but they like it. Hurry now, and don't look back."

He had touched her cheek, and Marguerite's face flushed scarlet now at the recollection of the brief pressure of his calloused hands against her skin. She shook her head hard, to chase away the memory and the sensation and turned to see her fellow sisters.

Marguerite leaned forward and rested her hands on her thighs gathering her thoughts and her strength. Mother Monica Maria had dragged her into this mess with sentiment and cajolery.

*"Are you watching all this, Mother, from some soft place in heaven? I should never have fallen for that deathbed last wish nonsense. What have you gotten me in to?"*

And she shook off that memory too and found a wide place in the trail where she summoned the young sisters who had led each group to come for instructions. As they arrived she saw a fascinating mixture of trepidation and exhilaration on their faces.

"Well done, Sisters! Well done! We have managed the impossible, thanks to you. Now I ask more impossibilities from you."

Sister Agnes, as it turned out, was from a farm in this valley. Proving herself resourceful yet again, she spoke up.

"Mother, are we seeking shelter on the valley farms? My family is a walk of a few short hours from here. They would see us safe."

"Thank you, Sister. But with the daylight, I don't want to draw anyone into danger, should they be seen as supporting or protecting us. We need to head for the forest and travel through the trees to our sister convent at Carcassonne."

"Our farm abuts the woods, Mother. I know the way," Sister Agnes said calmly.

"Thanks be to God and His Holy Mother," Mother Marguerite exclaimed before she even thought. "Then you, Sister Agnes shall guide us through the wilderness. Lead on, Moses!"

At the bottom third of the mountainside, the pine and fir trees made for some shade. By the time they had reached the valley floor, the leaf canopy of newly unfurled beech and oak made a blessed relief from the now midday sun. Marguerite felt the breath of the hellhounds so brutally painted by Juan Miguel's words on their heels, but agreed to let the company rest at high noon to eat and recover.

So far from Mater Misericordia, they could no longer hear the bells for the holy offices. Marguerite had never been prone to prayers of supplication. In her years she had felt God to be a benign and disinterested force of the nature around her. But today, on this arduous trek, she said a constant stream of prayers for Sisters Helena and Martha Mary, that they were safe, that the artifice of normalcy was still upheld, that Juan Miguel was safe, and...pleased that he had been correct about the need for this desperate escape.

# SASKATCHEWAN
## 1915 CE

On the night before he was set to leave, Tom was restless. The moonlight flooded into his room and shook him by the shoulder. He got dressed quick and carried his shoes downstairs so he wouldn't wake his folks. Once outside he felt like he could draw a full breath for the first time in days. Run. He had to run.

He started off with an easy lope, through the town and out into the country. It was a full moon and it seemed as light as day with the shadows making monsters out of cornstalks. Without deciding to, he picked up his pace and lengthened his strides, eating up the miles like they was nothin'. About a mile shy of the turnoff for Sally's cabin he felt a pull, like a fishhook in his middle, and wound his way through the bright lit woods down to the river with the clearing surrounded by beech trees He heard them before he could see them. The voices, the rattles, the sound of feet pounding into the earth. Stopping short of the clearing, he watched as silhouettes circled the small fire over and over.

Sally called out, "Come on, Tom! We know you are there!"

He felt a bit sheepish, like he had been eavesdropping, but walked slowly into the smoothed circle. Sally and her brother Walter came toward him and each took an arm, leading him toward the center and the small fire pit surrounded by river rocks. As the others watched on, Walter lifted Tom's shirt up over his head, Sally bent down and took off his shoes, and they set about painting his torso with the red clay and black ash mixed with tallow. Zigzags, and arrows and the shape of the sun as it breaks over the horizon. Walter, who stood a full foot taller than his sister Sally but looked cut from the same bolt of cloth, began spreading the black paint over the left side of Tom's face. As they did so, an elder, a tiny woman with a deeply lined face began to sing the warrior song. Her voice was thin with age, but steady. The words pierced Tom's skin and marked him on the inside, like the paint was marking him on the outside. When he was fully adorned he started to dance too. He could feel the power of the earth rise up through his feet, and the starlight sprinkle him with blessings. He danced. They all danced. They danced together until the moon shifted so far in the west that the clearing became too dark to see. It was as it had been, in the times long past, when the dancing raised the power of the earth and the Great Mother had held them all tenderly.

One by one the people left the fire, slipping off into the darkness without a word of farewell, until it was just Sally, Walter, and Tom left. Walter used his knife to cut a small piece off the bottom of Tom's shirt. Then he cut the pad of his own left thumb and let drops of his blood fall onto the small piece of cloth. He undid his braid and cut a length of his hair, then wound the hair round and round the cloth till it made a tiny bundle. He reached out and placed that into the medicine pouch resting on Tom's chest, and his hand clasped the back of Tom's neck hard. Without a word he turned and disappeared into the woods.

Sally was poking at the fire with her big staff, spreading the wood to ashes, so it would be safe to leave it. "You best go rinse off in the river. You go home lookin' like that and your Ma will have a conniption fit."

"Sally, I..."

"No, boy. No words. Words don't work for the likes of us. Go. Wash."

Tom felt his way down the small incline and slipped into the water. It had been so hot lately, and the shallows felt almost warm. When he went back up into the clearing, Sally was gone, and his shirt and shoes were laid out for him by the fire pit. All the way home he followed the setting moon.

# RUPERTSBERG
## 1121 CE

During the next three days, Giuseppe met with the others of the Thirteen, sometimes one on one, sometimes in small groupings. He found the frequent shift from present day personhood with their age and gender and social standing to their past identity sometimes disconcerting, sometimes alarming, and always exhausting. It was a violent swing between a deep and authentic knowing of their former selves and a distance and formality between the people they were now. He knew them, and yet they were strangers.

This startling yank from then to now was most severe when he spent time with Alejandro. The sculptor was unable to hide the ache and longing he felt for his twin, and at moments Giuseppe could respond in kind. The easy, nonverbal love and dedication that had been their bulwark flooded back into him, and he felt at peace. And then something, anything would shove the now into focus. He would see the pale blond hair curling across Alejandro's forehead and withdraw, recoil. Just a fraction of a moment earlier he had seen – no, felt – that the hair was mahogany, and now it was flaxen. How could he have been in communion with this…eunuch-like fellow? He couldn't feel the ground steady beneath him, and a sense of vertigo would sweep through him with physical magnitude.

From time to time Hildegard would find him staring into a fire or rubbing his temples as he struggled to weave together what was then and what was now.

The snow finally stopped falling on the third day. The Abbey was completely buried in almost four feet with drifts that reached up to high clerestory windows along the outside walls. With the blizzard had come a kind of quiet, a complete blanketing of outside noise and interference that was rare, even for an Abbey. It was as if they were all wrapped in cotton wool and the rest of the world had fallen away.

On the evening of that last day of snowfall. Hildegard had been working, without much success, on her latest treatise on women in the church, admitting to herself that her concentration was not what it could be. Her mind would wander, seeing those sculptures, speculating on what Giuseppe was thinking, watching Alejandro pine for his lost soul mate.

Giuseppe knocked and joined Hildegard in her study. He looked troubled and yet resigned, and she steeled herself to hear from him what would happen next.

"Hildegard."

"Giuseppe."

She gestured for him to sit on the settle by the fire, and poured them both some of the mulled wine that was warming on a hook near the flames. They sipped in an amiable silence for some minutes, neither wanting to break their companionship with the realities of what would transpire next. Finally, Hildegard spoke.

"Tomorrow will see the clearing of the roads. I expect you will want to send word to your entourage of your wellbeing."

He said nothing, just looked down at the cup resting between his hands. His lips twisted, as if the words poised to flow from them were bitter.

"I have a life in Rome."

"Yes, yes you do," Hildegard replied matter-of-factly. If she held a private sorrow at his words she didn't reveal it.

"If I were to not return to that life, there would be serious inquiry made as to why and wherefore."

"Yes, I imagine that the Pontiff would be curious."

He turned to face her suddenly, gripping her hand so tightly that the bones squeezed together.

"If I go back to Rome, I can protect you, protect all here. If I stay, I put you all in danger."

Hildegard found she couldn't reply. She pressed her lips together, shook her head slightly and tried to avoid his gaze.

"Hildegard! Look at me. Look on me! Know that I do not wish this."

She shifted her eyes back and saw the desperation on his face, the longing, the, dare she think it, love. She saw the love there.

She leaned forward and slowly, gently let her lips fall on his. She felt the rightness, the homecoming, the rising heat between them and let the kiss linger. At last they sat back and looked deep into the other's eyes.

"I'll be ready to depart in the morning," he said as he stood to leave the room.

Hildegard reached out and took his hand, linking her fingers into his. Without saying a word she led him into her sleeping chamber and closed the door.

Jeanne — *Maia*
John Somerset — *Eiofachta*
Friar Isambert de la Pierre — *Atvasfara*
St Michael — *Ni Me*
St Catherine — *Io*
St Margaret — *Uxua*

# ROUEN, NORMANDY (FRANCE) 1431 CE

The constant icy drip down the stone walls had sped up, telling Jeanne that it had warmed outside. But inside her cell, it was still the bone-chilling temperature that kept her with a constant low-level shiver. They had given her back her men's clothes last week, and those trousers, stockings, and tunic kept her marginally warmer. And of course, that garb made it much harder for those English pigs to rape her. But warmth, true warmth was available to her only in her visions. She still had daily visitations from St Michael, St Margaret and St Catherine, those brilliant beings of light who held her and supported her courage and her faith. She knew she would not waver with their sustaining presence. These days they looked younger and younger and wore different garments. These days they looked to be dressed in animal skins like the way folks described the Old Ones who lived in the mountains. But they were her dearest companions. They had promised that they would be with her up until and through the end.

Jeanne heard footsteps in the corridor outside her cell. Slow, almost hesitant footsteps. *"Sweet Mother of Baby Jesu, may it not be that pig of an English lord!"* She had told the judges in the court about his assault on her, and since then she hadn't seen him. She felt St Catherine's arms around her, heard the whisper in her ear,

*"All is well, my little sparrow. All is well. A friend comes."*

The footsteps stopped right outside her door and the tiny square of light that shone into her cell from the corridor was blacked out. She could hear breathing, rapid and catarrhal. The minutes stretched out long and fraught. Finally, Jeanne broke from the tension.

"Who is it? What do you want? If it is fornication you are after, I have my trousers on!"

"Hush! Don't raise a ruckus. I don't want to ravage you!" a man said.

The voice from behind the closed door of solid walnut was muffled, and sounded a bit embarrassed.

"Don't scream. I am opening the door. I brought you something."

The key turned in the lock, the hinges protested, and the door swung in, blocking the man from Jeanne's sight. He closed the door and turned to face her. She recognized him, He was small in stature and slight of frame, and looked young, about her age. She seldom paid attention to the English pig soldiers. They moved her around at spear point, threw food into her cell, called her a whore. But she refused to acknowledge their presence, and only prayed louder in her Occitan dialect to blot them out. However, this fellow had drawn her attention. She remembered his eyes. He had been staring at her at the last trial with those wide-open gray eyes like an owl. Now, he had that same, not blinking stare directed at her, and she saw that he was trembling with a light sheen of perspiration trapped in the scanty whisper of hairs atop his lip. He was holding a rough blanket in one hand, and a small bowl of something that had steam rising from it in the other.

"I have brought you soup, and a blanket," he said.

"Why?"

Jeanne's voice was laced with suspicion. At every turn the English pigs had tried to trick her, lure her into heretical statements, lull her into bad action.

"You must be cold…" he replied, with almost a question.

"I have been cold for these last nine months!" Jeanne snorted.

"I saw you last week. I was stationed in the courtroom. I saw you then."

"And so?"

Jeanne took another long look at the young soldier. He seemed familiar to her.

"Do I know you?" she asked.

The soldier cleared his throat and swallowed with what looked like some discomfort.

"It feels like I must. But how can that be? Have you ever been to Kent?" and his voice squeaked.

"No. Never. Were you at Orléans?"

"No. I arrived in the months after with a troop with the Duke of Wessex. I know this sounds strange...but...I have seen you in my dreams...riding the oddest of creatures." He looked at her and then directly away, as if what he was saying was too ludicrous to entertain.

Jeanne felt the abrupt cessation of sound that came with her most potent visions. The young man before her seemed to alter, to shift. Jeanne saw his face, then the face of a young girl with long tangled hair in a green cloak, then his face again. With a deeper urgency she asked,

"And again, why did you bring me soup and blanket?"

"I don't know! I saw you, and all I could think to do was to help. If my officer finds out I have been here, I will get lashed. And yet... here I stand."

The young man's face blanched, and the bowl of soup wobbled in his hand.

"Would you like to sit then?" Jeanne asked with a hint of humor in her voice. The fellow looked down at the scum and waste on the stone floor and wrestled with the desire to be polite and extreme disgust at the thought of resting on that surface. He capitulated, but only half-way, handed Jeanne the soup, put the blanket in her lap, and then with his back against the damp wall, slid himself down to a squat and rested on his heels. Jeanne had watched this sequence of thoughts and events with the beginnings of enjoyment for every piece of his process had shown on his face. *"This one can't lie,"* she thought. *"His is a glass face."*

"What's your name, English?" Jeanne asked.

"John," he replied. "John Somerset."

"So, we are called the same then," Jeanne teased. "Want to change places?"

He blushed and shook his head.

"I had better go before I'm noticed," the young man said and stood quickly. "I am sorry."

"For what?" Jeanne asked, genuinely curious.

He struggled to find a response that made sense, even to himself. "Why don't you just tell them what they want you to say? Then they would set you free!"

Jeanne stared at him long and hard, seeing that he truly did believe she could, under any circumstances, be free of her imprisonment ever again. She broke the stare and took a long swallow of soup, knowing in that moment that it was the best soup that had ever been in the life of the world.

"Thank you, English John, for the blanket and soup. I think, perhaps, unlike the other English, that you are not a pig." She finished the soup and handed him back the bowl and blanket. "You had better take the evidence of your kindness with you."

"Keep the blanket," he implored.

"I know my way to freedom, English John. You had best protect yourself." And she turned partially away from him, afraid that she might waver and snatch the warmth back from his hands.

# RUPERTSBERG
# 1121 CE

Hildegard woke in a sweaty tangle of sheets. Her heart was pounding, loud thunder hooves in her ears. There it was, the dream, the vision, the foretelling of what was to unfold that had catapulted all of the Thirteen toward their destiny at the Isis Temple, her beloved temple, the home of her heart. She had had this same nightmare remembering in all of her previous lifetimes. It had served to guide her, help her make choices, and keep her focused on the path to search for her beloveds again and again. In this lifetime she had seen her past when she had been a very young child, and had moved with constant dedication toward creating a sanctuary – this sanctuary – where the Thirteen and the Companions could feel the pull of their shared history and seek succor and solace. And since coming here to Rupertsberg, she had never had this night terror again.

Until now.

So why tonight, of all nights, did she see the panic and destruction? She turned to look at the face on the pillow next to her. Dark hair falling over the shadows made by high cheekbones, the stubble of beard, almost blue against the linen. She and Giuseppe had walked into her sleeping chamber and fallen on each other as starving folks do on a feast table after famine. Never enough to touch and kiss and taste and smell. Their first coming together was an explosion of the senses, rapid and tumultuous, fevered and insatiable.

That first frenzied bout had led to several more throughout the next hours, each more tender and more measured than the last. When at last they had fallen into an exhausted half slumber, Giuseppe had asked, in a voice barely audible.

"Have you ever…before…?"

Hildegard's head had been resting below his shoulder, and she had rubbed her cheek against his chest, enjoying the rasp of hair and the smell of his sweat. She had looked up to see his eyes, shaded and half-closed.

"Have I ever what? Made love? Lain with a man? Felt so wonderful?"

Giuseppe had chuckled gently, and she had felt the rumble deep beneath his ribs.

"All three, or any of them, actually."

She had smiled and he had felt the movement of her mouth as she had turned her face to kiss him softly directly above his heart before she replied.

"I have always known the body to be a blessing. In my younger years I had a beloved, a beautiful soul named Jutta with whom I had entered the convent. We were together in body and spirit up until several years ago when she passed. I have never before been with a man in intimacy. And judging by tonight, I don't believe that the experience has been overestimated. And yourself?"

"I grew up in Venezia."

"What does that mean, exactly?" Hildegard had teased.

"In Venezia, flesh is like food. One learns to cultivate an educated palate." He had paused, and she had believed he was finished speaking when he had continued.

"But tonight belies all previous experience and all deeply buried dreams. Hildegard…"

She placed her finger across his lips.

"Language cannot suffice." And lifted herself above him, lowering herself onto his ready body.

An hour later, after falling into sleep so deep as to be bottomless, she was awake with all the threads of the dream pummeling through her blood. Was Giuseppe a threat to all she had built here? He had said he would return to Rome to be able to protect them all, and she had believed him when he had said it. So why now the dream?

She sat up, feeling the chilly air in her bedchamber bring gooseflesh across her naked shoulders. Thoughts like trapped hornets buzzed inside her head and made her restless. She tried to slip out of the bed without waking Giuseppe, and had one foot on the icy floor when he rustled and reached for her, placing a warm hand on her back.

"Is anything amiss? You tossed and muttered in your sleep."

Hildegard took a deep steadying breath before she replied. Whether he was friend or foe, trustworthy or not, he was a part of her now. He was a part of the problem and a part of the solution from here on in. She turned to look at him. He was sitting up leaning against the bolster and the sheet had fallen low across his lap. She felt his gaze more than saw it, with only the light from the small fire in the hearth throwing indigo shadows across his face and torso.

"In these last few days, the Thirteen, they have spoken to you of our past. Have they talked about the vision that was the catalyst for all that befell us?" she asked.

"Alejandro spoke of it, and I then remembered the night the vision had come to her, to him. That Winter Solstice night that fell with a full moon. Did you have a similar dream tonight?"

"Not similar, no, but that exact dream in all its terror."

He felt her shudder, and placed his hand on the bed between them, palm up, offering comfort if she so wished. She took the solace, placing her small hand inside his and felt his fingers circle around. She dropped her eyes and stared at their joined hands, as if looking for an answer. In a small voice, a confessional tone she continued.

"I have, in times past, often had this dream, but not since we came here to Rupertsberg. Since then I had thought myself free from the vision."

"And you are wondering if it is a warning, a foretelling, and that I may be the trouble that is being foretold. Am I correct?" His voice was even and low, but Hildegard could hear the hurt.

"No! I mean, perhaps for a moment yes, but no! Or, in truth… yes." Her voice dwindled away until the last word was softer than a whisper.

Giuseppe abruptly swung his legs across, scooted over the bed and came to stand beside her. He looked at her with a sharp, glittering look, what might be perceived as anger, but Hildegard said nothing. He suddenly dropped to his knees before her. She still had one leg draped over the side of the bed from when she had begun to leave it, and he leaned forward, placing his hands on her bare thigh and lowered his head to rest there. She could feel his breath against her skin and saw the rapid rise and fall of his back as he struggled to contain himself. She could barely hear him when he spoke.

"I swear, by all I hold sacred, that I will never act to harm you or those you love. I swear, by my own life to protect yours. I know not what the dream may mean, but I will spend the rest of this life ensuring that you are safe."

They didn't move, suspended in the power and the anguish of that moment. They looked like one of Alejandro's sculptures. Her pale skin shimmered dimly in the firelight; his back had flickering patterns of gold and amber. The only sounds were the cracking and popping from the fire and the light rasp of Giuseppe's breathing. The room, their cocoon of tenderness and passion, was all the more precious for its imminent end. Hildegard could smell him, smell them, and let that memory burrow deep into her heart.

When at long last he stood and slowly leaned forward to kiss her mouth, she didn't move. He gathered his clothes, dressed quickly, and, without looking back at her, let himself through the connecting door into her study. She heard the soft click of the latch on the corridor door when he left the study to return to his quarters.

Hildegard still didn't move, a study in alabaster and loss.

Three hours later, when Sister Delphinia came to bring her hot water for washing she found her there, half on, half off the bed, hands folded in her naked lap, staring into the fire.

# SASKATCHEWAN 1915 CE

Later that morning a small group stood at the train depot and watched three boys loading their gear onto the train. Samuel and Hannah Fletcher were stone-faced as Tom said his goodbyes. They could see he was itching to be on the train and gone. Sally Standing Bear Portreaux was off to the side drinking deep of the sight of him. Tom was surprised to see her there: she hated goodbyes.

Marianne and Pete Palmer were a few paces away. Pete was holding Marianne up and she wailed and bucked.

"Not both my boys! Not you both!"

Morris and Andy were looking at their mother with panic. Morris had one foot on the train stairs ready to bolt. Andy was crying.

"I'm sorry, Ma. Don't be sad. Morris says we'll be back before ya know it." His sweet broad face was worried at his mother's distress, and for a moment he seemed to be ready to fold back into her arms. But he looked at his brother and at Tom, and he wanted to be like them. To be brave. So he patted feebly on his mother's arm and turned abruptly and ran up the steps onto the train car.

Tom shook his father's hand, accepted the clutch of his mother's embrace and then walked over to Sally.

"You got my medicine pouch?' she asked so that only he could hear.

"Yep. I'll keep it. I promised ya."

"And when you need – you'll know when that is – when you need, you'll call for me." She sounded stern.

"I will. I swear it." Tom had a catch in his voice and shook his head once violently like he was shaking off a hornet.

"I'll find you again. That's my promise to you." Sally looked at him hard, willing him to understand. Her words troubled him and burrowed under his skin. She spoke as if against her will. "Do you still see the friends only you could see? I hope so." She grabbed his face with both hands and pulled him down for a quick brusque kiss, then she turned and walked away.

Tom bounded up the steps and found his seat by the window. He looked out on his folks as the train left the station, then faced forward, to war.

# RUPERTSBERG
# 1121 CE

The news spread fast.

The Cardinal had departed early through the snow and without goodbyes.

Hildegard was statue still at her desk. The events of last night kept shifting in and out of focus. But she had barely a moment to herself to reflect, as the morning was filled with a continuous avalanche of conversations with the Thirteen. Young Petyer arrived first. His feelings were bruised, and he was taking umbrage with the Cardinal's method of departure. He had found a friendship with Giuseppe that had been a sweet antidote to all the female energy that surrounded him at the Abbey.

"He just up and left? And he didn't leave me a message?"

"Petyer, the Cardinal has a life that presses obligations upon him. His friendship with you is real, however temporary his time with us."

Petyer wiped his nose on his sleeve, and Hildegard didn't admonish him as he stomped out of the study.

Sister Catherine of the Wheel and tiny Griseld asked to see Mother Hildegard to get her advice about how to deal with Alejandro who had been seen stalking the grounds of the Abbey without cloak or hat. They both still had snow clumped in their boots and were swathed to the eyebrows in cloaks and shawls, not having waited to discard outerwear before seeing Hildegard.

"When I approached him, Mother, he looked right through me. It was as if he didn't see me or know me!" Griseld cried. "He is bereft."

Sister Catherine rubbed the child's bony shoulders, offering a modicum of warmth and comfort.

"Truly, Mother, he seems deranged with grief. What shall we do?"

"Sister, have him brought to me here. Ask some of the more reticent sisters to help you. Perhaps it is best if all believe he is suffering from a fever and is delusional. I will see to him here." Hildegard was thinking quickly, assessing the options.

As soon as Griseld and Sister Catherine had left her study, Betterm the gardener walked in without knocking. His wispy hair was swept upright making him look frightened or astonished.

"Mother! It's true? The Cardinal, our Talo is gone? I found Maria Stella weeping in the greenhouse."

Hildegard saw the old man struggling mightily not to cry. His cheeks blew in and out and he was working his lips hard.

"My old friend, sit down and rest here by the fire. I hope you haven't been over-exerting trying to dig us out of the snow."

"No, Mother. I put the young nuns onto it. They enjoy the snow throwing as much as the snow shoveling."

As soon as he mentioned it Hildegard could hear the sound of laughter and squeals of mirth floating up from the courtyard and gardens below. After those early morning hours where she had been in a daze, now bit-by-bit her senses were returning to her. Now she could register the brilliant white blue sunlight refracting off the snow and flooding her study. Now she smelled the tang of vinegar water as sisters mopped the corridors in a futile attempt to keep the sloppy boots from messing up the floor. Now she belatedly tasted the bread that Delphinia had insisted that she eat this morning. Piece by piece she pulled herself back together and faced the world that had the Cardinal's absence as the focal issue of the day. She touched her heart where a deep bruise would forever remain, for in each lifetime she had found and lost so many, and the bruising never healed.

She turned to tend to Betterm who now had a single tear rolling down his left cheek. She gave him a cup of mulled wine and sat down at his side.

"This is very, very hard, is it not, my friend?" Hildegard patted him on the knee and looked into the fire so he couldn't see the intimate pain in her own eyes. "When we remember, and then find each other again, the loss…the loss feels unbearable."

Betterm took her hand in his. Her hand was small in comparison to his and had a permanent ink stain on the last knuckle of her middle finger. He smiled to himself to see this evidence of her left-handed nature. It spoke volumes to him that despite much castigation and punishment from tutors and teachers to change to her other hand, Hildegard had remained steadfast, claiming that God had made her such and as such she would stay. His hand was gnarled and calloused with small cracks made bloody by the cold. These days his hands never seemed to get warm, but he refused to wear the gloves that Hildegard kept gifting him.

"We are two of God's most stubborn creatures, you and I. Are we not?" he said.

Hildegard felt him squeeze her hand, looked down at their joined palms and caught his meaning.

"And today, are we classifying stubbornness as a virtue or a flaw then?" she asked. He didn't answer right away, but sipped the wine and sniffed heartily. When he did reply he went right to the center of the heart pain.

"Will he ever return, do you think?"

Hildegard felt herself pulled by the riptide of loss. She closed her eyes against the momentary vertigo, and pushed down the rising floodwaters of despair.

"No, I do not believe he ever will." she said quietly.

There was a rapid knock on the door, and before she could respond the door swung open. Sister Catherine and three other sisters were shepherding Alejandro into the study. His eyes were blank with the look of an empty house. They had wrapped him in a blanket, and his lips looked blue. Betterm stood abruptly, and the women sat Alejandro down on the settle. Two of the younger nuns knelt down and rubbed his feet with the rough wool. Hildegard was shocked to see that his feet were bare and that the toes were blanched as white as the snow. He whimpered softly as they rubbed the blood back into his feet. Delphinia, anticipating need as she always did, arrived with another sister carrying two basins and warm water. They gently placed his hands and feet into the water and he cried out in pain. Betterm stood at Alejandro's back and calmed him, holding his shoulders and saying, "There, man, there. Steady on."

All Hildegard knew to do was to pray, and when she prayed she sang. She started softly, and slowly filled the room with a chant to the Blessed Mother. One by the one the others in the room joined her. Alejandro's ragged weeping got softer and softer until it was as if the sounds of their voices raised in song were warming him as well, sinking into the internal bits of pain and loss.

"Leave him here, Sisters. Let's make him comfortable by the fire. I don't want any fever he may have to spread its contagion through the Abbey."

All the nuns nodded as if they tacitly agreed that this was a good enough story. Delphinia brought bedding, and they prepared a pallet right in front of the fire. They gently laid Alejandro down there and walked quietly out of the room as Hildegard thanked them and blessed them. Betterm sat back down on the bench. He looked up at Hildegard and saw her, pale as new milk.

"I'll stay and watch him. You look like you need to go lie down yourself."

She swayed slightly, feeling fatigue pull at her feet.

"I will, thank you, just for a few moments."

Hildegard walked without seeing into her bedchamber, and without even closing her door, fell across the bed as an old tree slowly embraces the earth as it falls.

Alejandro was slow to recover. He spent the next few days in Hildegard's study, barely eating and never speaking. On the third day he allowed the sisters to help him bathe, and on the fourth day he spoke to Hildegard.

"Is this the justice of the Goddess? Is this how the Companions felt, how he felt when we all disappeared from life? Did they feel their hearts being ripped out of their bodies too?"

"Yes, I believe their pain was of this sort, but no, I do not believe that we are receiving retribution for the anguish our deaths caused them. The Goddess does not desire that we suffer."

"Then why must we suffer?" he wailed.

"It is the price of love," Hildegard replied.

# COMTÉ DE FOIX
# 1079 CE

As the nuns rested and napped in the cool of the forest, Sister Agnes took off her identifying veil and hurried to her family's farm to secretly enlist their help. She arrived back with her father and brothers as well as two uncles and a sister-in-law, all carrying blankets and baskets of food.

Mother Marguerite greeted them and led the kind folk aside for a consult. After she had lain out their circumstances, they urged her to let the nuns find shelter at their farms, and she again declined.

"You need to not make enemies of these men. Neutrality is your only protection," she explained. "We are so deeply grateful for your help and your offer of succor, but needs must. We shall be away."

Sister Agnes's oldest brother drew a good map in the dirt.

"There is a small stream to the east. Stay along its shore till it forks. Cross the stream there, and head due north. The forest is thickest there, and it travels along a limestone cliff face that you should follow. It goes all the way to Carcassonne. But Mother, this is a journey of several days, more for you with your sick and elderly. How will you manage?"

"Thanks to you and the provisions your family has brought us, and with the help of the Blessed Mother, we shall endure. You should all return home now. And if anyone asks, remember, you have seen nothing of us."

Marguerite used her foot to wipe away any traces of the map. As she turned back around, she saw that the father and brothers and uncles and sister-in-law had knelt, asking for her blessing. She was momentarily stunned at the request, but after a gentle nudge from Sister Dolora, she placed her palms on their heads and asked the Virgin and all the saints for grace to be visited upon them. She turned to Sister Agnes.

"Sister, what lies before us may be treacherous. If you so desire, I would relinquish you from your vows, and send you home with your family."

The young nun went pale, so that the freckles across her cheeks stood in sharp relief. Her father moved at her left as if to reach for her. She turned her head to look at him directly.

"Papa."

He said nothing, but looked at her with tender love.

"I can't, Papa."

And the older man nodded slowly, reached out to touch her pale cheek, and made to leave with his kin. Sister Agnes watched them go, and then turned back to Marguerite after her family had disappeared into the deep green.

"I stay with you, Mother. My place is with you." And her voice held the cadence of a long ago time and a far away place. The scent of spikenard and river water hung between them. Agnes felt the power of a fierce feminine divine rise up through her legs. She heard a hawk's cry overhead, and, for a splinter of a second, she felt the bliss of holding the Goddess within her body. Agnes, who had been Badh, the Keeper of Wild Spaces, would stand true in every lifetime. For that fraction of a heartbeat she remembered, and she stood true.

Marguerite couldn't speak, and she only shook her head once, looked down, then lifted her gaze and spotted Sister Anna Sophia leaning into a circle of nuns, deep in the susurration of barely contained whispers. When they saw her, their conversation came to an abrupt end. Several of the nuns had the grace to look chagrined, which gave Marguerite a pretty good idea that she had been the topic of their words. Sister Anna Sophia straightened and looked at Marguerite with look of triumph and a slanted mouth, lip almost curled in contempt.

"Anything amiss here, Sisters?" Marguerite strode forward to the group.

"What is *not* amiss? We have abandoned our home, and are lost in the wilderness, all at your behest. And for what?" Anna Sophia almost crowed.

Again, as she so often did, Anna Sophia spoke to Marguerite without using her title, without the recognition of her position. It was rude, bordering on disrespectful. Noting that, and seeing how several of the sisters looked shocked by the abrasive manner of Anna Sophia's speech, Marguerite lowered her voice till it required them to lean in to hear her.

"Oh, ye of little faith."

Feeling a bit audacious to be quoting Christ but feeling like the situation demanded desperate measures, Marguerite waited until the full impact of that statement had registered with every nun in the cluster. Then she continued.

"Perhaps placing yourselves in service to those sisters who need assistance is a better use of your God-given breath than speculation and gossip."

Most of the handful of nuns scurried away, but Anna Sophia looked as if she had been slapped again.

"You question my devotion to our Lord? Me? Who has been a tireless worker for His will?" she asked Marguerite with a sharp-edged rise in her voice.

"I question which is greater – your devotion to our Lord, or your thirst for personal power. But for the good of all, I require your obedience now, and at least a show of civility and respect. Your whispers and malign ideas can only jeopardize everyone here."

Marguerite stared at Anna Sophia, looking in the dimming light for some hint, some softening, some wisp of connection. To Marguerite it appeared that Anna Sophia was at war within herself. Her eyes shifted back and forth, and she bit the inside of her mouth. She wrestled internally, until finally she spoke, so very softly as to almost be indiscernible from the rustling of the leaves in the eventide breeze.

"This entire misadventure is a mistake. Your decision to lead us in this folly was a mistake. And Mother Monica Maria was mistaken when she chose you to follow her."

A chasm of silence stretched between them. Marguerite spoke first.

"I have pledged to protect and serve you. And that I will do. But if you choose to leave us and go your own way, and if any others choose to do so as well, I will release you from your vows and you may go where you wish. If that is back to Mater Misericordia, where I swear to you I believe there to be danger, you can declare yourself Mother and no one will be the wiser. A Mother of none or one or three or twenty. It matters not, for in your heart you will know you have taken the road of pride and ambition. But it is your path to choose."

Marguerite turned and walked away quickly. For so many years Marguerite had felt the safety of her secret escape hatch. She had held on to the notion that she could leave the convent and the community of sisters and find her own peace. But now, at the threat of that same community fraying and dissolving, she felt how strong the fibers were that wove them all together.

Sister Anna Sophia shouted at Marguerite's back, "I am returning to our convent! This is sheer madness, this traipsing through the forest to escape from a rumored enemy. I will lead anyone who wants to come with me. What say you, sisters? Shall we go home? Shall we return to what we know? Shall I lead you?"

Her voice rose louder as she finished. And then there was silence, with only the songbirds in reply.

"I am heading north, my sisters, toward Carcassonne, and the safety of our sister convent. If you follow Sister Anna Sophia, you would do so against my judgment. But you would go with my love. Sisters, I have asked much of you in these last hours. And I will ask even more in the hours to come. Faith, that most potent quality, is what I need of you now. We left our beloved sisters, Helena and Martha Mary behind at Mater Misericordia. Sister Agnes, when given the opportunity to return to her family, chose to remain with us. I believe that Sister Anna Sophia has a decision to make."

"We believe that it is in everyone's best interest to turn around, all of us, and return to the convent," Sister Anna Sophia responded, looking to the women surrounding her for agreement. Some heads nodded, others looked terrified at the clash of wills playing out.

"That is too bad," Marguerite said, then crossed her arms and held still as a statue.

"All right, then. We shall return!" Anna Sophia exulted, unaware that this was too easy. Marguerite had not agreed.

"So, let us all go!" Anna Sophia said, more loudly this time.

"No!" Marguerite replied quietly but with firmness.

"But I said…" Anna Sophia began.

Marguerite cut her off.

"I am fully aware what you said, and I said no."

Three of the group of sisters around Anna Sophia began to edge away. Two of the women, one at her right and one at her left stood firm.

"You are free to go wherever you choose, Sister Anna Sophia. And if these sisters wish to follow you, I fear it is folly, but that too I will permit. But you do not speak for this congregation. You are not the Mother. We are not turning back. The Sisters of Mater Misericordia move forward, starting now."

Marguerite looked each of the women there in the eye. Only Anna Sophia could hold her gaze. The others looked down or aside and muttered, "Yes, Mother," under their breath.

Sister Dolora came up to stand at Marguerite's right shoulder.

"All are ready to begin, Mother."

"Well then, gather everyone and we shall all pray together as one community," Marguerite looked pointedly at Anna Sophia. "Perhaps for the last time."

Word spread swiftly and women moved forward and back, through the leaf mold and dappled light and toward Mother Marguerite. One hundred and eighteen women were poised in the cathedral of the trees. Marguerite spoke clearly and loud enough for every woman to hear, hoping that prayer as their common language, would be the glue to hold them all together.

"Blessed Mother and the multitude of saints. We trust in the mercy of Jesus Christ and ask the light of the Holy Spirit to protect us against our enemies. We ask for blessings on this community of women, sworn to walk in the light of the Lord. Amen."

But as fabric will fray, so shall the circles of women. And three women, Anna Sophia and her two faithful followers, began their journey back toward the Convent with the words of their sisters' prayers trailing behind them like the low mist of morning.

For those remaining one hundred and fifteen, the journey deep into the forest began. They walked through the rest of that day, found the stream branch and crossed to the north side. As it got dark early in the forest, Mother Marguerite decided to make camp for the night at the base of the cliff face. The nuns laid out bedding, rough blankets and rolled up rucksacks, against the limestone wall that still held the heat from the day's sun. Marguerite walked along the line of women, checking that all had food, all were as settled and as comfortable as could be. Later, Sister Dolora found Marguerite standing alone, looking into the deepening dark.

"What is amiss, niece?"

"What is amiss? Oh, by the heavens, everything?" Marguerite took a bite of mushy apple. "Sufficient unto the day is the evil within. Sister. We shall just have to wait and see what fresh hell tomorrow brings."

The two, aunt and niece in blood, sisters in vows, brides of Christ, friends from ages past, found what comfort they could on the forest floor and Dolora fell into the deepest of slumbers. Only Marguerite stayed awake, watching for any and all comers, man or beast. Finally, she was dragged under the wave of fatigue.

*She was racing through a woods of broad leaf trees, sand beneath her feet, trailing a heavy wool cloak. Just ahead skipped a young girl with skin so dark that she disappeared in the shadows and only the flash of brilliant white in her smile gave hint of where she was. It was dusk and the air was deliciously warm.*

*And then…she was standing before a large fire, blasts of heat pushing her backward as she swung the cloak, deep and green, over her head and flung it into the flames. It was rightly done, and she felt tears course down her cheeks. She had done right by Alama, the First Among Equals.*

*And then...she stood in a circle with other women around that fire.*

*And then...they were on the deck of a ship, chanting together as the world split asunder and the ship was yanked into the abyss and all the air was pulled from her lungs and the sea fell away...*

"Mother!" A hand roughly shook her shoulder. "Mother! You were dreaming!"

Marguerite fought her way through the cobwebs of images and faces and songs in an almost remembered language to see Sister Dolora's worried face inches from her own, and her hand over Marguerite's mouth. "Hush, child, hush!"

"What did I...?" Marguerite asked, needing to have any tiny bit of substance to hang onto what she had just experienced.

"You were singing. Then you screamed. Scared a year off my life, I swear by the Virgin."

The first hint of light filtered through the trees, women came awake and turned and moaned and shifted their sore bodies to rise and face what was before them. The night had been cold, and the older nuns felt it in their bones, the aches and sharp stabs of old joints. The morning held a hint of rain, with overcast skies of pearl and dove gray softly tempering the sun. Sister Agnes approached Marguerite and asked, "Mother? What do you require?"

"Well firstly, I would like a warm dry bed. And then, I would like to tell the Almighty that I am not seeing His sense of humor here."

The Sisters nearby felt themselves relax. If Mother Marguerite was being flippant, then all was not lost.

# RUPERTSBERG
# 1121 CE

A month later Hildegard received a letter from Cardinal Giuseppe Giardelli. The missive was written in his own hand, a sign that he did not choose to have the assistance of a scribe. He described the details of his return to Rome and expressed his gratitude at the hospitality he had received at Rupertsberg. The letter was polite and friendly and gave nothing away; this was correspondence that could and would be read by any and all. He asked to be remembered to "all the special friends" he had met at the Abbey, and specifically mentioned Alejandro, suggesting that the curator at the Vatican would be delighted to procure one of Alejandro's sculptures for the Papal chapel. He wondered when Hildegard would be submitting her next herbal treatise and promised to personally see to its approval. He closed by saying that he would welcome further communications with the Mother and inhabitants of the Abbey and wished them all the blessings of God and the Holy Father.

Hildegard read the letter several times, straight away. Looking for any hint, any clue as to his disposition. She sat back against her chair and breathed deeply. Was she sighing in relief that he seemed amiable and open, or sighing in frustration that he left no clue as to whether he missed her or no? As she searched her heart, she discovered that it was both, but that to ensure the safety of all she loved she would learn to lean more toward feeling relief at his apparent neutrality. Letting the paper rest in one hand, she turned her face to catch the last rays of gold that shone through the windows. She was sitting like that in peaceful repose when Sister Delphinia came into the study and stood in front of the desk, hands folded and hanging down low across her waist. Hildegard looked up at her and smiled with languid pleasure at the very sight of this faithful friend.

"We have heard from the Cardinal. He is back at the Holy See and sends his regards to you."

Hildegard reached the letter across the desk.

"Would you care to read it?"

Delphinia didn't unclasp her hands to take the letter. Instead she raised her eyes, looking at Hildegard with a kind of frozen panic.

"Delphinia, what is it? Is someone hurt or ill? Tell me!"

"Mother..." and she stopped. Her voice trembled as she continued. "Mother, your moon cycle, it is two weeks late."

The two women stared at each other as the sound of the bells for Vespers rang clean and bright.

"You are sure?" Hildegard replied in a calm tone that belied the racing of her heart.

"Of course I'm sure! Are you not?" Delphinia's voice rose in exasperation. "I tend to your laundry, do you not attend to your own body?"

"Infrequently, at best," Hildegard retorted.

Both women looked in the other's eyes at a stand-off. Hildegard broke first as her eyelids fluttered and she blanched.

"Great Mother, what am I to do?" and she let the letter from the Cardinal fall from her fingers onto the desk.

Delphinia sat down hard into the chair before the desk.

"What can be done?" she asked.

Hildegard let a small hysterical laugh escape her lips.

"Oh, so many things can be done. But should they? And will they?"

Delphinia took a moment to carefully craft a response. Her devotion to Hildegard wrestled with her anger that the Mother could have let this happen. A small thread of jealousy that the Cardinal had gotten that close to Hildegard wove around all her thoughts and whispered in her ear. Finally, loyalty won out.

"Mother, whatever you need shall be done. Tell me what you want."

Hildegard's breath caught in a small rasp as she gave Delphinia a sad smile.

"You are precious beyond rubies, my friend. But where do I even begin to decide what I want?"

The two women sat through the evening hours and made lists of options and their repercussions. Hildegard, gifted as an herbalist, could ensure that her moon cycle arrived quickly, obliterating any concerns for future consequences. All would remain as it was at Rupertsberg, and the Cardinal need never know there was ever any complication from his stay at the Abbey. Or, Hildegard could keep all evidence of pregnancy hidden under her voluminous habit until, in four months or so, she declared herself in need of a private retreat to a hermit's cabin. With that option further decisions would be necessary. Would, Goddess willing, after a safe delivery for mother and child, would that child be given to folks that could be trusted for rearing as their own? Or, would that child be delivered to the doorsteps of the Abbey, and raised within its walls as an orphan? Would the Cardinal ever need to be told about the parentage of this child? Would he, if that information was given to him, desire to claim the child and see to her or his upbringing? Would Hildegard be able to live with that? And if any of this ever got out to the outside world, what would happen to Hildegard and the Abbey, and all those who found a life of sanctuary within its walls?

It was even possible, dangerous but possible, that Hildegard could deliver the baby here at Rupertsberg, claim it, and that the child could be folded into the family of sisters. It would not be the first baby born here. A number of women had arrived at the Abbey doors over the years, alone, desperate and with child. They had always been welcomed and given safe harbor. Some of those babies lived within the Abbey walls today, tiny Griseld being one of them. Some babies had been adopted by trusted allies of the Abbey. And several women had found their resolution in the herbs crafted by Hildegard. Each decision was personal and honored. Hildegard knew that the sisters of the Abbey would protect her, but she wasn't sure she wanted to ask that of them.

"We have thought long and hard with our minds, my friend. But the mind can only take us so far. The heart, roaring like a mountain lion, can be listened to and acknowledged. But the one voice we haven't consulted is that of the life within me. I think I need to speak to that spark of life directly."

"Well you aren't doing anything until you have something to eat!" Delphinia admonished. "All work should be done on a full stomach."

Hildegard felt a small wave of nausea at the thought of food. How had she been missing these signals from her body? Had she known and not wanted to admit that she knew? She shook her head at her own foolishness and agreed to some supper.

"Something light, please, maybe soup?"

Delphinia lifted an eyebrow and left the study to go see to it. While she was gone Hildegard set about preparing for the deep work she would do tonight. She set out the small iron bowl and prepared some charcoal and the herbs necessary to facilitate her soul journey. She selected dried mugwort and balm of Gilead and placed them next to her scrying bowl. All of this sat upon a small table in front of the fire as she paced back and forth, restless to begin. When Delphinia arrived with a tray of oxtail soup and warm bread, she sat down and ate without really tasting, admitting that she needed the fuel, but her mind racing beyond and ahead.

With her hunger and Delphinia satisfied Hildegard bade her friend goodnight, sat before the fire and focused on her breath. Years of practice, lifetimes of practice, helped her ease swiftly into the deep meditative state. She lit the charcoal, sprinkled the herbs on it and poured water into the scrying bowl. She felt the presence of her Goddess and the support of her ancestors as she spoke softly aloud.

"I seek the voice of the one within. I call upon the spirit within me. I, who you have chosen to be your home, ask to be in communion with you. What is your soul's mission? What choice would you have me make?"

As Hildegard looked into the water its flat obsidian surface began to ripple and shimmer. The image of a face came clear as if walking out of a fog. It seemed familiar, that face, but it shifted from female to male and back to female. Then it came into sharp focus. It was a long translucent face with flowing white hair and eyes so pale a green as to be silver. The person smiled at Hildegard who could hear the musical voice as if spoken inside her head.

"Hello! At long last!"

"Ah, it's you!" Hildegard replied. "Ni Me!"

"Yes, Atvasfara. It is I, Ni Me of the Pleiades."

"Dear One, you come to me now? I have never found you in all the lives since Egypt."

"Have you not, Atvasfara of Isis?"

Hildegard had a sudden flooding of images, times, places, lives. In each life if she had incarnated as female she had been with child, early pregnancy in each case, and always lost the baby, sometimes without cause, and sometimes with. She remembered gripping pain and a gush of blood. She felt the abrupt loss of presence. She recalled times making choices and those times when choices had been made for her. Had each been the soul of Ni Me? As if she had asked the question directly Ni Me replied.

"I have always been that spirit visited upon you. And now you see me."

"What is it you want of me, Ni Me of the Pleiades? Do you seek a life walking upon this earth?"

"Each time that I have lived briefly within you, I had chosen to become embodied to teach you something, to remind you of who you are, to awaken your memories and your truths. I never was required to come into a walking, breathing body. I visited, I touched, and my mission was complete. Now, you and I can decide."

"Is your mission different this time, Ni Me?"

"You have been able to accomplish so much in this life, Atvasfara. I have volunteered to ensure that the world will always remember you as you live as Hildegard of Bingen. I could and would protect your legacy. Your wisdom should be preserved. It will be needed when we all meet again. But the fact of me presents difficulties for you. And it is your choice."

"Ni Me, how brave you are to seek to take a place in this world! In so many ways, it is a harsher world than when we stood together before. I am deeply grateful for your offer. And yes, the very fact of you is problematic." Hildegard gave a wry smile, and she could hear the high descending bell tones of Ni Me's laughter. "The question is thorny. I carry the weight for the safety of many."

Ni Me's face began to fade and her voice became softer and softer.

"The Goddess knows that your decision will be made with heart and mind. Whatever you choose, know that you are loved. All will be well. All will be well. All manner of things will be well."

And the vision evaporated. Hildegard sat, staring into the scrying bowl which now only held water. She floated in indecision until sunrise, when a middle path became clear to her. All, indeed, might be well.

Five months later Hildegard, claiming a state of physical and spiritual exhaustion, left the Abbey at Rupertsberg with her faithful attendant, Sister Delphinia. They made their way to a small cabin high in the mountains that was maintained by Delphinia's family as a hunting lodge.

Every week Sister Delphinia's cousin would arrive with supplies of food and charcoal for heating. He often brought the letters from the Abbey that the Sisters there had deemed urgent or personal. He always spoke to Delphinia in the pretty little garden on the southern side of the cabin. Of Hildegard he saw nothing. When asked about her welfare Delphinia always replied.

"She is better and better."

In those letters were several from Cardinal Giuseppe Giardelli. He would write about the events political and intellectual from within the Vatican. He never failed to ask after his "special friends" and send them blessings from the Holy Father. His letters were warm and congenial. Hildegard had written to him of her "retreat", but never attributed its true cause to her condition. He sent along learned treatises for her to read and packages of special foodstuffs reputed to build strength and purify the humours. Hildegard read the books and tossed the cures into the pigsty.

On the night of the ancient feast of May Eve, Hildegard was delivered of a baby boy with only Delphinia in attendance. Since it was a first birth for both of them, the night was fraught with pain and worry. But as Ni Me had promised, all was well.

Hildegard named the boy Theoderic – coming from God. Delphinia's cousin's wife had recently given birth as well, and she agreed to wet-nurse the "poor abandoned babe" when she heard from Delphinia that they had come upon the child in the woods, nestled under a tree wrapped in a blanket with only a ruby ring tied to a piece of parchment with his name writ upon it to give clue to his identity. Arrangements were made that when the baby could eat solid foods he would be brought to the Abbey to be given all the care the sisters could provide.

Hildegard's return to the Abbey coincided with the Summer Solstice. The sisters had wreaths of flowers over their veils and a large feast was laid out upon the grass. Each woman took time to kiss Hildegard's hands and exclaim their joy at her return. Sister Catherine of the Wheel gave her a look that spoke volumes and Hildegard promised.

"Later."

That night the members of the Thirteen met at the gazebo where only one year before they had been introduced to Petyer Fieldenstarn and he to them. In that year Petyer had shot up at least a foot in height and his voice had dropped almost an octave. Betterm the gardener now needed a cane to walk. His voice was thin and his speech was short. Sister Maria Stella was constantly at his side and had dark shadows under her eyes, as if in anticipation of the grief to come at the loss of him. Alejandro, after months of barely eating or talking to anyone, had finally emerged from his shadows to spend more time with tiny Griseld whose cough was worse and worse. And Sister Catherine's beloved dog had had a paroxysm two months past and was buried in the gardens under the irises. She hadn't cried when anyone could see, but her eyes and nose were always red.

When Hildegard joined them they all thought her different. Something had shifted within her, under her skin. It was like looking at a familiar pond and now you could see the movement of fish deep in the water. They all stood in a circle, their community of the re-incarnated, and clasped hands.

"Beloveds, I have something to tell you," she began.

Khadee — *Kiyia*
Samuel — *Badh*
Grandmother Prudence — *Maia*
Juba — *Parasfahe*
Bonnie — U*xua*
Homer — N*i* M*e*

# OSHUN VILLAGE, UPPER CANADA (CANADA) 1812 CE

Khadee sat at her desk, looking out the window at the women of Oshun gathered on either side of plank tables set up in the commons. They were doing the fruit canning for the early harvest. The peaches and cherries had been especially bountiful this year, and the jars of brilliant blush and scarlet were shot through with sunlight. It was a beautiful day. Not too hot, with a light breeze. Perfect to keep off the flies and waft the heat from the cauldrons away.

She knew she should go join the women, but her heart was heavy, and she really wanted to get this letter to Master Farley off with the post rider. So she bent to her work.

*Dear Friend,*

*I was aggrieved upon receipt of thy last letter to hear of our Thomas's passing. I know he is held in the arms of those who have gone before. But as in death there is life, I must tell thee that I have been in the safe delivery of a baby, a girl again. We are calling her Joan, after the saint and after thy mother.*

*The news that thee and Martha would not be able to come visit us this year at Harvest Festival brings me much sadness. I am angry at the workings of men and governments that keep us and our lands apart. I know that conflict is a fearful thing to thee and thy Society of Friends.*

*And I have in my life also seen the ferocious consequences of violence. And so, with great reluctance, I must share with thee something that I am hesitant to convey.*

*My husband Samuel has decided to enlist in the Coloured Corps and go fight. I have argued myself breathless at him, asking why he feels the need to fight this white man's war. Why would he leave his wife and children and risk his life for them? In all honesty, thee and thy father are the only decent white folks I have ever known — with the exception of that sailor boy on the slave ship. Samuel's only answer is that it will prove to the provisional governor that we are equal, that he is a man like all other men. What foolishness!*

*Our neighbors, the Seneca, have also decided to fight for the British and believe in the promises of secured lands and fair treatment. I despair at their naïveté.*

*I take solace in the company and comfort of our special friends here. Thanks to thy family's decency and generosity our Sanctuary for friends from ages past can rest in our time together in the here and now. Bonnie and Homer have had their third child this past month, a boy with a powerful set of lungs. Grandmother Prudence's mind slips more and more since her Juba passed in the spring, but her memories of our home across the ocean grow stronger and are a comfort to her and us. And my Samuel is as pig-headed as ever was. I am well, though missing thee and Martha most sorely.*

*I must haste to finish this as the post rider is saddling up.*

*With thee always in friendship and constancy,*

*Khadee Farley*

Setting the wax seal on the paper, Khadee walked outside and handed the missive to the weathered fellow sitting atop a giant bay.

"May thee have safe travels. Will there be trouble at the border, does thee think?" she asked.

"I knows my ways. I'll go through the Iroquois lands and follow along Lake Champlain. The Americans avoid the Indians." He chortled, tipped the brim of his hat at her and kicked off down the dusty road.

"Mama!" Khadee's eldest, a girl of four ran up, lifted her arms high, asking to be picked up.

"Oof, child. Thee is as heavy as a calf." But she laughed and swung the girl high up into the air. She carried her daughter over to the long tables, and soaked in the sounds of talk and laughter and song as the women worked together.

A hawk sounded high above and Khadee lifted her eyes to spot him. She smiled to think that from his viewpoint, her world, her village, her sanctuary was a green and vibrant place, a place where songs and drums kissed the land, a place where bounty and respite were found. She could hear the men coming back from the fields; she could feel the sun bake deep into her bones. She felt peace descend upon her, as Alexander Farley would say. And because it was right, and because she could, she touched her heart and prayed aloud to her ancestors. All those around her fell into a quick and easy hush, as the language of the Fulani and the Fante and the Mandinka rose skyward.

# RUPERTSBERG
# 1122 CE

At the time of last harvest when the days were growing short Sister Delphinia met her cousin at the Abbey gate. He had brought a wagonload of bounty from the mountains. There were baskets of mushrooms and bushels of nuts, acorns, filberts, and chestnuts. He even had a small woven carry of truffles covered in a plain white cloth. Tucked up on the wagon bench beside him was a larger basket that held the boy, Theoderic, who had thrived on rich mother's milk and mountain air. Delphinia climbed up onto the bench so that the child was nestled between them, and directed her cousin to drive the wagon around to the kitchen yard. With a held breath and a racing heart she pulled back the blankets cocooning the child and took a peek at the sleeping baby. He was sturdy and plump with a shocking amount of black curly hair and extraordinarily long black lashes resting on those rounded cheeks. As if he could feel her gaze the baby opened his eyes and looked directly at her. Tawny golden eyes. Mother Hildegard's eyes.

"Jesu Cristi!" Delphinia exclaimed.

"I can assure you, he has more devil than Christ in him," her cousin chuckled. "Now that he is crawling, he is into everything: the butter churn, the coal scuttle, the dung heap. And he just laughs when we find him slathered in all substances. You sisters will have to keep a close watch on him."

Delphinia, pale and stunned, replied with a quaver in her voice.

"Oh cousin, rest easy. We will keep the closest of watch on this child."

Baby Theoderic became toddler Theo and everyone's darling. Only Hildegard held back. The Sisters devised a soft fleece-lined harness with a long rope attached so that they could save him from falling down staircases and into privy pits. Theo sat on any lap that would have him and would sing along in the divine offices and music rehearsals, first with his own special gibberish, and then in the several languages spoken at the Abbey. He was bright beyond measure and a delicious mix of affection and mischief. And the winter passed with no severe storms like the one the year before.

As spring found its way to Rupertsberg, Theo was often found in the gardens with Betterm. The old gardener spent his days sitting on the benches there, directing the Sisters what to plant and where to weed, and soaking up the sun. Theo could walk through flowerbeds, dig up bulbs, squash tender shoots with his firmly planted little feet, and Betterm never scolded him. The boy would bring his treasures back to show Betterm, crawl up onto the bench, and plop onto the old man's lap with a solid little thud.

"See, Betta? Wha' dis?"

"That was to be a daffodil, my little urchin. Go now and put it back in the ground where the sun can make it grow," Betterm would reply, with a sweetness in his voice that few had ever heard.

Theo would scramble down, and steady on his little legs, go back to some spot of dirt and plant the bulb again. It was in this way that Betterm felt he was saying goodbye to all the green life of Rupertberg, and passing his knowledge along. By late summer Theo was always running, never walking, along the garden paths, and the sound of his high tripping laughter and the low rumble of Betterm's voice could be heard lifted on warm updrafts.

It was at the end of one especially golden day in late September that Hildegard found them near the pear orchard. Betterm had his face turned up to the sun and Theo was sound asleep, sprawled across the gardener's lap. Hildegard walked up quietly, and Betterm, hearing her, turned his head slightly and opened one eye. She stood a few paces away with hands folded, looking at them both with love. And yet, Betterm sensed her reserve. He steeled himself, for he had been the one appointed by the others of the Thirteen to address her on this issue.

"You can come closer. He won't bite. Well, at least, he won't as long as he is asleep!" Betterm chuckled softly and that started a cough that ended in a wheeze.

"You shouldn't let the child overtire you, Betterm. There are many that can help you care for him," Hildegard said, not answering his previous comment.

"I know that, Hildegard. But you see, he is forcing me to rest right now. He is as heavy as a ham, and I couldn't get up even if I cared to." He reached down and brushed Theo's black curls back from his face to reveal sun-kissed peach fuzz on his cheeks. "And he is the delight of my last years. Hildegard, why do you avoid him? Does his resemblance to his father pain you?"

Hildegard took a half step back involuntarily, as if struck by Betterm's words. Her voice grew fainter.

"He does look like Giuseppe, doesn't he? More and more every day. And I don't choose to avoid him, as much as seek to shield us all. You have seen his eyes, have you not?"

"Your eyes, you mean?"

"Yes! By all that is holy! Why couldn't the child have brown eyes like half the world!"

Betterm's mouth twitched, and seeing it, Hildegard's did too.

"Does everyone here at Rupertsberg know, do you think?"

"Unless they are blind," Betterm retorted.

"Well, by Hatshupt's cats, what am I to do about that?"

All here know whose child he is, Hildegard. You don't accentuate the risk of people knowing by getting close to the boy. He is the perfect blend of his mother and father, and you should let yourself love him for his own sake."

He watched the war within this woman, their beloved Hildegard who carried the weight of their lives and their secrets. Betterm saw her blink back tears hard, and as if in sudden victory or capitulation she knelt down before the man and boy and carefully lifted the small and surprisingly heavy sleeping body up and over her shoulder. She stood with some effort.

"Heavy as a ham you think? I'd say heavy as a calf, myself!" Hildegard felt crashing waves of love and longing and something that trembled between fear and bliss. Betterm stood slowly with a groan and a hand at his back, and the three walked back to the Abbey along the garden's paths drenched with slanted molten golden light.

# COMTÉ DE FOIX
## 1079 CE

Three days passed in relatively easy travel. The days stayed dry and gradually warmed. They were far enough away from Mater Misericordia that Marguerite felt less fear and allowed the women to travel at a more decorous pace. Nights came earlier as they stopped before dark, and in the safety of the deep woods they built small fires, warmed water for tea and roasted the small rabbits that Sister Agnes and a couple of other young resourceful nuns were able to capture with snares. In the early soft light Sister Agnes and her closest friend, Sister Theresa a young woman of spindly body and blinding intellect, had gone a distance away from the slowly awakening women to check on the snares that they had set the night before. They came close to the edge of the woods where the trees thinned and the low brush made good rabbit hunting. The two young women looked warily, and saw no one in the meadow before them. It was so tempting after the day in the deep woods to feel the direct warmth on their faces! They took tentative steps out past the treeline to watch the sunrise.

As if from nowhere three men on horseback broke through the tall meadow grasses and spotted the two women.

"Ho! Look what's here!"

"Females! Before breakfast? Why not!"

The horses were urged forward, and the men galloped toward Agnes and Theresa who stood frozen for five interminable heartbeats and then broke and ran back into the woods.

"Hey! Come back!"

"Are we not to your liking? Tomas is ugly, but I'm good looking!"

"Only your mother thinks you are good looking!"

The third horseman edged close to the trees and could hear the snapping branches and rustling of leaves as the women escaped.

"Did you see the veils? Those were the nuns!"

He had smelled their fear and he liked it.

Up ahead Agnes and Theresa ran full tilt until they came to the women in their camp, stirring with first light. Mother Marguerite had heard their thrashing and was standing at the edge of the group, poised for danger. She broke into a deep sigh and flashed a brilliant smile when she saw that it was Agnes and Theresa crashing through the underbrush. Then she saw their faces and was alarmed anew.

"What is amiss? Has something happened?" she said in a rough whisper to them.

The two young nuns, their faces a study in contrast were breathing ragged. Agnes was beet red, and Theresa was as pale as new milk. Agnes spoke first.

"Mother! Forgive us! There were men! They saw us!"

"Have you been harmed?"

"No, Mother. We ran away. They came toward us, and then stopped"

"How did they see you? In the woods? Are they in these woods?" Marguerite's voice was rising in volume and panic now. Theresa hung her head and spoke.

"No, Mother, we stepped into the meadow to check the snares. And they appeared as if right up from the earth!"

Marguerite compressed her lips to hold back the retort. Foolish girls! They knew better! She shook her head hard to clear it, and asked.

"Did they come from behind us? From the west?" *Had the soldiers from Mater Misericordia followed them here?*

Agnes found an answer.

"Yes, Mother, from the west.

Marguerite's heart raced like a hummingbird's. It was the men that

Juan Miguel had warned her against. How had they found them so quickly? And then, with a certainty that stunned her, she knew. Sister Anna Sophia had pointed them the way, and no doubt felt satisfied in her own dire predictions coming true. Marguerite was frozen in fear. Then a vision came to her and she felt suspended in crystal.

*She was sitting high in a beech tree, having conversation with the tree and her sisters. It was so easy to understand them, and such a feeling of peace. Beautiful creatures of cobwebs and moonlight with multi-hued hair that lived and danced all around them floated toward her and rose effortlessly up to her level on the high branch. They were the Fey, and to be with them again was such joy! The Queen of the Fey spoke into Marguerite's head in a language that she didn't know how she knew.*

*"The time is near, Little One. Stand ready."*

*"Ready for what?" she cried, but no sound came from her mouth. And the harder she tried the more desperate she became for an answer. She tried to climb down out of the tree, but the branches grasped at her clothes and there was the sound of rending cloth and snapping branches and crying…who was crying?*

Marguerite came free of her vision as a sword hilt slammed into her back. She rolled to her knees and saw hell before her. There were men everywhere, shouting and twisting arms and pushing faces of her beloved women near the still smoldering coals of last night's fires.

A tall man with the marks of smallpox across his cheeks strode into the middle of the chaos. He pulled a small sword and shoved it into the abdomen of the nun closest to him, Sister Agnes. She looked directly at Marguerite with compassion as the light left her eyes. The women screamed and wailed.

"Where is the treasure you have taken from the Convent?" he roared. "Give us the treasure, or you all die! I have little patience this morning."

Marguerite pushed forward and raced to stand before this man.

"We have no treasure! We have nothing!"

The man swung his arm across his chest and back-handed Marguerite so hard that she flew back onto the ground.

"Anders! Come here!"

The man who had tracked them, the poacher, the man who hated nuns, stepped forward and approached his Capitan.

"What did that woman, that other blasted nun, the one on the road what did she say of treasure?"

"She said that all that was precious had gone with these," the poacher replied, and he remembered the twisted smile on that other's face when she had said it, just before they had killed her.

Marguerite's ears were ringing. She looked around frantically and could see men with swords pointed at her sisters. She made herself look at the body of Sister Agnes, blood pooled inches deep on the earth around her.

She struggled to her feet and implored the Capitan.

"We have no worldly goods! The only treasure we have is our sister-hood!" In a frantic attempt to make them understand she gestured to where Sister Perpetua was lying. "We treasure this, our aged Sister"

The poacher, Anders, walked to the stretcher where Sister Perpetua was deep in dementia sleep wrapped in two blankets to keep her safe from the elements. He ripped off the covers and pulled back in disgust when he saw the old woman there.

"It isn't here. They must have it hidden somewhere!"

The Capitan held his short sword under Marguerite's chin.

"We shall see for ourselves."

# RUPERTSBERG
# 1141 CE

Cardinal Giuseppe Giardelli stood looking at the latest in the series of sculptures that had come from Rupertsberg. Over the last two decades the sculptor, Alejandro de Marsitel had sent one piece a year to the Cardinal who had procured the art works for the Vatican. In each piece there had been a boy featured prominently. In the first sculpture he had been the baby Jesus held by his Blessed Mother. In the next, he was a small child reaching for the tablets of the Ten Commandments. Every year, the same child, older and more formed.

On this day the Cardinal, alone in the foyer to his chambers, held his hand over his mouth as if to hold back sound. The statue was of David, arm lifted back and high, preparing to let loose the slingshot toward an unseen Goliath. The young man was lean with defined musculature and had a mane of curls that flowed to his shoulders. He came to an abrupt halt as he looked up into the face of this David poised larger than life above him.

"Jesu Cristi!' he exclaimed aloud.

It was his face! The face he still saw in the mirror as he shaved. The face that had been his and showed little aging since he had been twenty years old himself. And by some artist's magic, Alejandro had made it obvious that the young David's eyes were light in hue, a message across the miles of golden hawk-like eyes.

Giuseppe sank to his knees, pressing his hand to his heart as he felt it break. Such pain!

"Hildegard!"

Hundreds of miles away, over mountains and rivers and valleys, Mother Hildegard of Bingen, Abbess of Rupertsberg, heard that wail. She had been walking along the corridor, heading for the chapel for Vespers. She staggered and leaned one hand against the wall to hold herself upright. And in the face of that anguish she allowed herself the open connection to him that she had withheld these twenty years. With the power of her spirit she called to him directly because the physical miles meant nothing to the power of love.

*"Giuseppe?"*

*"The boy. He is ours?"*

*"Yes, my love. He is ours."*

*"He is with you?"*

*"Yes, he is here at the Abbey."*

*"And you never told me."* Giuseppe's words held the hurt.

*"Did we not, my love? You saw him grow through Alejandro's work. He is healthy and well-formed and as beautiful as you."*

Giuseppe thought he could hear laughter and the catch of tears in the voice in his head.

*"What is he called?"*

*"Theoderic, but all know him as Theo. And perhaps, not strangely, he is a brilliant scholar and a gifted musician."*

*"Does he know of me?"*

*"Oh yes. He is also one of the Thirteen, once Ni Me of the Pleiades. His soul has always known his physical origins. And we here have all given him the true value of his father's name."*

*"I have missed you, Hildegard."*

*"And I you, Giuseppe. My longing has been eased and increased by seeing you in him every day."*

*"I so wish…"*

Hildegard felt her own longing rise up and threaten to overcome her. She stilled her mind and asked him what needed to be asked.

*"Giuseppe, your heart?"*

*"It pains me. I want to see you before I die. May I?"*

Hildegard's eyes filled up and spilled over. She had kept the distance between them all these twenty years as a safeguard against rumors and accusations that could threaten all here. But in the end, she had to follow her heart. She said what needed to be said.

*"Come to us, my love. Come to us."*

# COMTÉ DE FOIX 1079 CE

"No!"

The sound of Marguerite screaming abruptly cut off as he flicked his sword sideways and slit her throat. She fell to her knees as her life's blood pumped between her fingers. All around her she saw her sisters stabbed and their clothes ripped from their bodies. The screams they made seemed miles distant. She saw spirits, dozens of them, rising from the now slumped bodies of the nuns of Mater Misericordia led by the spirit of Sister Dolora. The physical shells were discarded, and the spirits were rising, up through the branches of a giant beech.

Marguerite had one final thought as the carnage around her piled up as the men, like mad dogs, kept up the vain search for treasure. The words wailed in her mind as she took her final breath.

"I have failed!"

# RUPERTSBERG
## 1141 CE

Three months later, as the orange and gold and scarlet colors of autumn ran riot in the forests, Cardinal Giuseppe Giardelli arrived at the Abbey at Rupertsberg with only a single manservant in attendance. He was met at the gates by Mother Hildegard, Sister Delphinia, and young Theo.

Giuseppe swung a leg over his horse's back and came to stand before the party assembled there. To Hildegard's eye he looked gray of pallor and his once brilliant black hair was shot with white. But to her heart he was still so very beautiful. He looked at her as if drinking her in, and then let his glance shift to the young man with raven hair beside her. He kept his hand on the horse's neck to keep himself upright.

"Your Eminence, the Abbey welcomes you," Hildegard said with layers of meaning woven into and inbetween her words.

He smiled a smile of inestimable sweetness at her, and sank in a heap at his horse's feet.

A cry for assistance, a scramble to carry the Cardinal inside, a flurry of worry and fluster, and then he was settled.

"Why, by She of a Thousand Names, did you drive yourself so hard?" Hildegard spat the words out, shooting them between pursed lips as she held a cup of hawthorn berry tea to Giuseppe's lips. He tried to answer but she shushed him and tipped more tea into his mouth.

"It was pointless to arrive here so quickly, if in doing so you arrive three quarters dead!" Her voice rose an octave on the last three words.

Sister Delphinia moved quietly around the edges of the room assessing that Hildegard had everything she would need to tend to the Cardinal. There was water on the boil hung on a hook over the fire, wood in abundance to throw off extra heat. A small table stood ready with herbs in muslin pouches: hawthorn, cinnamon, rose, and motherwort, and a set of lancets if bleeding was necessary.

The windows were open to let in the last of the warmth of the day, and the slightly tangy smell of fallen apples wafted in from the orchards. Hildegard would allow no one but Delphinia into this room that had been especially prepared on the ground floor so that the Cardinal would not have to navigate a staircase.

After receiving another mouthful of tea poured into him with some force, Giuseppe clasped Hildegard's hand and gently held the cup away.

"You are the bossiest, most opinionated woman I have ever known. And I couldn't wait one more day to…hear you berate me!" Giuseppe needed to take several breaths to finish his thought, and that very fact destroyed any hope that Hildegard had harbored that he might be cured. This was that progressive malady of the heart that made strong men weak as babes. It brought shortness of breath and a racing, skittering pulse that she was feeling under her fingertips. He would have increased angina, and need to be propped up at an incline to help him breathe.

"Delphinia, we need more bolsters."

The two women brought his shoulders forward and placed pillows and rolls behind his back. Almost immediately his breathing eased and some color returned to his face.

"Will you stop fussing and physicking me. Come and sit and let me look upon you."

Hildegard felt herself blush, shot a sideway glance at Delphinia who tried to make herself invisible, and then drew up a stool next to his bed.

"You haven't changed a tot. If anything, how is it possible, you are even more beautiful?" His voice was low and raspy, but less labored.

"Aging must have affected your eyesight, my love. Time has danced with me; you just don't see it." Hildegard smiled sadly and wiped his forehead with a cool cloth.

Giuseppe chuckled, a low jagged sound, and continued.

"My vision is always perfect when it comes to you, Hildegard. And you are truly even more radiant than ever."

She tutted and smiled more deeply. Sister Delphinia cleared her throat.

"There are two waiting in the corridor, if you feel up to it."

Giuseppe sighed, wishing for more moments alone with Hildegard, but feeling the urgency of Theo and Alejandro to see him, and his own need to do what he needed to do in the time remaining to him.

"Of course. Bring them in. Shall I see them together, or one at a time, do you think?"

Hildegard smiled with true mischief and her gold eyes flashed.

"I am guessing that they are needing each other for courage right about now. Let me bring them both to you, and perhaps later they will request private audience." She motioned to Delphinia who moved smoothly to the door, the skirt of her habit shushing along the floor.

Alejandro and Theo entered side by side. They were a study in contrasts, like the angels of light and dark. The last two decades had been kind to Alejandro. His hair was still thick and curly, shot with sunlight and flashes of silver. He wore it even longer now so that it flowed past his shoulders. He was still slight of build and eccentric of dress. Today for this momentous reunion he wore a tunic of periwinkle silk that came to his knees with a scarlet vest and turquoise trousers that ballooned and then gathered at the ankles. His face, with barely a line upon it, was set in a façade of calm but his eyes were hungry.

Beside him and towering a good ten inches taller was the dark angel, Theo. His hair was so black and shiny as to give blue hints from the sunlight. He was lean but powerful of build, like a soldier masterful in swordplay. Black slashes of brows arched above those golden eyes he had received from his mother. And he looked at Giuseppe with an expression of curiosity mingled with recognition. Theo looked quickly to Hildegard to check how she was faring. When he saw her calmly nod, he looked back at Giuseppe.

"Your Eminence," he said in a beautiful melodious baritone as he

217

made a sweeping bow that would be the envy of far more practiced courtiers.

Alejandro, shaken from his reverie made a similar bow but said nothing.

"My full heart is now overflowing," Giuseppe said, as his eyes filled and he reached both hands out to the two men standing before him. They came forward, one to each side of his bed and took the offered hands. Hildegard closed her eyes and said a prayer of gratitude to her Goddess for the sight before her. As Alejandro and Theo settled on stools by the bedside, Hildegard kicked off her shoes and climbed up onto the head of the bed, nestling in beside Giuseppe. She allowed herself the luxury of stroking his hair. The four stayed thus as Giuseppe's eyes drifted slowly shut and Hildegard's fingers slipped through the waves of silken silver over and over again.

They took shifts staying with him as he slept for a continuous eighteen hours. Hildegard was loathe to leave the room, but was eventually convinced to rest on a pallet on the floor near Giuseppe's bed. When Alejandro sat vigil, he softly told the tales of their lives together as brother and sister, speaking of all of the shards of loss and anguish that he would not be able to say if Giuseppe had been awake.

"I have had dreams recently of the woman and man who were our parents. They were very small – you and I grew to be much taller than them. She smelled of mangoes – it is a sweet orange fruit of that place."

"When we left our temple to travel to Egypt, I knew we would never return together. Did you ever make it back home?"

"I begrudged you the love you felt for Pel. Did you know that? I wanted you to only care about me. How could I have been so petty? I hope you had each other in the days after."

When Theo sat next to his father he spoke of his life and interests here at the Abbey.

"I have been working to compile all of Mother's music. It is very convenient, is it not, to be able to call her Mother and those of the outside world think I am referring to her as the Abbess!"

"Mother was bolstering her courage to ask you if I could come and study with you in Rome. But as I look upon you, I can see that there would be no hiding our relationship. Best to stay here where no one can be threatened by the fact of me."

"I find myself studying the stars and remembering the wisdom of my home world. As Ni Me I came from a place now called the Seven Sisters. I see that place in my dreams."

And when Hildegard sat beside him she sang, she whispered songs of Egypt,

*"Isis, Isis Glorious One!*
*You are the Source of all life."*

And she crooned the hymns she had crafted in this lifetime,

*"Spirited light! on the edge*
*of the Presence your yearning*
*burns in the secret darkness,*
*O angels, insatiably*
*into God's gaze.*
*Perversity*
*could not touch your beauty;*
*you are essential joy.*
*But your lost companion,*
*angel of the crooked*
*wings – he sought the summit,*
*shot down the depths of God*
*and plummeted past Adam –*
*that a mud-bound spirit might soar."*

She composed love songs that poured out from her like water tumbling down a mountain brook.

*"My Beloved is divinity sculpted of flesh and bone.*
*He looks upon me and my heart gallops.*
*His touch upon me quickens my breath.*
*I hunger for his kisses."*

After the day and long night, Hildegard had been finally taken into a long, deep sleep leaving Theo to watch over their patient. Giuseppe's lashes lifted and his eyes looked upon his son. Theo squeezed his hand and turned to call Hildegard to wakefulness, but Giuseppe pulled his hand back so that Theo would look at him again.

"Water..." His lips moved and barely a sound escaped. Theo lifted the cup from the bedside table and gently lifted his father's head and held the cup to his cracked lips.

"Mother will be furious that I forgot to put unguent on your lips and they chapped. Here, let me," he whispered. The young man took the small clay pot of beeswax and calendula and so very gently smoothed the salve on top and bottom lip.

"She says I have your mouth too, although she is usually referring to my inopportune speech more than the shape of my lips." Theo smiled a crooked smile that reminded Giuseppe of Hildegard when she thought she was being clever. "More water?" Giuseppe nodded.

"I did not know of you, not until the last sculpture...I... I would never have stayed away."

"I know that. And she knew that. Hence, the secrecy. Too many lives were at stake to threaten this sanctuary. But you must trust that that decision tore at her." Theo set down the cup and wiped beads of moisture from Giuseppe's chin with a chamois cloth. He heard Hildegard turning on the goose feather pallet at the foot of the bed.

"Brace yourself. She awakes." And again, that crooked grin lit Theo's face and he looked all of six years old not twenty.

Giuseppe stayed bedridden for several more days with Hildegard never leaving his room except to bathe and change garments. Sister Delphinia brought their food, Alejandro sat in the corner through much of the daylight hours and made sketches on sheet after sheet of parchment, and Theo would rush in bringing the smells of autumn with him. When Hildegard finally deemed Giuseppe strong enough to venture out their first walk was to the small burial plot that ran along the west side of the chapel.

"Here they are, here on the right," Hildegard gestured with her hand toward three gravestones that seemed to be leaning in as if to listen to each others' secrets. "Tiny Griseld only lived one year past your visit here. She lingered so as to see baby Theo, and then proclaimed herself right and truly finished with all she needed to do. It was a gracious reprieve for her to be free of her body; she suffered so in her last months and struggled to breath."

Hildegard felt her voice catch and tears threaten as she heard the rasp in Giuseppe's breathing from this short excursion. She stopped in front of the next stone.

"Betterm was like a grandfather to Theo. They were constant companions. Frequently Sister Maria Stella had to send him back to the Abbey for his meals so she could get some private time with Betterm." Hildegard's voice was a broad stroke of sadness with the splash of humor shining through. "He was bedridden the last year of his life, and between Theo and Maria Stella the man had such constant nursing that it could drive a person mad. But he never wanted it different. He told me that for so much of this lifetime he had been lonely, so a surfeit of company felt like a blessing. He died when Theo was twelve. We worried for Maria Stella for a bit. She seemed inconsolable. But the garden, and Theo brought her back."

They walked to the third grave marker that had two small rounded stones alongside it.

"Sister Catherine of the Wheel, the dog you knew, and her next companion, also a small yappy creature with an underbite. I never could understand where she found those dogs. They would just appear at her heels one day and never leave, with no apparent local parentage. They were her magical friends, make no mistake."

Hildegard led him to the bench that allowed them to sit and see their friends' resting places.

"Catherine died just last year, and her dog died the day after."

"And the rest of the Thirteen? Have any others come to find you here?" Giuseppe's voice was low, but sounded easy enough that Hildegard stopped worrying for a second.

"Not here, no," she shook her head slightly. "But you remember our Petyer Fieldenstarn? He stayed with us for ten years and then returned to his home. He is now the Burgermeister of Wiesbaden like his father before him, married and with three small children. He wrote to me recently to say that his second child, a girl named Bettina has flaming red hair though he and his wife do not. The child is horse mad and is always sneaking away from her studies to then be found in the stables, frequently astride some draft horse or another. He is overjoyed to be reunited with his Kiyia once again. Although as a parent he finds her willfulness challenging to say the least!"

"Kiyia, again and in the flesh!" Giuseppe barked a short rough laugh. The two old friends and lovers laughed at the then and the now, overlapping like the current of two rivers coming together where they meet.

# TORONTO, CANADA/ SALISBURY PLAINS, ENGLAND/ YPRES, BELGIUM 1915–17 CE

When the train arrived in Toronto the boys were herded onto lorries and taken out to the base camp for the Canadian Expeditionary Force. That first night in the barracks Tom could hardly sleep with the sound of Andy Palmer crying.

The next day at dawn their training began. Marching, drills, gun training, slogging through mud, climbing over obstacles, and the long runs. Tom put up with it all with a stoicism that his grandmother would have recognized. And then, when they got to run, he felt like he slipped from his too tight skin and found freedom. His drill sergeant spotted his speed, and noted to his lieutenant that the boy could be a messenger runner.

Morris excelled at sharpshooting and that too was duly noted by their superiors. Andy, though, was having trouble. He startled at the sounds of the artillery, he balked at heights, and he seemed ready to weep when orders were barked at him. The sergeant knew Andy for what he was: cannon fodder. Morris gave little effort to help his brother and Tom tried to ignore Andy altogether.

"Why'd he have to come along anyway?" Tom grumbled for the umpteenth time, and Morris just shrugged.

When their training was deemed complete, the recruits were taken to the docks at the river where the transatlantic boats moored and they were directed onto the big transport ships. The lines of men shuffling forward reminded Tom of the days on the farm when the calves were castrated and he felt his balls shrivel up to his body. This wasn't exciting yet. But Tom knew that adventure would come. It just had to.

The trip across the ocean was hell. Rough winter storms made a six-day journey last eleven days. Almost all the soldiers suffered terrible seasickness, and the quarters below decks were the rankest thing Tom had ever smelled. They finally disembarked at Plymouth, got on trains for the Salisbury Plains, and started training some more.

Tom knew bad weather: Saskatchewan was a furnace or an icebox. But he had never encountered the British wet. Everything was mud, and rain, and nothing ever got dried out. The three boys were still bunked together, but Andy had stopped trying to get his brother's attention.

Christmas came and went, and the Canadian boys sang songs from home and had wrestling matches in the mud. In February they all boarded troop ships again and made for Belgium. Once there they were marched toward Ypres. It was a rubble of a town – there had been two battles over it already, but an HQ of the British forces was there and it needed defending.

*March 1, 1916*

*Dear Granny Sally,*

*I can't tell you where we are, but we are someplace new. I hope you all had a nice Christmas. I miss the woods in winter. Ma says you got a couple of blizzards. I hope you can get supplies in. How are the goats?*

*Tom*

Days were filled with trainings, chores, and guard duty. Latrines constantly needed tending and more ditches dug. Barracks needed scrubbing. Tom thought he could have stayed home if all he did was chores. Guard duties were the toughest for him because he was required to just stand still in one place. He would dream about running, about speed, about the wind pushing against him as it roared across the prairie. He and Morris still found ease with each other, but Andy had sunk into a kind of stupor; he went about with his head hung low and was the object of a lot of bullying in his barracks.

As spring turned into summer the rumors started flying that they would be moved soon closer to the front. Tom could barely contain himself. Movement! Motion! Something happening!

When they did move east, Tom got split from Morris for the first time since they had signed up. Morris was assigned to an artillery group and Tom found himself as a runner between the trenches at the Front and the Operational HQ.

*August 15, 1916*

*Dear Granny Sally,*

*I hope you are getting my letters. I sure would like to hear from you. Did you get your garden in? If I was home I'd help you with the three sisters.*

*Love,*

*Tom*

The pounding of the shelling was constant. After the first week Tom didn't even duck anymore. The really scary sound was the tiny whine of a single bullet. It came flying by like a mosquito, but the guy next to you could be alive one minute and then lose half his face while he was talking.

They hadn't even been at the Front for five days when Tom saw that happen to Andy. He had been there saying, "Hiya Tom!" with that goofy smile of his and then his head exploded. Tom wiped the brains and blood off his face and turned and retched. *Stupid Andy. He shoulda stayed home! Why'd he have to come along anyway?* Tom thought and didn't even realize he was crying.

"Soldier! Message! Get this to HQ!" And Tom would take off running. Dodging shells, tripping over bodies, falling into the deep wagon ruts that scarred the roads. Back and forth between the HQ at the village of Ypres and the Front.

"Soldier! Message! Captain Alistair needs this!"

"Soldier! Message! Give this to those idiots at HQ!"

After one trip away from the trenches Tom made a detour before heading to the mess tent. He went looking for Morris at the rear artillery formations. The sun was setting and the earthworks that protected the big guns looked like sleeping dragons in the shadows.

"Morris Palmer?"

"Never heard of him."

"Morris Palmer?"

"I think he shipped home, maybe."

"Morris Palmer?"

"Last bulwark past the fire tower."

Tom trudged forward, his feet feeling like lead. He hadn't seen Morris in over a month, and now he dreaded bringing this news. As he approached the last earthwork on the northern most end of the battery he could see the outlines of a handful of men around a small low fire and he could hear the whinny of the artillery horses corralled off in the darkness. The men were talking low with the occasional bark of laughter. They tensed as they heard Tom's footsteps approaching. Several men stood as if expecting to need to come to attention for an officer.

"I'm looking for Morris Palmer," Tom called out before he could be seen in the firelight.

"Tom? Is that you, buddy?" Morris leaped forward and clasped Tom's arms hard. "Guys! This is my best friend, Tom Fletcher. We grew up together. Our folks farms are back to back." Morris drew Tom closer to the fire and grabbed him a bottle of lager from the metal tub.

Tom didn't say anything and sat down hard on a campstool taking a big drag on the beer.

"Gee, Tom it sure is good to see ya!" Morris said in an overly loud voice.

"You keeping safe, Morris?" Tom asked.

"Yeah, fine. Just going a little deaf, I think."

"I can hear that!" Tom replied and couldn't help the grin from breaking out on his face. Morris punched him in the upper arm and the war fell away and it was like they were back home. Tom let the moment stretch out. And then he took a deep breath and said,

"Morris, I got some tough news for ya."

Morris's face got tight and he blinked hard twice.

"It's about Andy..." Tom said through his tight throat.

Morris shook his head no, but Tom kept talking.

"He's gone, Morris. I saw it. He got sniper shot."

"No, he can't have..." Morris cried. "What am I gonna tell my Ma?"

Tom gulped audibly. "Tell her he's a hero."

"Is he? Did he go over the top? How the hell did a sniper get him?"

Tom struggled with himself whether to tell Morris the truth or not, but he just couldn't bring himself to lie to his friend. "He just stood up tall in the trench. He said hi to me and then stood up like an idiot and the sniper got him."

Morris started crying and then laughing. Tom joined him. They clinked their lager bottles together. Morris wiped the snot off his nose on his sleeve.

"And yeah, I'll tell Ma he was a hero."

*September 20, 1916*

*Dear Granny Sally,*

*I saw a place that had fields of marigolds for healing potions. It made me think of you. I offered some tobacco at the Moon. Maybe you did too.*

*I signed up a year ago today. Maybe we'll be home by this Christmas.*

*Morris is at a field hospital. He got shot up, but will be back in uniform soon, so you can let his folks know he is OK.*

*I started seeing my invisible friends again out of the corner of my eye. You can write me if you want. We get letters here.*

*Love,*

*Tom*

*PS. If anybody's dog has a litter this winter, maybe you could save me a pup. I'm thinking I would like to have a dog when I get home.*

The winter came in and the mud froze. Tom still struggled and slipped as he ran messages back and forth, but now it was the ice that got him. He snapped an ankle just before Christmas and spent the holiday in the hospital. Morris came to visit him on Christmas Day and they played euchre and shared the small tin of pulled taffy that Morris's ma had sent him. Morris had an angry scar that ran across his left cheek where a fragment of a bullet had ripped across his face and took off most of his ear. His smile was more crooked than ever, but he was in high spirits, and told Tom about the pretty English nurse he had fallen in love with.

"Cassandra," he said in a loud and yet reverential tone. "Ain't that pretty? Cassandra is her name." Tom's response wasn't required as Morris very loudly expounded on her virtues.

It was warm in the hospital barracks, and if you blocked out the constant moans of pain and the smell of blood it was almost cozy. The boys tried hard to forget the war for one day. After the evening meal, the doctors brought out a bottle of a fine scotch whisky and all the soldiers that could swallow were allowed a Christmas dram. One fellow from Inverness who had lost the lower half of his right arm stood, held his glass high in his left hand and toasted.

"To all our fallen comrades!" And all who could speak replied. "To all our fallen comrades!"

The whisky was gulped or sipped or coughed about, and Tom and

Morris felt the shade of Andy slip between them.

"Sorry about your brother, Morris," Tom said softly, and Morris mostly read his lips.

Morris only nodded and then took a bigger sip of whisky.

*January 1, 1917*

*Dear Granny Sally,*

*Happy New Year. I got the package from home and it sure was nice to get. Ma knit me socks and they are always welcome here. Please tell Uncle Walter that I really like the moose hide moccasins. I got a bigger pair of boots and now I can wear the moccasins inside them. I know you heard about my ankle. It is healing up good, and I will be running again soon they say.*

*I have been having those dreams again like I had when I was a kid, the ones with the fancy palace and where my legs are crippled and hurt something fierce. Maybe it's just the morphine they give us, but sometimes I hear your voice in those dreams too.*

*Granny, why won't you write to me? Are you still mad I signed up? Even Ma writes, but not you. I feel like something is tearing in me. The priest here says I am just homesick. Would you do a spirit healing? Just don't tell Ma or she will have a conniption.*

*Your loving grandson,*

*Tom*

February found Tom back on his message runs and thanks to his family he had warmer and drier feet. The soldiers all worried about their feet. Always wet and cold, their boots were disintegrating, and frostbite and fungus were a real concern. More than one fellow Tom knew had lost toes this winter. Tom ran messages and only felt a little twinge on his bum ankle. The infantry fighting was less constant in the winter, but the flashes of shelling and counter shelling never seemed to stop. Tom started finding ways to get off to himself when away from the trenches, and he began to make small ceremony at dusk when he could. He would lift a pinch of tobacco up to the seven directions and call upon his ancestors. Sometimes that's all he could do. Then he would get flashes of what felt like a memory of something like incense… He could hear women singing and feel like his legs were on fire. The memories – if that's what they were – weren't a comfort exactly, but he felt like he was getting close to something real important.

# RUPERTSBERG
# 1141 CE

Autumn lingered that year, as if to offer Giuseppe a last look at her splendor. His health rallied with Hildegard's love and care, and he found his rhythm in the Abbey as the year's wheel turned into winter. Hildegard was finally convinced that he didn't need constant monitoring and moved back to her rooms. She was swept back into the thousand details of running her spiritual community, keeping pace with the torrent of information that she needed to get onto parchment, and assuaging her own deep hunger to spend time with her beloveds.

One afternoon near Martinmas, after a long time spent counseling two sisters who were finding cohabitation particularly challenging, she gave herself the gift of a quick visit to Giuseppe's room for sweet conversation and the precious treat of just looking upon him. She tapped softly on his door and heard the deep reply.

"Come in, Hildegard."

"How do you always know it is me on the other side of the door? Does high position in the Vatican confer the ability to see though walls?" Hildegard's tone was light, but Giuseppe could hear a thread of frustration and could see the furrow between her brows.

"Who needs extraordinary vision when the susurration of rapid footsteps is always followed by a peremptory one-two-three of knuckles on wood? God's teeth, Hildegard, you even knock like an Abbess!"

Hildegard laughed and felt the weight of her position fall away.

"The 'Abbess knock'. Yes, well, we train for that, didn't you know?"

Giuseppe grinned and patted at the seat next to him. She came to sit down, exhaling more than just a breath's worth of air.

"Are the two Sisters Elizabeth at each other again? One day you might simply let them scrap it out instead of standing between them."

"There would be blood on the floor!" Hildegard replied and leaned into him. "What are you reading?"

"With an enormous pride to which I have no true claim, I am reading the newest treatise on medicinal herbs written by the brilliant Abbess of Rupertsberg and compiled by an equally brilliant scholar of the same Abbey, a young man called Theoderic."

Hildegard felt herself blush and looked up at him shyly from under her lashes. "Do you think it good?"

"I think it a great contribution to humankind. But you know that, surely?"

Hildegard coughed into her fist. "For some reason, you seem to carry the imprimatur of Rome and I always seek that with trepidation."

He nudged her gently with his elbow.

"Since when have you cared about what Rome thinks?"

Caught out with her deflection, Hildegard threw back her head and laughed heartily for the first time in days. "In truth? Probably never once in this lifetime. I only care what you think, Your Eminence."

They looked at one another and deep in each other's eyes they saw the most profound joy and sadness.

"Hildegard, I must broach a topic that you keep avoiding." She stood abruptly to move about the room, but he clasped her wrist and held her there. She resisted the slight tug, and then folded back down onto the settle. "I have had a reprieve due to your ministrations, but it is but temporary." She shook her head, but he continued. "We both know that to be true, my love." Giuseppe reached for her chin to turn her face to him, and saw that her eyes were flooding over. "Hildegard, you of all people…" And he couldn't continue, so she did for him.

"I, of all people, know that this life is but a small piece of who we are. I, more than anyone, know that a single lifetime is but one brief fraction of our journey, and that we cross and intersect with those we love over and over again. And so? And so I must never grieve? Am I not entitled to cling to those I love for one more week, one more day, one more precious minute?" She was crying freely now and wiped an arm furiously across her nose. "I don't want to let you go!"

They tipped forward and rested their foreheads against one another. Eyes closed, drinking in the smell of the other's skin, coming to breathe in synchronicity, they stayed thus while the fire snapped in the grate and the call for Vespers came and went. Finally, in the stillness, Giuseppe spoke so very softly as to be almost indiscernible.

"When I die, I wish to be laid at rest here in Rupertsberg so that my bones shall remain as close to you for as long as can be. And in my hubris, I wish that you could someday be interred nearby. I sound selfish to mine own ears, but I speak from my heart."

Hildegard said nothing and the silence stretched and stretched. Finally Giuseppe could bear it no longer.

"Hildegard? I speak from my poor, pathetic, struggling heart." He teased. "Have you no answer, be it yeah or nay?"

She lifted her eyes and drank in the sight of him. "Your body shall be buried here, and your boney remains shall be nestled close to mine" She smiled weakly with a slight wobble to her lips, and Giuseppe leaned in and kissed away the tracks of tears down her cheeks.

"Then they shall be the happiest bones in Christendom," he replied.

Two days later, twenty-one years to the day when Hildegard and Giuseppe had conceived their beautiful son, the Cardinal of Venetzia, the Right Eminent Giuseppe Martinelli's spirit left his body. As that spirit lifted up and away from the shell that had encased it, he saw a beautiful woman, Hildegard of Bingen was sitting at the head of the bed, legs to each side of that body that had been his, holding that torso up at an incline to ease the last few breaths he had taken. The room was filled with those who loved him. Theo, raven head lowered, held one hand and Alejandro, clasped the other, his face was turned away as he laid his head upon the bed and wailed like a wounded animal. Petyer Fiedenstarn was there with his flame-haired daughter, Bettina, and both were weeping softly. Sister Maria Stella was singing songs of a distant land and time.

Hildegard took no pause for grief but let the memories of Atvasfara, High Priestess of Isis, rise to the fore. In a language no longer spoken on this earth she said the prayers of transmutation to speed the soul onward to the Hall of Ma'at for judgment. Clasping Giuseppe's body in her arms, circling his body with hand gestures of blessing, Hildegard/Atvasfara prayed with all the intensity of dozens of lifetimes.

*"Anubis asks 'Is this heart pure? Is this heart lighter than Ma'at's feather on the other side of the scale? Might this soul fly onward to life after life?'*

*And the sweet, scarred heart of Giuseppe/Talo was lighter than that feather, and all of the Goddesses of the times before said 'Yes!'"*

# ROUEN
# 1432 CE

The hearings continued and the evidence against Jeanne became more and more fabricated and fantastical. Only two men defended her, both clerics. One, a Dominican friar, was the most vocal. At one of her hearings her attention drifted as the small dark-skinned Dominican with odd golden eyes, Isambart de la Pierre, spoke passionately, claiming Jeanne's innocence and the illegality of the very trial under the auspices of the English and Burgundian lords.

Jeanne appreciated the friar's attempts, she liked him even, and trusted him though she seldom trusted anyone these days but her saintly friends. She knew he was risking censure and his own life by trying to save hers. But Jeanne had been told her fate. Saint Catherine had given her the gift of a foretelling.

*"Little Sparrow, soon you will be with us. Fear not. They cannot destroy the essence of you. That will live on and on."*

She knew the Friar was wasting his breath, and her mind drifted. As she looked over toward the window, she saw John Somerset, pale as milk, his eyes never leaving her. She winked at him with the eye turned away from the court, and he couldn't help himself but smile in return.

The final time Jeanne saw John Somerset was on the day of her execution. She had asked, and it had been permitted, for Friar Isambart to be with her to say Holy Offices as she was tied to the stake. John pushed his way through the avid throng, and walked right up to

235

Jeanne. He had fashioned a cross out of straw, and handed that to Fr. Isambart who stretched his arm up to where Jeanne was standing on her pyre. She placed the cross inside her tunic, next to her heart and with a trembling smile spoke a coded blessing to the young Englishman, an expression of gratitude that would not indict him.

"Now I know that you are not a pig."

The fire was lit, and Jeanne's mind flew from her body. Poised above, she saw the Friar and heard him saying prayers, not in Latin, but in an even older tongue, calling upon ancient goddesses to guide this soul onward. As Jeanne watched, the Friar shifted shape and became a woman of amber skin and small stature with a diadem of jewels woven though her glossy black hair. John Somerset's form shifted also, into the young girl he had once been. She heard him sing to the wood, summoning the spirits of the trees to burn fast and hard to speed the end to her torment. As she ascended, she could hear multitudes chanting.

*"Kali Ma, Goddess of the Fire. Kali Ma, Mother of the Bones. Kali Ma, Mistress of the Dying. Kali Ma, Daughter of Reborn."*

Her beloved saints, Michael and Catherine and Margaret, surrounded her and their forms shifted as well until she could see their true essence. She saw how they had been: a shimmering tall woman in flowing lavender, a tiny girl with wild curls, and a beautiful woman with snake tattoos running up her arms. She remembered how they too had been with her before time. And with the help of those below her and those around her she lifted quickly and effortlessly, and knew that she was home.

# YPRES
# 1917 CE

As spring pushed up from the frozen mud, he would see small signs of life and hope: a feather from a nesting bird, a wildflower, a tiny bee... He would draw a circle around himself with his pointed finger and feel like he could find that quiet part of himself that could connect with the old Tom and with Granny Sally and Uncle Walter and the woods back home.

May, June July, and the heat brought the smell of rotting bodies and flies. Word was spreading that a big campaign was in the works. Reinforcements came in from England and Canada. To Tom they looked like babies, and therefore fools, and he tried to avoid getting to know them or rely on them to cover him when he made a break from the trench to run back to HQ. By the end of July, the British troops had started trying to inch forward toward the ridge near the ruined village of Passchendaele, trying inch by inch to break through the German lines that had stood solid for three years. In September Tom had a fright when he went looking for Morris only to find out his artillery unit had been moved forward to support the Brits.

"Goddammit. Morris! You'd better stay alive!" Tom said to himself as he skirted around the corpses of three dead horses. He took a detour back behind some officers' tents and made an offering of tobacco to Spirit to keep his friend safe. A rabbit hopped up, appearing suddenly from a ditch that had once served as a latrine. It stopped and looked right at him.

"Granny Sally?" Tom said, real quiet. The rabbit took two hops closer and Tom knelt down slowly onto one knee. Barely breathing he reached into his message pouch and took out a bit of bread he had been saving for later. He lay the bread down on the dirt before him and sat back on his heel and waited. Very softly he began singing in Cree the song of the rabbit moon that Granny Sally had taught him when he was a little boy.

*"Heya, Spirit Moon*
*Rabbit, son of the Sun*
*Hey Heya, Spirit Moon."*

The rabbit came forward and nibbled on the bread, and Tom very slowly reached out to rub its head. A single tear slid down his face and fell onto the ground between them. Time was suspended and Tom could feel his granny's fingers, roughened from work and weather, gently wiping the track of his tear.

*November 1, 1917*

*Dear Granny Sally,*

*Things are getting pretty lively here. That's what the officers say. I woke up last night when a shell fell pretty close. That rabbit was there right by the edge of the trench. Was that you?*

*Tom*

On November 6 the Canadian forces were ordered to take the ridge. It had been raining hard for two days and by morning as they were told to go over the top, the rain was so steady that you could barely see the man in front of you. Tom went with the wave of troops as they crawled forward over No Man's Land and headed east toward Passchendaele ridge. The German shelling was relentless, and soon they were struggling over piles of bodies and equipment mired in thigh deep mud.

"This is suicide!"

"We can't stay here. We'll get picked off!"

"If we go up, we'll die for sure!"

The two officers, aged by war into old men, looked at one another with flat eyes.

"Fletcher!"

"Yes, Sir." Take a message back to FOP. Tell them we are all dead men. We can't move forward. Can't stay still. Can't retreat." The Lieutenant drew a deep breath, "And Fletcher."

"Sir!"

"Don't come back here! No matter what they tell you to do. Do you understand me, soldier?"

Tom dove into the man's eyes and saw his fate.

"Yes, sir, I understand! You are a brave man, sir!"

"Go with God, Fletcher!"

Tom turned and started to fight his way back across the churned earth tossed with body parts and old rifles. He winnowed his way through the rest of the Canadian force that was moving forward like a glacier toward that hell-spawned ridge. He was bending over to drag a boy no older than seventeen up to his feet when he felt a stab like an icepick into the back of his left knee. He gasped and let go of the young man who now had a spreading crimson rose across the front of his chest. Tom felt another stab into his right thigh and pitched forward face down into the mud. He reached into his shirt and grabbed Granny Sally's medicine bag. His legs were screaming in pain. It was a pain like he had never felt before and yet it was so familiar like in his dreams. He called for Sally with all the power of his spirit and he heard her respond immediately.

*"Tom, boy!"*

*"Granny, I'm hit."*

*"It's bad."*

*"It is real bad. It's my legs."* He turned to look down and saw that the bottom half of his left leg was gone and was laying about two feet away with the boot pointed toward him. The ground around him was warm and he realized that it was flooded with his blood.

*"Tom, Listen to me. I will find you again. Do you hear?"*

*"I hear ya, Granny."*

*"I am sending you help, Tom. Do you see them?"*

Tom saw a handful of forms, mostly bright light but they seemed solid. They moved toward him as if they floated over the ground and surrounded him. It was his friends, his invisible spirit friends from his childhood! He felt safe, and the sounds and screams of the battle around him disappeared.

*"I see 'em."*

*"Go to the Goddess, Tom. Go to Her and don't be afraid. I will find you again. I will always find you."*

Tom felt her breath on his face and felt a gentle kiss on his lips. He lifted up and saw the mangled body that had been his on a field of mud and carnage. His helpers escorted him higher and higher. He saw a brilliant light of rose gold, and heard the word.

*"Beloved!"*

# RUPERTSBERG
# 1179 CE

Theoderic sat at his desk overlooking the gardens at the monastic school at Rupertsberg Abbey. It was a glorious day with a startlingly blue sky that pierced the heart, one of those autumn days where life seemed suspended in fullness. He was tired, so very, very tired, but the life force outside his window gently, slowly caressed his spirit. His mind was full of song, the songs that Hildegard had brought into the world, and they soothed his tattered heart.

The last week had been a time of exquisite pain and joy. Hildegard, at the age of eighty-one had had a precipitous decline in health. She had been busy dealing with the myriad loose ends from the latest scuffle for power with the Archbishop of Mainz, dictating her correspondence to Theoderic as a small concession to the arthritis that had plagued her of late. One day, hale and hearty; the next, taken to her bed. Her private chamber had been filled with those closest to her, the corridors outside were lined with the nuns of the Abbeys. Open windows allowed the prayers of those filling the gardens to float in to her.

As the day edged into twilight, she opened her golden eyes wide for the last time. It was as if a string had been plucked, and a single clear tone rang through the air. One tone became two, became thirteen. The primordial chord. Celestial music began to swell and soar. It was heard and unheard. It was pressing on the eardrums and thrumming in the bones. It was Hildegard's final gift to them all – her soul song. It was the essence of her being and it moved beyond all containment.

No one remaining could ever remember that melody, and it was an ache of longing that was never to be assuaged.

And then suddenly, all the sounds except that first single tone disappeared, and Hildegard was called home. She lifted effortlessly from her body into the arms of her beloved beings of light. As graceful in death as she had been in life, present in all her glory and generosity of heart, she had given them the song of all her lifetimes. And then Hildegard, she who had been Atvasfara, She of a Hundred Names, was gone.

There had been a short-lived tussle between the two spiritual communities of Rupertsberg and Eibingen as to where her remains would be interred, but Theoderic had been the deciding vote and he was able to express Hildegard's wishes to be in the ground and at rest as soon as possible. What he hadn't said to anyone but Alejandro and Sister Maria Stella, was that the Mother had desired to be with Giuseppe. In the darkness of night he had placed her body and Giuseppe's skeletal remains into the same grave, high up the hill beneath Grandmother Beech.

Theo had seen Alejandro to his studio where the old man insisted on continuing his work on the tombstone for Hildegard's now empty grave in the communal yard. Maria Stella had gone for a midday nap, and Petyer Fieldenstarn and his still fire-haired daughter Bettina had left to travel back to Wiesbaden.

Now Theo was truly alone for the first time in eight days, and the letter that lay in the drawer of his desk was calling to him loudly. Hildegard had whispered to him in her last hour.

"I left you something in your desk. Read it when no one else is there. It is for you alone."

So now he hesitated. When he read this letter it would be his last conversation with her, their time together in this life would truly be over. He didn't feel ready for that, but he felt the shades of his parents granting him courage.

Hearing his mother's remonstrances for 'caution' in his head, he cast a protective circle around himself. He drew a deep breath, took a sip of the summer's elderberry wine, and pulled the parchment out of the drawer.

He cracked the wax seal with Hildegard's triple moon emblem with his thumb and unfolded the single page, seeing her meticulous, back-slanting script.

*My son,*

*It is thrilling to put those words on paper, if only for your eyes. In all my lifetimes, you are the only child of my body that has been gifted to me, and our years together are richer than anyone has a right to expect. I know you will well steward the writings that I channeled, and we can only hope that the wisdoms of our Divine Mother will be able to be heard and interpreted for the greater good.*

*Know that I have seen this vision – that the rivers of the Goddess's love will become thinner and thinner, rivers to streams, and streams to tiny creeks. We, the Thirteen, as we re-embody, will look for safe harbors in more and more remote places: in groups of the disposed, the marginalized, the persecuted. We carry Her in our hearts, and we will need to be more and more unseen and hidden. But keep faith, my son. When giant silver birds fill the skies, when people can see one another across oceans and hear each other's voices in other continents, when humanity is killing its own home – then – we shall all be together again. The Thirteen shall hear the call, shall find one another, and we shall revive all those truths we so long ago buried. We shall return when again the world is in crisis, to give our all to save what might be saved.*

Theo tipped the parchment toward the candle, and watched as the flames ate the page and the smoke spiraled out the window.

# HISTORICAL NOTE

## HILDEGARD OF BINGEN
### 1098–1179 CE

The remarkable Hildegard, born of lesser nobility and pledged at the age of eight to the religious life, was known within her lifetime as an Abbess at Rupertsberg and Eibingen, a theologian, composer, philosopher, artist, biologist and polymath. She suffered throughout her life with painful maladies and experienced revolutionary visions. She composed over one hundred and fifty liturgical pieces of music and is known for the first medieval morality play. In her life she corresponded with popes, kings, and queens as well as prominent theologians such as Thomas Beckett and Bernard of Clairvaux. She received approval from Pope Eugenius for the publication of her writings, and traveled on speaking tours throughout Europe. The foundation of her philosophy centered on the concept of Viriditas – the greenness of earthly and spiritual life force, and the inspiration of Caritas/Divine Love and Sapientia/Divine Wisdom, forces of the Divine Feminine. She is considered the founder of scientific natural history in Germany and was known as the Sybil of the Rhine.

How was a woman, limited by her society and education, able to command such respect and autonomy in medieval Europe? How was a woman able to chastise popes and kings and establish flourishing communities for women of intellect and artistry? Perhaps she carried the wisdom of many lifetimes. In my herstory of Hildegard I have played a bit fast and loose with the known timeline of her accomplishments, but I haven't diminished their impact in her world. There was a Jutta who was Hildegard's first spiritual mentor. Hildegard's nuns wore white and didn't suffer the torments of the flesh; she believed that suffering made it harder to connect with spirit. Her abbeys were filled with music at every hour. And she did have correspondence and influence within the Vatican. There was indeed, a Theoderic who compiled her works during and after her death. And, her remains are not in the grave specified by her tombstone.

The majority of the other characters are fictional...though you may have spotted some other people from history:

Li Er, better known as Lao Tse/ Lao Tzu,

Hypatia,

Jeanne, better known in English as Joan of Arc,

Juana de la Cruz.

As for the rest...

# ACKNOWLEDGEMENTS

I am deeply grateful for my teachers, for the wisdoms they convey, for the patience they demonstrate, for their generosity of spirit.

I have not nearly enough words of gratitude for the Monday Night Scribes – Jess, Judi, Linda, and Naaz – my bulwarks, my peeps, my constancy.

I am blessed beyond all deserving with my family. Rick, Eliza and Malcolm. The laughter and love that fills our house is the best medicine.

I have spiritual mentors and fellow travelers that have made these stories better and richer. In deepest gratitude to Triple Spiral of Dún na Sidhe, Beverly Little Thunder, Lushanya Echeverria, Sappho Morisette, Sharynne NicMhacha, Rachel Ginther, Adhi Two Owls, Elizabeth Nahum, Marie Nazon, Marian Zeitlin, Dalia Basiouny, Tashi Dolma, ALisa Starkweather, Scot AnSgeulaiche, Reggie Ceasar, Lee Hancock, Ginny Brook, Laura Delano, and Jeffery Yuen.

For the hardworking, multi-tasking, multi-talented team at Womancraft Publishing who make beautiful books out of, literally, thin air.

For Lucy H. Pearce – for being Lucy.

And to my ancestors – I hope I do you proud.

# ABOUT THE AUTHOR

Gina Martin is a founding mother and High Priestess of Triple Spiral of Dún na Sidhe, a pagan spiritual congregation in the Hudson Valley. She is a ritualist, teacher, healer, mother, wife and writer of sacred songs. She has helped to create RISE (Revivers of Indigenous Spiritualities and Eco-systems), an organization dedicated to protecting and promoting indigenous and pagan belief structures and the lands that support them.

Gina is a practitioner of Classical Chinese medicine and a Board-certified acupuncturist.

She lives as a steward of the land that previously held a village of the Ramapough Lenape where people can come together now to remember the Old Ways. She is kept company by her husband and dogs, as well as the Sidhe who live in the hills.

**www.ginamartinauthor.com**

# SHE
## IS HERE

## GINA MARTIN

### THE FINAL BOOK OF THE
### *WHEN SHE WAKES* SERIES

Their journey began with a nightmare.

It was held and protected throughout centuries with private visions.

And now it comes to manifestation with thirteen, dreaming the same dream.

In a world embroiled in climactic crisis, pandemic, and global political upheaval, thirteen people awaken with the knowledge that they must converge to witness the rebirth of the Goddess. The forces organized against them are well-funded and intent on protecting their own dominance.

Everything is at stake – the life of the planet, the wellbeing of all that dwell on her, and the reassertion of balance. The Thirteen feel the stirring of their destiny, and give everything they have so that She can be here.

# ABOUT THE ARTIST

Iris Sullivan was born in Australia, lived in the UK and settled in California to raise her four children. She now lives on Maui teaching art therapy, and the understanding of color in relation to the soul to international groups. Iris strives to reveal the invisible transparent soul movements through her art.

**movingthesoulwithcolor.com**

# ABOUT WOMANCRAFT

Womancraft Publishing was founded on the revolutionary vision that women and words can change the world. We act as midwife to transformational women's words that have the power to challenge, inspire, heal and speak to the silenced aspects of ourselves.

We believe that:

+ books are a fabulous way of transmitting powerful transformation,

+ values should be juicy actions, lived out,

+ ethical business is a key way to contribute to conscious change.

At the heart of our Womancraft philosophy is fairness and integrity. Creatives and women have always been underpaid. Not on our watch! We split royalties 50:50 with our authors. We work on a full circle model of giving and receiving: reaching backwards, supporting TreeSisters' reforestation projects, and forwards via Worldreader, providing books at no cost to education projects for girls and women.

We are proud that Womancraft is walking its talk and engaging so many women each year via our books and online. Join the revolution! Sign up to the mailing list at womancraftpublishing.com and find us on social media for exclusive offers:

 womancraftpublishing

 womancraftbooks

 womancraft_publishing

# SISTERS

*of the*

## SOLSTICE MOON

### GINA MARTIN

## BOOK 1 OF THE
## *WHEN SHE WAKES* SERIES

On the Winter Solstice, thirteen women across the world see the same terrifying vision. Their world is about to experience ravaging destruction. All that is now sacred will be destroyed. Each answers the call, to journey to Egypt, and save the wisdom of the Goddess.

This is the history before history.

This is herstory, as it emerged.

An imagining… or is it a remembering… of the end of matriarchy and the emergence of global patriarchy, this book brings alive long dead cultures from around the world and brings us closer to the lost wisdoms that we know in our bones.

*Sisters of the Solstice Moon* is a story of vast richness and complexity, in the tradition of speculative historical novel series, *Clan of the Cave Bear* and *The Mists of Avalon*.

## THE OTHER SIDE OF THE RIVER: STORIES OF WOMEN, WATER AND THE WORLD
Eila Kundrie Carrico

Rooted in rivers, inspired by wetlands, sources and tributaries, this book weaves its path between the banks of memory and story, from Florida to Kyoto, storm-ravaged New Orleans to London, via San Francisco and Ghana. We navigate through flood and drought to confront the place of wildness in the age of technology. A deep searching into the ways we become dammed and how we recover fluidity. A journey through memory and time, personal and shared landscapes to discover the source, the flow and the deltas of women and water.

## BURNING WOMAN
Lucy H. Pearce

A breath-taking and controversial woman's journey through history – personal and cultural – on a quest to find and free her own power.

Uncompromising and all-encompassing, Pearce uncovers the archetype of the Burning Women of days gone by – Joan of Arc and the witch trials, through to the way women are burned today in cyber bullying, acid attacks, shaming and burnout, fearlessly examining the roots of Feminine power – what it is, how it has been controlled, and why it needs to be unleashed on the world in our modern Burning Times.

*A must-read for all women! A life-changing book that fills the reader with a burning passion and desire for change.*

**Glennie Kindred, author of *Earth Wisdom***

## THE MISTRESS OF LONGING
Wendy Havlir Cherry

The Mistress of Longing is an invitation to listen
and trust the deep feminine that longs to be heard.
A love letter from, and for, devotion.
A prescription for a passionate and creative life.
A sacred reclamation.
A liberation of desire.
A hymn to kindness.
The voice of a modern mystic.

*The Mistress of Longing is like the fragrance and softness of rose petals offered
to our collective hearts. Wendy speaks directly to the Soul and whispers to our
fear and hesitation, beckoning us to live the fullness of ourselves. She not only
inspires but also offers concrete, potent exercises to help guide our journey.
Don't miss this bounty.*

**Heidi Rose Robbins, The Radiance Project podcast**

**shop.womancraftpublishing.com**

Made in the USA
Coppell, TX
29 May 2022

78265447R00155